CONTEMPORARY AMERICAN FICTION

IVORY BRIGHT

Elaine Ford graduated from Radcliffe College. She received grants from the National Endowment for the Arts in 1982 and 1986, and was a fellow at Yaddo in 1983 and 1984. Author of *The Playhouse* and *Missed Connections*, she now teaches writing at the University of Maine.

IVORY

BRIGHT

Elaine Ford

PENGUIN BOOKS

PENGUIN BOOKS
Viking Penguin Inc., 40 West 23rd Street,
New York, New York 10010, U.S.A.
Penguin Books Ltd, Harmondsworth,
Middlesex, England
Penguin Books Australia Ltd, Ringwood,
Victoria, Australia
Penguin Books Canada Limited, 2801 John Street,
Markham, Ontario, Canada L3R 1B4
Penguin Books (N.Z.) Ltd, 182–190 Wairau Road,
Auckland 10, New Zealand

First published in the United States of America by
Viking Penguin Inc. 1986
Published in Penguin Books 1987

LIBRARY OF CONGRESS CATALOGING IN PUBLICATION DATA
Ford, Elaine.
Ivory bright.
I. Title.
PS3556.069719   1987   813'.54   86-22645
ISBN 0 14 00.8497 5

Printed in the United States of America by
R. R. Donnelley & Sons Company, Harrisonburg, Virginia
Set in Electra

For my father, Jack,

and in memory of my mother, Ruth

IVORY BRIGHT

One

....

FOGEL POLISHES THE LENSES FOR HER, even though she's
not going to be able to see out of them. The prescription is for
an unknown rich person, long deceased. The gold frames were
what she fell in love with, the moment she spotted them in
Fogel's junk shop window. She craved them for weeks, and
haggled, and finally met Fogel's price. Carefully she tucks the
tissue-wrapped package into her raincoat pocket.

"Don't rush off," Fogel says, digging into a musty cardboard
carton. He pulls out a paisley shawl, the kind that goes on a
piano. "A present."

"You never gave me anything for free before," Ivory says.
"Maybe you feel guilty because the glasses aren't worth nine
dollars."

"You, Miss Bright, are a crabby and suspicious individual."

Ivory looks the shawl over. Two moth holes. And a raveled
hem. "At least you're not feeling *very* guilty."

"You don't like it? Don't take it."

"Thank you, Mr. Fogel," Ivory says, stuffing the shawl into
her tote.

In her crepe-soled canvas shoes she lopes along Somerville
Avenue, past the Portuguese fish store with the front half of
a pink fish in the window—all that remains late in the day on
a Friday—and the Continental Unisex Salon. Fogel is wrong,

Ivory thinks. She is not a suspicious person, or a crab either. All of her thirty-one years she has been a romantic person, in spite of the fact that, on account of her looks, romance is not a practical hope. She has an asymmetrical face: one hazel eye bigger than the other and the mouth skewed slightly to one side. It's as though God found two half faces left over at the end of a working day. "Waste not, want not," He said, clapping them together and fitting the creation out with a pair of pointy elbows and some unruly dark hair He also had lying around.

Once in the library when nobody was looking Ivory made a photocopy of her face, her eyes squeezed shut and her nose flattened against the glass. The photocopy came out looking like the pictures the hospital took of her brother's kids, Arlene and Diane, when they were newborn. Nobody could fall in love with a face like that.

As she walks Ivory's hand is in her pocket, touching the eyeglasses. For some reason they *feel* like gold, even through the tissue paper. She shivers with pleasure. She turns the corner onto Granite and begins to walk uphill on the asphalt sidewalk. Clumps of weeds grow out of the cracks. The houses are triple-deckers, jammed close together, most of them not very well kept up. If you held a competition to pick the Neighborhood Tree, the tree of heaven would have to win by a mile. Nobody planted those trees; they just grew wherever they found a hole in the cement, and they didn't notice that the soil is practically as hard. The name "tree of heaven" makes Ivory laugh. Granite Street is not exactly heaven, and none of the landlords or tenants try to pretend it is. Except for the Portuguese, who string up colored lights in their alleys and yards with desperate homesick optimism.

Since no teenagers are hanging out in Osgood Park, Ivory stops to have a smoke before going upstairs to fix supper for

Diane and Arlene. Calling this place a park is another joke; she hopes that whoever Osgood is, he is dead, so he can't see how his name is being taken in vain. The park is no more than a house lot, asphalted over and surrounded by a chain-link fence. At one time there were swings, but they were yanked out by vandals, so only the maimed metal stumps remain. Ivory sits on a bench and drags on her Salem. She sees that somebody has recently spray-painted the asphalt in a weirdly graceful alphabet, like curlicues. Sri Lankan, maybe. Also spelled out in the same blue paint is the word *killer*.

A squat brown dog comes through the gap in the chain-link and begins to sniff at an empty pizza box.

"Hello, dog," Ivory says.

He watches without much interest as she crushes the butt under her crepe sole.

"What's your name, dog?"

He sits on his haunches and scratches his flank with a hind leg.

"Mine is Ivory. Like the soap."

He opens his mouth in a yawn.

"Yeah, that's what they all say."

She drapes the paisley shawl around her shoulders and makes a fat knot over her heart. Then she takes the gold eyeglasses out of her pocket, unwraps them from the tissue paper, and hooks them over her ears. "Pay attention now, dog. Tell me what you think of my new image."

Blurrily he scratches himself. He bites the itchy spot with his teeth.

"Well, just thought I'd ask," she says, folding the eyeglasses and putting them back in her pocket. "What do you think, dog, is it going to rain?"

She hopes so. A hard rain keeps the bottle smashers out of the park, and Friday nights are the worst.

. . . .

Ray sits down to a cheese sandwich on seeded rye. He removes the top slice of bread and spreads a thin coating of mustard onto the cheese with a small wooden scoop that came with the mustard jar.

"You didn't want lettuce in that, did you?"

Lillian sits tentatively on the edge of the needlepoint upholstered chair at the far end of the table. The indecisiveness of her manner, Ray knows, stems partly from the fact that she is still nominally a servant in this house, even after thirty-odd years. Nevertheless, from time to time it gets his goat.

"It's fine the way it is, thank you."

Lillian frowns. "Because iceberg was eighty-nine cents at Star Market last week and I simply can't bring myself to pay that kind of money."

"I don't even *like* lettuce in cheese sandwiches."

"It's just as well, then," she says, either failing to notice or pretending not to notice the shortness in his voice.

He feels a minute pang of contrition. "Aren't you going to eat something?"

"I don't believe I care for anything right now," she says with a meaningful look, from which he is supposed to understand that the unnamed condition that occasionally disrupts her internal organs is doing it again.

Ray chews steadily and gazes at the window. It has begun to rain, and the acacia is rattling its long black pods against the outside of the glass, reminding him that he ought to do some yard work before winter sets in.

"I took Sammy to the vet this afternoon," Lillian says, picking up one or two stray crumbs from her place mat and depositing them inside her folded napkin.

"What did he say?"

"It isn't a BB shot wound after all. It's an abscess."

Ray takes a swallow of beer and waits for her to go on.

"From a cat fight, he says. We shouldn't let Sammy get into cat fights, Raymond."

"Fighting is in the nature of male cats."

"But he's fixed."

Ray shrugs.

"The vet put some ointment on the sore. He licked it right off again."

Lillian is now removing a speck of lint or a loose thread from the front of her dress. The shiny material, a sort of imitation silk, clings to her lumpily structured undergarments. Even at this end of the table Ray catches the characteristic scent of her: underarm odor unsuccessfully dry-cleaned, overlaid with garde-nia bath powder.

"Are you sure one sandwich is going to be enough? It wouldn't be any trouble to make another."

"Please don't bother, Lillian." He will be obliged to eat sheet cake later in the evening, squandering his self-imposed calorie allotment.

"It would have killed your mother," Lillian is saying, "to think of somebody in this neighborhood shooting at cats with a BB gun."

"You told me it wasn't a gunshot wound," Ray says pa-tiently.

"It very well might have been. Somebody from Somerville Avenue or the other side of Central. Those people cut through Westwood Road all the time."

Ray sighs inwardly and drains his beer glass.

"Is this retirement party going to be a big affair, Raymond?"

"As far as I know, the same as usual."

"All the bank employees, including the secretaries?"

"I assume so."

Lillian pats her permanent. The color her tight curls are dyed makes Ray think of the way people do up unfinished furniture, in unconvincing shades of walnut or mahogany.

"Then Miss Neely will be there?"

"Muriel has moved to Phoenix," Ray says, looking into the jar of bread-and-butter pickles and spearing a slice with a little silver fork.

Lillian cannot conceal her astonishment. "Why in the world would she do a thing like that?"

"For her mother's arthritis, I am told." .

"Well, think of that. Way out there in the desert with the cactuses. That will be quite a change for her."

At one time Ray considered marrying Muriel Neely, the gentle and gently spoken secretary to one of the vice-presidents. Not that he ever confided his thoughts to Lillian, but no doubt she had her suspicions. Since the move it has occurred to him to wonder whether the deed wasn't some sort of unvoiced ultimatum to him. Well, if so, it didn't work, and on the whole just as well, though he does feel somewhat melancholy to think of Muriel so far away. Out there with the cacti. The retirement party will be even deadlier than usual without someone to smile at his small jokes and asides. Feeling rather sorry for himself, he folds his napkin and goes upstairs to bathe.

Ivory Frances Bright lives on the top floor of an avocado-green three-family house on the corner of Granite and Osgood, within walking distance of Union Square. The family moved to Granite Street when Ivory was twelve and her brother Richie fifteen, the year their mother died. Since the apartment had only two bedrooms, Ivory's father fixed up the back porch for her. He replaced the screens with odd pieces of plywood and windows rescued from a demolition site, stuffed the cracks with strips of pink insulation, and strung an extension wire out from the kitchen to power the electric heater. A hasty and half-baked alteration, no question, but no use improving a landlord's property if the tenancy is only going to be temporary. They'd moved every year or two during her childhood; Ivory had no reason to guess she'd end up living on that porch, with its view of a vandalized park and a vacant lot, for nearly twenty years.

But Richie graduated from high school and was hired by the city. Soon afterward he started going steady with Roselle Fletcher, and then he and Ivory really dug in their heels about staying in one place for a change. Not that Ivory loved Granite Street, but she didn't love moving, either.

Ivory graduated three years after Richie did, and it turned into one of those summers when everything happens at once. Roselle got pregnant. Bill Bright had to go into the V.A. hospital in Worcester to have three toes on his right foot amputated. Roselle moved into Richie's room and had morning sickness. Richie had to do a lot of overtime.

So although Ivory had been planning on renting a little room in another part of the city and getting her hair cut in the kind of shop where you have to make an appointment in advance, what she actually did was go out to buy pints of strawberry ice cream for Roselle at all kinds of strange hours and take the bus back and forth to Worcester. Before Diane was born Ivory had found a job working at a dry cleaner's in Union Square, so she just stayed on with the family. Nobody did anything about making the back porch any more watertight or winterized, because living there was still only temporary for all of them. Roselle was talking about a little house in the suburbs for her and Richie and the baby, and Bill Bright, out of the V.A. hospital, was weighing the advantages of a move to California. He claimed he knew somebody out in L.A.

In the end, none of them went anywhere. Just when he'd definitely made up his mind to buy an airplane ticket, Bill fell into a hypoglycemic coma and didn't come out of it. Roselle put up new wallpaper in Bill's room for Diane. Richie found a two-bedroom Cape in Pinehurst for which he could just about afford the down payment, but Roselle wasn't crazy about that particular house, and besides, she was damned if she was going to leave brand-new wallpaper behind for some new tenants who wouldn't even appreciate it. Not to mention how handy it was having Ivory right there in the apartment in case she and Richie felt like seeing a movie. In Pinehurst they'd have to hire a sitter.

By the time Roselle's second baby was born, Ivory was three years out of high school. She'd quit the job ticketing soiled clothes and become the assistant in a watch repair shop around the corner from the dry cleaner's. She worked there for five years, and then the woman who sold blouses and lingerie in the little shop between the watch repairer and Wallpaper World gave up her lease and went out of business.

Well into the tail end of that winter the store stayed empty, except for some bare shelves and Final Sale signs and a tangle of hangers on the ill-fitting carpet. Its derelict state made Ivory uneasy. Small-time vandals would begin to attack it, and the pox would spread.

On a drizzly afternoon in February the watchmaker went home early with a bad back, leaving Ivory alone with the watches and clocks and gold-filled birthstone rings and Speidel ID bracelets. She was out of cigarettes and half-asleep. The clocks made whiny chewing noises, numbing her brain.

Then she seemed to be in the abandoned shop next door. But now it was night. Dreamily she moved across the carpet and opened a Lucite box on one of the shelves. Inside, instead of bras or slips, she found a baby. It was wearing a thin white cotton gown with a single row of crochet work around the armholes. It wasn't alive. Or dead, exactly, either. The open eyes looked like glass, with crumpled blue irises.

Soon after her vision, or whatever it was, Ivory started arguing Richie into lending her part of his mortgage money to set up a toy store. Hell no, he said. Union Square's on its last legs. Nobody shops in town anymore, they're all out at the malls. She must have gone bananas. She'd lose her shirt. Correction: his shirt.

But she and Richie had always been close, especially after their mother died. The time Ivory was in a bad jam they didn't tell Roselle; he mentioned to a buddy at the DPW that his girlfriend was in trouble—which was the reverse of the story the guy usually heard—and the guy came up with a doctor out in the suburbs who did it in his office on a Sunday morning. Richie paid the fee without asking Ivory any questions. It wasn't just that he owed her for two years of free baby-sitting. They were each other's only blood relation, and blood is thicker than water.

She wore him down about the toy store. She got her way.

Two

. . . .

IVORY IS CUTTING A RECIPE for Señor Pico chicken out of the newspaper. On the back of the recipe, she notices, is part of a story about a plot to shoot the mayor of Chicago.

Arlene yanks open the porch door. "Nothing's cooking in the kitchen. There aren't even any pots on the stove."

"Really?"

"I'm starving."

"I'm busy just now."

Arlene unzips her jacket and flops onto the other end of Ivory's bed, which is covered with a crazy quilt made of pieces of panne velvet sewn together with gold thread. "Busy doing what?" The bedsprings squeal, and shreds of newspaper float down to the hooked rug.

"This is a very interesting article about a plot to shoot the mayor of Chicago. Would you like me to read it to you?"

Arlene doesn't bother to think up a smart reply. She removes a sneaker and sock, lifts a Band-Aid from her heel, and examines the scab of an old blister. She rubs some skin and fuzz from between two toes, rolls it into a ball, and drops it onto the rug. Then she picks up Ivory's scissors and begins to trim the nail of her big toe. "These sure are dull," she complains.

"They aren't meant to be manicure scissors."

Arlene goes on using them anyway. "You got any nail polish, Ivory?"

"No." She has taken off her blouse and is sorting through a tin cough-drop box full of odd buttons. "I'd just as soon not draw attention to my toenails."

"What's the matter with them?"

Ivory selects a pink button that is surprisingly close in color to the ones on the blouse. "This is what they call a cautionary tale, Arlene. If you bite your toenails they grow back in at peculiar angles."

"You bit your *toe*nails?"

"When my fingernails were down to the quick I'd go for my toes."

Like her mother, Arlene has a bland, egg-shaped, nearly eyebrowless face, but she manages to look impressed even so. "How did you reach them?"

"I'm double-jointed. Did I ever show you this stunt?" Ivory forces her thumb down toward the inside of her forearm until it meets the skin. Some bone in her wrist makes a cracking sound.

"About a million times."

"I can't do it as easy as I used to."

"That's because you're getting old."

"Thanks a lot," Ivory says, licking the end of a length of pink thread and putting a knot in it. The only needle she could find has a blunt point from being held over a stove burner to sterilize it for purposes of splinter removal. She squints to thread it.

"You know what, Ivory? That blouse belongs in the ragbag."

Ivory ignores her.

"This girl I know in school, her sister was done over by *Glamour* magazine. In the magazine they had pictures of her,

Before and After. Maybe *Glamour* would do you, Ivory. You could write in and ask."

Ivory punches the needle from the wrong side of the cloth into the hole in the button. "Arlene," she says suddenly, "how do you think I'd look in gold eyeglasses?"

Arlene pauses in her pedicure and thinks this over for quite a long time. "Do you need eyeglasses, Ivory?"

"Not that I know of."

"I never heard of anybody wearing glasses when they didn't need to."

"These aren't just any old glasses. They're antique. They'd make me look unusual."

"You already look unusual."

"I don't know why I bother to ask *you* for advice," Ivory says, winding the thread around the button six or seven times and breaking it off with her teeth.

Arlene has removed the other sneaker and is operating on the left set of toes. "Ivory," she says, "do you think Mom and Dad still do it?"

"Do what?" Ivory asks absently, her mind still on the gold eyeglasses.

"*You* know."

"Oh, *it.*" She pushes her overlong brown bangs to one side of her forehead. "Well, I'd say they probably do it quite a lot."

Arlene drops a toenail paring onto the rug. "Have *you* ever, Ivory?"

"That's a pretty nosy question." She pokes the needle into a matchbook cover and packs it and the cough-drop tin into her sewing box. She puts the blouse back on. It is pink, rather rumpled, with a scalloped Peter Pan–type collar. The button she sewed on doesn't match as well as she'd hoped.

"But have you?"

"Maybe."

"Did you like it?"

"It was all right. I have to go cook."

"What are we having?"

"You'll find out. All in the fullness of time."

A new stain has materialized, Ray notes, on the dull-gold carpet near the counter where customers endorse checks and fill in deposit slips. It is at least the size of a dinner plate. The sight depresses him, and he prefers not to speculate on what accident or act of social irresponsibility might have caused it. Immediately taking matters into his own hands, Ray hefts a large foliage plant—a weeping fig, Muriel once told him it was called—from its accustomed position next to the receptionist's desk and places the plant, in its wicker basket, on top of the stain. An improvement to the casual bank customer, perhaps, but Ray will not be able to help remembering what is under the basket.

Briskly he walks past the fish tank and through the low swinging gate into the Life Insurance Department. Sometimes he feels like a tropical fish himself in his so-called office; there is no real escape from the public. Any Tom, Dick, or Harry is free to lean over the divider and, ignoring Ray's secretary, bellow for the attention of the manager, no matter if the manager is in the middle of writing a policy. Of course, after all these years Ray could easily write the most complex of policies in the express line at Star Market, but that isn't the point. Flynn and Hooks, the two other assistant treasurers—mortgage and loan officers—have the option of going into their private offices and shutting their doors and reading the newspaper or damn well picking their noses if the spirit so moves them.

But not the Life Insurance Manager. The bank does what it can to maintain the illusion that in granting loans and mortgages it is doing customers a favor; the men who negotiate them act with a sort of noblesse oblige. Selling life insurance, on the other hand, is still selling, however genteelly it is carried off, and a salesman must be at the public's beck and call at all times. Well, at least Ray is spared going into people's homes and smelling what they had for dinner and raising his voice over some quiz show on their television set while endeavoring to persuade them of their mortality. For that much, he is grateful.

As usual, the bank is stifling: the furnace going full blast even on this bright morning in Indian summer. Ray removes his herringbone sports jacket and turns each cuff back twice. For a bank officer, he has hairy forearms. A hairy chest, too, though few people know about that. Ray considers the hair on his body some small compensation for the relative sparseness of it on his head. The hair is finely textured and, in spite of his fifty-three years, hardly gray at all. On the first day of his vacation the previous summer he embarked on the cultivation of a beard, an undertaking he had contemplated for some time. But the beard came in dismayingly coarse and springy; after ten days he shaved it off again. Lillian remarked then that she'd thought the beard was a mistake from the beginning but hadn't wanted to say so. She expressed the opinion that only men with weak chins have any excuse to wear beards. Ray rubs his chin thoughtfully. No, his isn't weak, and the flesh on his jaw is not particularly slack, either; still, he's disappointed the beard didn't work out because he would have liked some sort of change.

He looks with irritation at his watch and then remembers that Madelyn, his secretary, will not be in today; she is in the hospital having periodontal surgery performed under general anesthesia. Ray politely did not let Madelyn know what he thinks about hospitalization for a gum operation, although that is the kind of nonsense that makes the cost of medical insurance outrageous for everybody. He'd concede that some people have low pain thresholds, and Madelyn is undoubtedly one of them. A silly, brainless girl who cannot spell to save her soul and whose most serious crises in life, up to now, have been split ends—whatever they may be. At once Ray feels guilty for his thoughts. *Judge not, that ye be not judged.* He believes in the principle, though the practice is often difficult.

Amid the clutter in Madelyn's desk he locates a container of fish food; he gives the fish in the tank a modest pinch. He suspects Madelyn of overfeeding them, which is why there is occasionally a small corpse floating on the surface of the water when he comes into the bank in the morning. He is sensitive about these deaths; they tend to get the day started off on the wrong foot. Well, for these few days at least, the fish will be on a strict regimen, willy-nilly.

"Excuse me," a voice says, as Ray is capping the fish food container. "You seem to be out of slips."

"Slips?"

"The yellow ones, for taking out money. There aren't any."

Ray starts to tell the girl that the manager of the Life Insurance Department is not in charge of replacing withdrawal slips and then realizes that since she found him feeding the fish, in his shirt sleeves, she can't really be blamed for presuming him to be a low-level employee. "Mrs. McElroy," he calls to one of the tellers behind the glass partition, "withdrawal slips, please."

He watches, standing by the fish tank, as the girl moves back to the slip-filling-out counter. She accepts a slip from Mrs. McElroy and bites the end of the pen chained to the counter. Something about her odd little asymmetrical face with its pointed chin, or perhaps the faded shawl knotted around her shoulders, makes her seem not quite to belong in a savings bank on a sunny Monday. She looks, it occurs to him, like one of those people you meet in the woods while gathering mushrooms or twigs for kindling and they grant you three wishes. Or turn you into a toad.

He returns to his office and opens a file drawer. With nimble care he sorts through the folders, discovering that several have been misfiled by Madelyn, and when he looks up again the girl is still at the counter. She has picked up a leaflet from the rack and appears to be studying it with more than casual interest. As though she'd been able to feel his eyes upon her she glances up at him and smiles a crooked smile.

> . . . *found a crooked sixpence against a crooked stile;*
> *bought a crooked cat, which caught a crooked mouse,*
> *and they all lived together in a little crooked house.*

Quickly he slides the file drawer shut and turns away.

Ivory hangs her raincoat on a nail in the stock room and, on impulse, drapes the paisley shawl over her wood table. The effect isn't bad. She runs water into her mug, plugs in the coil water heater, and sticks it into the water. She has, she decides, enough time for a cigarette with her tea. Not that customers will be banging the door down right on the dot of ten—or any other time, for that matter.

She dangles a tea bag into the mug by its string, twirls it around, and deposits it on the edge of the chipped saucer she uses for an ashtray, away from the butts. She'll brew tea out of the same tea bag three or four more times during the day, unless she happens to be feeling unusually low in the middle of the afternoon, in which case she'll treat herself to a fresh one.

Making a hissing tune in her teeth, she carries the mug and

ashtray to the table and sets them on the shawl. Then she lights a Salem and pokes through the contents of her cloth tote until she finds the by now rumpled leaflet. *Savings Bank Life Insurance Rates and Information* it says on the cover. *The Buy of Your Life.* Taking a medicinal drag on the cigarette, Ivory turns the leaflet over. *Union Square Savings Bank* is stamped on the back, and underneath that, *Life Insurance Dept. Raymond Bartlett, Mgr.*

Now she knows his name, the man behind the swinging gate. She's observed him countless times giving instructions to the girl with the frizzy perm, leaning toward the girl's desk and holding his tie against his shirtfront with a flat palm. Or scanning a computer printout. Or talking into his beige Touch-tone telephone, pensively depressing and retracting the button on the end of a ball-point pen. Never before has she seen him feed the tropical fish, however. She liked that: the quiet attentive gesture.

Ivory blows a ragged smoke ring and opens the leaflet to an inside page. *Straight Life* is printed in bold green letters above eight columns of figures. It is stupefying just to look at all the numbers; her own talents do not include mathematics. Nevertheless, she has an intuition about this Raymond Bartlett, Mgr. In spite of his competence with numbers and manifest competence in general, she feels he is a sensitive person. Maybe it's the way his ears, as delicately formed as the insides of snail shells, lie so close and modestly to his head.

She swallows the rest of her lukewarm tea and puts out her cigarette. Then she reaches for the telephone directory and locates his address.

Later on, as she's prying the staples from a cardboard case of tiddlywinks sets, it occurs to her how odd it is that already she knows so much about Raymond Bartlett and he knows nothing at all about her.

Three

·················

DIANE AND ARLENE are down in the front room squabbling over which program to watch and Roselle is in the bathroom with the water running. Richie has gone off to a union meeting. Leaving the supper dishes in the drainer to dry by themselves, Ivory shuts herself in her room. She puts on a Turkey-red challis skirt printed with black flowers that she bought for two dollars in the thrift shop across from City Hall. It comes almost to her ankles. On top a cream-colored blouse with fake pearl buttons and on top of that a black bouclé sleeveless sweater that comes down far enough to conceal the lapped-over and pinned skirt waistband. Then her beaver jacket, a flea market find, and a peaked wool cap discarded by Arlene that more or less matches the red in the skirt.

As quietly as she can manage in clogs she goes down the back steps, past the trash cans in the entryway, and along the skinny alley between the side of the next house and the park fence. In the park a couple of kids hunch over a joint under the basketball backboard. The backboard says *Sixers* in foot-high roughly painted letters, but it has no hoop, hasn't for years. Those Sixers may be dead or in jail or owners of fast-food franchises by now, but whoever they are, Ivory would bet they don't think about Osgood Park with much nostalgia. Or maybe they do, at that. It's amazing what the mind can accomplish.

"Hey, lady. Halloween's over."

Ivory pays no attention. Across from the park a few pigeons peck at the weeds and gravel in the big empty lot that is actually the bottom of a defunct quarry; lights are going on in the frame houses that line the top of the stone outcrop, thirty feet above her. Damp leaves stick to her clogs as she walks along, past Blaisdell's slate and roofing yard and through an opening in the rusty chain-link fence to Laurel Terrace. On account of the fence you can't drive to Laurel Terrace from this end; Ivory figures that the residents of Laurel Terrace hope Osgood Street decay will spread westward less quickly if it comes on foot. For a moment she feels perversely gratified to be violating this slightly better neighborhood, if only by tracking tree of heaven leaves onto its sidewalk.

At the corner of Summer and Central, in front of the Home for the Aged, she stops and lights a cigarette. It's not very far now to where she's heading, and she needs to calm her nerves, though really she has no plan in mind. There is a smashed jack-o'-lantern in the gutter, run over by a car, maybe, or just flung there by some prankster. The sight saddens her, even though, as the kid said, Halloween's over.

Westwood Road runs to the west off Central, one way the wrong way, with the Historical Society building on the corner. It's a wide street lined with some kind of prickly tree bearing feathery leaves and stiff black pods. The houses are old, built for just one family: still mostly used that way, Ivory guesses. She grinds the Salem out and begins to look for the number.

She finds it near the end of the one-block street. The house is gray stucco with peeling bottle-green trim, and a small porch, and a balcony supported on wooden pillars that look as though they have knees or elbows. Somebody is home: there is a light in a downstairs window, a bay window with many panes and with miniature cactuses in clay pots on the sills. Even on tiptoe she can't see inside; she'd have to climb the crab apple tree in the yard. Except for a light in the back of the house all the other windows are dark, and their shades are drawn.

Ivory crosses to the other side of the road and sits on a low brick wall in the shadow of some evergreens. She watches. The light in back may be a kitchen. Does a kitchen mean a wife?

Nobody has pruned the crab apple for a long time, and the puckered fruit still clings to the branches; the hedge is scraggly and has gaps where possibly animals or children have broken through. Raymond Bartlett's children?

She lights a second cigarette and ponders. When he fed the fish in the tank he did it with such attentiveness, as though he's not very used to feeding things. And although Ivory herself approves of the overgrown vegetation in the yard—she likes privacy and mystery and abundance—she knows she's not like other women, or at least the kind of women who live on Westwood Road, who are respectable and think about keeping up their property. So she finds it simple to expunge Raymond Bartlett's wife and children, as simple as cropping extraneous passersby out of a photograph.

A cat now emerges from behind an iron urn on the porch and walks stiff-legged down the steps. It is large, its black-and-white coat is patterned in random spots and splashes like camouflage, and its cheeks are so fat it might have mumps. Ivory wonders what appealed to Raymond Bartlett about this cat as a kitten to make him choose it. Or perhaps the cat was a stray who chose him? The cat pauses on the sidewalk to lick a white patch on its breast.

Ivory draws on her cigarette. The cat smells the smoke, perhaps, or has seen the lit end move in a jagged arc and suddenly flare. Its ears twitch; it is puzzled to see a person sitting on the brick wall, puzzled and curious. Heading toward Ivory it mews, a very faint sound for such a large beast, and crosses the road. It rubs its heavy skull against Ivory's skirt.

Without a second thought Ivory picks the cat up and begins to clop along in the direction of Central Street, quite casually, as if the cat were her own.

"He's come to grief. I just know it. I feel it in my bones."

Ray nips off the top of his soft-boiled brown egg with gilt chicken-shaped egg scissors. "I doubt that, Lillian."

"You never cared for Sammy the way your mother did," she says, her lips puckering reproachfully. "You just put up with him."

Lillian is, of course, talking about herself more than the cat, but Ray pretends not to be aware of the double meaning. "He'll turn up," Ray says, spooning some egg onto the corner of his toast.

Lillian dabs at her mouth with her napkin. "Perhaps not. And then you may find you miss him more than you ever dreamed."

"You could be right. But that's human nature, isn't it?"

"What is?" she asks after some thought.

"Only appreciating things after you've lost them."

"*I* appreciate things right now."

"Well, good." Ray scoops out the last of the egg. "I'm glad you're happy, Lillian."

He means it. He'd be pained to think she is dissatisfied with her life: other people's grievances, whether reasonable or not, tend to discomfort him.

He cuts a piece of toast in two and spreads some damson preserves on one of the halves. "If you're really worried about Sam, why don't you put an ad in the *Journal*?"

"That's quite a good idea, Raymond."

"You could offer a reward."

She considers, nervously fingering the hem of her napkin. "Do you think twenty-five dollars is enough?"

"More than enough," Ray says, pushing back his chair. He feels pleased to have solved the missing-cat problem, at least temporarily, and to have given Lillian something positive to do.

He puts on his reversible topcoat, tweed side out, and sets off for the bank. The walk, along Summer Street to Bow Street and into Union Square, can be done in twelve minutes if a person doesn't dawdle. The convenience is one of the reasons Ray never sought a position in a Boston bank; he could go home for lunch if he wanted to, though he rarely does.

Overnight the weather has turned chilly and overcast: the end, he fears, of Indian summer. Ray pulls on a pair of hand-knit gloves that Lillian bought for him at some church fair or other. She failed to notice a knobby blunder at the tip of one thumb. He sighs, thinking about her.

In Ray's sixteenth year his father died, and his mother, exhausted with mourning and with the effort of coping with a succession of unreliable local cleaning ladies, hired Lillian Dunlop to live in. She had the attic room papered for her, some linoleum laid down. The girl was barely twenty, the daughter of a house painter who had fallen on hard times during the Depression. She'd come up on the train from the small manu-facturing city southwest of Boston where she was born, glad to be given a job, compliant and eager to please. From the begin-ning she copied Bartlett ways as best she could. Her hair was long then and light brown, mousy. Out of Lillian's hearing Mrs. Bartlett referred to her as The Mouse. Yes, she was timid and also rather stupid; she did not seem conscious of Ray's fascination with her extraordinarily generous and at the time virtually unfettered bosom. He had never seen a woman's un-clothed body, except on trips to the Museum of Fine Arts with his mother, and for several years when he imagined one, it was Lillian's he imagined.

He still finds it embarrassing that he ever had those fantasies and he doesn't like to think about it.

Before his twenty-first birthday Ray went to live in New York City in order to attend the American Institute of Banking. That year he lost his virginity to a stenographer from Staten Island named Janeen. She soon rejected him in favor of a television repairman; in 1951 the jokes from Texaco Star Theater were on everybody's lips.

With his AIB certificate in his suitcase he returned to Westwood Road. His hair was already thinning at the temples and the crown. One night he collected Lillian from choir practice in his mother's car and Lillian let her gloved hand come to rest on his overcoated shoulder. He went on driving, pretending not to notice, and nothing like that ever happened again. If she had a crush on him then, or even if she is in love with him now, it isn't his fault. Nobody can claim with justice that he encouraged her in any way.

Madelyn comes in late with a mouth full of pink packing that looks disgustingly like bubble gum. He is kind to her, even though she makes more mistakes in the typing than usual and he is obliged to answer his own telephone.

At twenty minutes past nine in the morning Ivory unlocks the rear door of the toy shop and switches on the overhead bulb in the stock room. The tiddlywinks carton, lined with her paisley shawl, is empty. Perhaps it has all been a dream, like the vision of the doll in the plastic underwear box. No, the big mottled cat gazes at her from the wooden shelf above the sink; he has knocked her mug into the sink, breaking the handle off.

"Looking for something to eat, I bet," she says to him. "I brought you some cat food." She opens the can, dumps the food into her saucer ashtray, and sets it on the floor. "Cape Cod Style Platter. Doesn't that sound good?"

The cat mews softly but stays on the shelf.

"Maybe you found a rat and ate it for breakfast, tail and all. I wouldn't be at all surprised, though I've never actually seen one in here." She rips open a bag of litter and pours some into a foil roasting pan. "That's so you won't have to go outside. Union Square is awfully busy compared to Westwood Road. You wouldn't like it, take my word for it."

She sits at the table, once more minus a cloth, and lights a cigarette.

"Hoo, cat, looks like somebody was using you for target practice," she says, noticing for the first time the small hole in his chest. "That doesn't surprise me, either. Have you heard they were plotting to shoot the mayor of Chicago?"

The cat jumps down from the shelf via the edge of the deep sink and sniffs politely at the fish dinner. He doesn't eat any.

"Cats on TV chow that stuff right down. I hope you don't think I'm trying to poison you."

The cat pads away from the saucer and examines with interest various objects in the stock room: a snow shovel, a dented forty-cup coffee maker, a sack of rock salt, a dry mop, a toy one-armed bandit missing the arm. At the door leading to the front of the shop he stops and mews.

"I wouldn't mind letting you in there, but supposing Raymond Bartlett should take it into his head to buy a yo-yo or something. Then the jig would be up." Ivory brushes her bangs to one side. "Not that it's very likely, I admit. He's not really the yo-yo type," she says, putting out her Salem in yesterday's tea bag.

The cat returns to the fish dinner and again elects not to taste it.

"You certainly are suspicious. Come to think of it, that's what Fogel said about me. 'Discriminating' is the word I would have used. Maybe you are, too, but hell, the can cost forty-three cents. The least you could do is try it."

He licks the fur around the hole in his chest.

"In fifth grade I was class yo-yo champion. We lived in Taylor, Michigan, at the time, and I was the same age Arlene is now. I find that amazing. I was a smart kid but I didn't know much about how the world works. Arlene is the exact opposite.

"I was an expert at loop the loop, skin the cat—pardon the expression—and rock the baby. I was very good at taking tests, too. The right answer would just pop into my head at the crucial moment and then pop right out again after the test.

"I may have known how to skin the cat, but I didn't have too many friends. No sooner would I make one than my father would decide to move someplace else. I was an ugly kid, too. You know how in the funnies a roast chicken looks after the cat has got to it? That was me: all bones. My ribs looked like they'd been picked clean.

"Now I'm not quite so skinny and I can blow smoke rings and cook chili and drive a car with a standard shift. Listen, cat, this is a secret between you and me. Even if he's not the yo-yo type, I think I want him, your Raymond Bartlett."

Four

. . . .

ON THURSDAY, after Raymond has set off for work, Lillian brings the *Journal* out to the kitchen and spreads it out on the enamel-topped kitchen table. She pours herself a second cup of coffee. Taking the hankie from the sleeve of her morning glory–patterned housedress, she blows her nose, first through one nostril and then through the other. She puts on her reading glasses, the pair with the old prescription; the new pair she saves for more public occasions.

All her movements are slower than they would have been only a few years ago; in the mornings, especially, she feels sharp little twinges in her neck and left knee and a troublesome stiffness in her fingers. Still, she was fifty-eight last August and, unlike poor Cousin Flo, has never had a major operation. She supposes she should not complain about joint pains and digestive upsets and the occasional dizzy spell. The only thing to do, as the doctor says, is to take her time about things; she's not on her way to any fire.

She opens the newspaper to the classified page and reads through each item in the Lost and Found section. A Syrian lost his passport in Kennedy Airport on July 7 and prays the finder will be so kind as to return it to him. You have to feel sorry for the man—perhaps he is unable to return to his homeland without it—but whatever makes him think that a Somervillian might have found his passport in New York and kept it for four months? Lillian sighs. Lately the world seems full of desperate people with inexplicable things going on in their heads.

The last item in the column is the one she herself placed. Perhaps, she now thinks, she ought not to have included the line about answering to the name Sam Walter, since he doesn't even answer to Sammy. He arrives and departs with very little attention to the wishes of anybody else, certainly not Lillian. And yet he's never gone very far before, never been away a whole night, and now it's been three. That's what makes her so convinced something dreadful has happened to him.

Feeling rather sad and under the weather, Lillian pages through the rest of the newspaper. She has recently noticed that she doesn't enjoy it as much as she used to, the same way that the food she cooks doesn't taste as good, even though she uses the same recipes. Just the other night she made chicken tamale pie, which has always been such a favorite of Raymond's, and it came out tasting downright odd. Not that Raymond complained; when she brought it up he said it tasted the same as ever to him. But she knew different; he just wasn't paying attention. They do things to the ingredients. The canned corn or the stuffed olives. And how can a chicken have any flavor when it spends its whole life on a conveyor belt and never sees the light of day? She's read that's how chickens are raised nowadays.

The *Journal* isn't the same, either. You never read about anybody you know anymore. The ladies who belonged to Mrs. Bartlett's literary circle and came to the house in rotation every eight weeks for tea are either deceased or in faraway retirement communities; their names don't even turn up in the obituary column. And the youngsters who win prizes in the science fair or at graduation all have strange unpronounceable foreign names. Not that Lillian objects to that; she thinks it's wonderful when those boat people or whoever they are manage to get a good education and make something of themselves. That's what America is all about. Still, it *is* disappointing to feel so cut off from the place she's lived for thirty-eight years. And worse than useless to expect any sympathy or help out of Raymond. The tidbits he learns about customers at the bank are privileged information, as he calls it, and he is just as secretive about his social life. As secretive as a wombat. Lillian does not know a great deal about wombats—some kind of bat, she supposes—but somewhere she must have heard that they keep to themselves, and that would definitely describe Raymond. He's hardly any company at all.

Lillian folds the newspaper and puts it on the mail table in the front hall, where Raymond will see it when he comes in. She hopes he won't laugh at *Answers to the name Sam Walter.*

The *Journal* is on the table in Ivory's stock room, opened to the classified section and now embellished with tea rings, ashes, doodles, and cat prints. An unusual name for a cat, Ivory thinks. There must be, she decides, a quirky sense of humor in the man, disguised by his serious bankerly bearing.

Sam Walter does not seem to mind being a hostage. He plays with the Styrofoam peanuts that toys come packed in, a pink rubber rat, and a Ping-Pong ball. Ivory can hear his wild solitary games when she's out in front with the customers. It's the plumbing, she explains to them. The pipes have lately taken to making that hollow sort of bouncing sound. Yes, it *is* kind of like a Ping-Pong ball, now that they mention it. Staggering how gullible people can be. No wonder the quacks who sell snake oil and copper bracelets have no trouble unloading their wares. She's probably in the wrong business entirely.

The fact is that even if copper bracelets did ward off arthritis, you still wouldn't know what else was going to get you, or when, or where. Jam jars fall from airplanes and crash through windshields; the papers are full of things like that.

Ivory's mother died in a Laundromat while doing the family wash. It happened the year they lived in Niagara Falls, in February, and Ivory was not yet thirteen.

Two days after she died they found a folded note in her billfold, barely legible because of the creases and the red dye rubbed on it from the worn leather. It was a sort of will, leaving her add-a-pearl necklace to Ivory and her wedding ring to Richie, for the wife he'd someday marry. The part that surprised them was the last sentence: *If it's not too much trouble, I'd like to be buried at sea.*

In spite of all the moves the family made over the years she'd never lived anywhere near any ocean, never even seen one as far as anybody knew, but for some reason she'd had her heart set on it. Ivory and Richie kept pestering their father until he had to give in. No, Lake Erie wouldn't do. So the three survivors boarded a bus to Boston, which was the nearest place on an ocean that Greyhound went from Niagara Falls, carrying Frances Bright's ashes in a small white cardboard box. From the bus terminal, asking directions along the way, they walked to Boston Harbor and emptied the ashes into the black oily water. Well, maybe it wasn't exactly the burial her mother had dreamed of, but Ivory feels they did the best they could for her, considering.

On this trip Ivory's father met a man who told him about a job opening in Somerville, just outside Boston, and since he was unemployed at the time, they went back to Niagara Falls and packed up and moved East. Right in the middle of the school term, as usual.

"And that's how I ended up in Somerville," she says to S.W. It's nice to have somebody to talk to besides Roselle and Arlene and Diane, who are a lot more interested in the plot of some television serial than in Ivory's ruminations on fate.

Richie is always saying she ought to take an inventory so she'll know what in the name of God she *has* in that pack rat's nest she calls a store. Actually, Ivory does have a pretty good idea what she has and where, but she has to admit it's not all neatly written down in columns with numbers and prices and dates. Richie says that one day the little men from the IRS are going to come and cart her away and she shouldn't expect Richie to rush to her rescue. Ten days after the kidnapping of Raymond Bartlett's cat a sudden organizing mood comes over her, which occasionally happens when she is premenstrual.

"Okay, S.W., today is the day," she says, opening a newly purchased ledger to the first page.

She puts a hand-lettered sign in the display window saying *Closed for Pre-Christmas Inventory* and drinks two cups of tea from her handleless mug. Since there is now no danger of Raymond Bartlett bursting in by some act of God or fate, she lets the cat into the front of the store. He seems too dazed even to mew.

"It's true," she says cheerfully. " 'Pack rat's nest' hardly describes it."

Ivory stocks all kinds of toys, as many as she can cram into the little shop: stuffed animals jumbled together on the shelves; board games and jigsaw puzzles stacked from the top shelves to the ceiling; kites rolled up and stored in a wastebasket; kiddie cars and tea sets and steam shovels on the floor; party favors and penny toys in egg boxes on top of the counter. The counter is a glass display case she bought when a bakery on Bow Street went out of business. Inside are the dolls.

One wears a skating costume with rabbit fur trim on the skirt and a muff and tiny white leather skates with knife-sharp runners. Next to her is a wooden marionette in a silk Harlequin outfit. There is a boy doll wearing a hand-knit sweater and corduroy pants, and a bisque doll with real hair, and a life-size baby doll in a christening gown with a misshapen skull and a self-absorbed expression.

Children make breath marks and fingerprints on the glass, but their mothers don't buy the dolls in the case. They are expensive, for one thing. And Ivory doesn't encourage it. If somebody asks the price of one of the dolls she says she isn't sure, she'll have to look it up, and in the meantime the kid's attention will usually be diverted by a mechanical bank or stuffed penguin. Ivory holds a low opinion of the care children take of toys, rooted partly in the way Diane and Arlene dismantled and mangled theirs. Chinese checker sets with half the marbles missing; Legos scattered; dolls abandoned naked, their wigs matted and peeling loose from the scalp.

Ivory now recalls that taking inventory tends to remind her how the toys she sells will most likely end up. Maybe Raymond Bartlett feels that way, too; death is what those columns of figures in his tables are about, after all.

She decides that the vaguely uncomfortable feeling in her gut must be hunger. Leaving a stack of magic kits half-counted, she pulls on a baggy cardigan and goes out to Union Square in search of food.

It is a raw day, overcast, with gusts of wind blowing dead leaves and submarine sandwich wrappers about on the sidewalk. A sub, Ivory realizes, is exactly what she craves. Fried baloney and egg with hot relish and onions. It is her own invention. One day she talked Sally at the Triple A Sub Shop into making it for her, and now other people order it, too. Ivory sometimes urges Sally, half-kidding, to spell out *Ivory's Special Egg and Baloney* with the white plastic letters on the menu board behind the counter. (Sally is a man, christened Salvatore.) But Sally says he can't waste that many letters on one sandwich and besides he has only two *v*'s, which he has to use for cold veal loaf and liver and onion. Her one opportunity for fame and immortality, she complains to Sally, sabotaged by the stingy number of V's that come in a lettering set.

The Triple A is mostly empty when Ivory comes in and sits at the counter stool: too late for breakfast, too early for lunch. Sally isn't there, either. Shirley McWeeny, the other cook, explains that Sally is out sick. Sprained his arm bowling. Since Shirley's version of the egg and baloney special is only a limp imitation of the real thing, Ivory settles for a pepper steak.

The thin little frozen strips of beef curl and begin to turn gray on the grill next to the half-cooked green pepper dice. Somebody down at the far end of the counter orders an English, no extra butter, and a cup of coffee. Shirley slices the muffin open with a butcher knife and pushes the halves face down on the grill; after a minute or so she picks up an iron weight and flattens the halves down farther into the sizzling fat. Like a medieval torture, Ivory is thinking, and then she sees that the person awaiting this martyred muffin is Raymond Bartlett.

He looks only slightly out of place on the stool, and that more because of his pressed gray suit and general formal appearance than on account of any obvious unfamiliarity with the Triple A. In fact, Ivory thinks with a jolt, he's probably been coming to the Triple A every morning at eleven for years. Decades. If things had worked out differently, he might have noticed Ivory's Special up on the menu board. He might even have asked Sally who (or what) this Ivory is. "Oh, oddball girl runs the toy shop over by Wallpaper World," he'd say. "Toyland, she calls it." "But she ain't no babe," one of the regulars would say, cracking up.

Ivory feels a sudden relief and gratitude that the veal loaf has taken precedence, that her name is not up there spelled out in little plastic letters. How could any man possibly take her seriously if he connected her in his mind with a baloney and egg sandwich?

She swivels her stool so that he'd be unable to see her face if he looked her way, though actually he seems fully absorbed in something he is reading, and an obese mail carrier has planted himself on an intervening stool. Depressed, she waits for Raymond Bartlett to eat his English and drink his coffee and depart. When Shirley finally gets around to serving the pepper steak Ivory finds that the funny feeling in her gut wasn't hunger after all.

Ray hangs his topcoat on the oak coat tree in the hall, glances at the mail—an electricity bill and an L. L. Bean Christmas catalog—and goes into the lavatory to wash his hands. Several small brown blemishes on the back of his right hand seem to have gotten bigger. His mother had them in her old age: liver spots. She rubbed them, he remembers, with a cut lemon in the vain hope of fading them.

He pulls the rubber plug from the drain and the water seeps slowly into the hole, leaving a gray soapy scum in the bowl. The old pipes beginning to back up again, he thinks with irritation. No doubt he's gradually being poisoned with lead and God knows what other heavy metals and chemicals sloughing off the insides of the pipes. The entire plumbing system ought to be ripped out and replaced.

Same with the wiring, he thinks gloomily, reminded by the electricity bill; the whole thing is an inefficient and dangerous tangle liable to burst into flames any day and fry him in his bed. The problem is, you can't trust a contractor to do anything right and they charge an arm and a leg to do it wrong. He has half a mind to sell the damn house and move into an apartment.

There is no reason, he thinks, drying his hands, that Lillian couldn't move into an apartment, too—some *other* apartment, of course. Just because she's fifty-seven, or is it fifty-eight, doesn't mean she isn't capable of changing her life. It would be better for her, actually. She wouldn't have to cook for him, or clean a big house. These days her cleaning leaves something to be desired anyway; she doesn't seem to be able to see cat hair and dust balls anymore. Her cooking never was something to rush home to.

She could have her friends in for canasta or whatever. She must have *some* friends, people she knows through the church she goes to. Though come to think of it, she hasn't been getting out to church much lately. And she gave up going to choir practice ages ago. She didn't care for the new choir director, she explained, though Ray suspects what really happened was the new choir director had been courageous enough to weed the tin-eared old ladies out of the choir.

Ray sighs. He knows in his heart there's no hope of selling the house, at least as long as Lillian wants to live in it. And he's not so sure he'd like apartment living anyway. No matter how respectable and modern an apartment house, you'd still be subjected to other people's noises, other people's odors. He remembers the times he visited Muriel and her mother in their quite nice apartment on Highland Avenue near the library. A dog somewhere on the same floor yapped throughout one entire Sunday dinner, and on another occasion, when Ray was helping Muriel clear the table, the Disposall sludge from the apartment overhead suddenly gurgled up into Muriel's kitchenette sink. Ray shudders. At least whatever backs into *his* sink is his own.

He emerges from the lavatory and nearly bumps into Lillian in the hall. He feels a stab of remorse, as though she could have overheard his reflections on the subject of sending her off to fend for herself. On the other hand, he wonders if she was lurking there outside the lavatory the whole time he was washing, eager to pounce on him with some piece of bad news.

"Somebody telephoned," she says. "A woman."

Muriel? he thinks fleetingly.

"About Sammy."

"Has he turned up, then?"

"I don't know if it's Sammy or not. The woman says he's big and has spots."

"Sounds promising," Ray says, starting down the hall to the kitchen to get himself a drink.

Lillian follows. "She's on her way over. I suggested you could go wherever she is to make the identification, but she wouldn't listen to me."

Ray opens the cupboard over the refrigerator and takes out a bottle of blended whiskey. "I'm just as glad," he says, relieved he will not have to go into some woman's house and listen to a lengthy saga about how she rescued his cat from a terrible fate.

"Well," Lillian says hesitantly, tugging at the neckline of her dress. "Well, I suppose so."

The way her plump hands fumble with the cloth and with various straps or whatever just inside makes Ray uneasy; the exposed flesh above her bosom is reddened and loose, full of embarrassing little puckers.

"Is something wrong, Lillian?"

"I thought you wouldn't want a strange person coming into the house and looking around."

He measures an ounce and a half of whiskey into a glass and

adds some soda from a quart bottle. "That's going to extremes, isn't it?"

"You never know," Lillian says, beginning to lay strips of processed cheese on top of a casserole in an almost touching attempt at decoration. Before he can escape into his study with his drink she starts to tell him about a suspicious odor she noticed when hanging a dish towel out on the line. It was like something rotting. A fault in the gas main? A new pollutant released into the air by the plastic foam company over on Vernon Street? A dead mouse under the garage?

The doorbell rings.

Ray goes to answer it, happy to be spared, at least for the moment, having to speculate on Lillian's phantom odor or investigate its source. The person at the door is a skinny little thing, oddly dressed in a peaked red cap pulled low over her forehead and a moth-eaten beaver jacket. She stands on the jute mat, Sam in her arms, blinking awkwardly in the light from the hall.

"Where have you been, you wicked cat?" Lillian cries at Ray's elbow, reaching for Sam.

"We're very grateful to you," Ray says, trying to recall where he's seen this person before.

"That's okay." The girl shifts the cat in her arms but makes no move to hand him over. After a pause she says, "There was something in the paper about a reward?"

Ray feels at a disadvantage, not having remembered the offer of a reward. People have sometimes accused him of being a tightwad, a criticism he knows is unfair, and he resents it when he is inadvertently made to seem like one. "I'm afraid I keep very little cash in the house as a rule," he says. "Do you mind taking a check?"

"That's okay. I trust you."

Ray winces. "Please come in, then."

His checkbook is in the cherry secretary in his study, just off the hall. The girl follows him, still carrying the cat, and Lillian crowds in after them. He opens his checkbook and unscrews the cap from a fountain pen. "And your name?"

"Ivory Frances Bright."

"Ivy, is that?"

"Ivory. Like the soap," she adds, with a lopsided smile. He sees now that she is not really a girl, though he'd be hard-pressed to guess her age.

As Ray fills out the check she looks at things in the room: the miniature cacti on the sills, the oriental carpet, a framed steel engraving of Mont-Saint-Michel at high tide, a title or two in the bookcase, his leather armchair with its cracked seat and tarnished brass studs.

"We were so worried," Lillian is saying. "Was he a long way from Westwood Road?"

Sam nonchalantly stretches his forelegs.

"Not such a long way."

Ray detaches the check from the stub along the perforation and folds it crisply. "You've been very kind," he says, in a dismissive tone of voice. He does not want to know where Sam has been.

Afterward, though, he finds himself wondering who exactly she is, this Ivory Frances Bright, with her peaked red hat and downright spooky smile.

Five

....

IVORY DOES NOT KNOW what to do next.

She had visualized the return of the cat coming to pass in
a mood of quiet celebration. Raymond would, she had imagined, have difficulty finding just the right words to thank her.
He'd insist on giving her a glass of sherry, and sit with her on
a little sofa in the room with the cactuses, and begin to talk
about this and that. Lonely, he would think up ways of prolong-
ing the conversation—with anecdotes about Sam, perhaps, and
with small personal confessions and gentle probings into her
life. After a while he would pour more sherry into their glasses.

Instead, that awful woman shoved her great bust into the
doorway and tried to grab Sam out of Ivory's hands before
Raymond had a chance to say one word. Ivory had no choice
but to bring up the subject of the reward; she might as well
have been peddling megavitamins or collecting for the cancer
drive for all the chance she had to get past the woman and into
the house otherwise. Asking for the reward put Raymond off,
she knows that. As if she cares two hoots about the twenty-five
dollars.

No sherry, no little sofa, just that peculiarly shaped woman
bustling around asking idiotic questions. Could she be his
mother? It scarcely seems possible that Raymond Bartlett's
mother would henna her hair in such a tacky way, but Ivory

would not wish to be judged by the things her own relations do, either.

Ivory drops the folded check onto her panne crazy quilt and lights a cigarette. Not one single thing has gone right. And now she won't have the cat to greet her and keep her company in the shop. It would have been better to keep him.

She paces on the oval hooked rug, smoking and thinking. It is worse than being back to square one because now Raymond will be bound to recognize her, be wary of her, suspicious of her motives.

Outside, in Osgood Park, a man in an overcoat big enough for two of him is settling onto one of the splintery benches, probably for the night. Ivory can see a fragment of moon above Landers Street, at the far end of the vacant lot. A set of concrete steps goes up to the Landers Street level, the lip of the old quarry, from Osgood Street. A long time ago, also in November, Ivory sat on those steps with a boy. He was staying with a cousin in the neighborhood because of some trouble at home, wherever he lived; he was overweight and heavy-lidded, with black hair like porcupine quills and a five o'clock shadow even at the age of thirteen or fourteen. She let him poke around inside her clothes and touch her breast so she could find out what it felt like. Such a puny little breast under those, cold, thick, clumsy fingers. No good-looking boy ever wanted to do that to her, no boy at all ever bothered to ask her out on a date in order to negotiate the right.

She put out the cigarette.

What made her think anything had changed? What made her imagine that even out of loneliness Raymond Bartlett of Westwood Road, Manager of the Life Insurance Department and Assistant Treasurer of the Union Square Savings Bank, might be in the least likely to take an interest in Ivory Bright?

And he isn't lonely, obviously. There is that woman who

dyes her hair for him, and doubtless many friends and col-
leagues. He was probably on his way out to some social engage-
ment the very moment she arrived on his doorstep with his
stolen cat in her arms. No wonder he unscrewed the cap from
his fountain pen and made out the check so briskly.

She unfolds the check and looks at it. The handwriting is
self-confident and fluid, very different from her own left-
handed scribble, and his name is perfectly legible. This is a
person who knows who the hell he is.

Sighing, she chews on a cuticle. In the morning she'll find
the cat's china dish with food crusted in it and his soft belly
hair clinging to the paisley shawl, but no Sam. Lighting another Salem, she scoffs at herself for being sentimental over a
cat; she must really be losing her marbles. They say that happens to old maids.

She supposes she should just give up on Raymond Bartlett
and preserve what shreds of pride she still possesses. But she
knows she won't. She feels about him the way she did about
the gold spectacles in Fogel's window.

She gets the spectacles out of the tin repoussé box where she
stores her favorite odds and ends, and puts them on. The colors
in the room meld and soften. She hardly hears Diane calling
her to come eat.

Something about that girl made Lillian nervous. It wasn't only
that she looked like some kind of leftover hippie, and Lillian
never approved of hippies. Or that she examined so carefully
the things in Raymond's study, in particular the William Dean
Howells first editions that came down from Raymond's grandfather on his father's side and are said to be quite valuable.

No, Lillian decides, it was more the way Sammy acted. He
was as calm and placid in her arms as a rag doll. Almost as

though . . . *as though he had been drugged.* What if Sam was never "lost" at all? What if the girl is a member of a ring of house burglars who kidnap pets as an excuse to "case the joint"? Lillian has read about such schemes. Thieves who study obituary notices and then drive moving vans up to the homes of the deceased and empty them down to the floorboards while the relatives are attending the funeral. These days absolutely nothing is sacred.

Lillian, down on her knees and running a damp dustcloth along the rungs of the dining room chairs, imagines these very chairs carried roughly out to a moving van while the girl in the pixie hat gives orders. Lillian almost weeps. The needlepoint upholstery on these fine mahogany chairs was worked by Mrs. Bartlett herself. Well, nobody is going to carry off these chairs if Lillian can help it.

She hoists herself to her feet, using one of the heavy chairs for support. Oh, how that knee does ache. She might even need an operation, but she is certainly not about to submit to surgery while the house is in danger of being burgled.

If only she could share her anxieties with Raymond. But she knows very well what would happen if she tried that. He'd say she's "going to extremes" or smile and pretend to agree with her but actually be thinking about something else altogether. The trouble is he doesn't take her seriously, never has. Her kind of loyalty can't be bought with money, and Mrs. Bartlett appreciated that, but not her son. It isn't Christian to hope that one day he'll be sorry, but she can't help herself. She's only human.

She lifts a cut-glass candy dish on the sideboard to dust under it. The dish in fact belongs to Lillian; Mrs. Bartlett always said she was going to leave it to her in her will because it is Irish glass and Lillian is also Irish. She is, in a manner of speaking, though of course not one of those ignorant peasants from the south. When the will was read it appeared that Mrs. Bartlett had neglected to mention the dish specifically, but Raymond quite rightly said that it belonged to Lillian anyway. She left it on the sideboard rather than taking it up to her room because it had occupied that spot for generations and it seemed a shame to move it. Besides, the whole house is as much Lillian's home as it is Raymond's, not legally perhaps, but morally, and there is no reason why her candy dish should not sit on the sideboard, if that's where she chooses to keep it.

Sadly and slowly she lifts and dusts under the other decorative pieces on the sideboard: a three-tiered lazy Susan; a glass decanter one-quarter full of shooting sherry, the level of which has changed in the three years since Mrs. Bartlett's death only by evaporation; a pink and gold vase that Mrs. Bartlett considered not in the best of taste but displayed on the sideboard because the late Mr. Bartlett had acquired it in his travels. The girl can take *that* away if she wants. Probably knows no better. Taste is the last thing that girl would have, dressed the way she was.

Lillian goes out to the kitchen, limping a little, and opens the back door. It is a chill day, looking like rain; the odd odor Raymond refused to take notice of lingers in the damp air, clinging to unraked leaves and pods. As Lillian shakes her dustcloth over the stoop, Sam pops out from the barberry hedge and scoots past her through the open door. Thinking of the girl, Lillian scowls. What a nuisance cats can't talk.

Muriel Neely has sent a picture postcard from Arizona. On the front is a giant cactus, shaped like a pickle but more garishly green, covered with spines, and with a large white waxy flower erupting from the crown. On the other side Muriel has written in her neat Palmer Method handwriting: *This one is a little bigger than yours.*

Ray flushes and laughs and tucks the card into his pocket. Surely she could not have realized what she was doing; even in her disappointment—and Ray is ready to acknowledge that she was, in all probability, somewhat disappointed—Muriel would never wittingly have been so vulgar. One of those Freudian things, no doubt. Poor Muriel: such a quiet, shy, kind person. He hopes she will find a husband in Arizona, but he fears she will not. A cowboy would be even less likely to figure out how to deal with her.

Ray courted Muriel for six years and never went to bed with her. Well, "courted" does not accurately describe the situation, perhaps. Although he thought about marriage, and even went so far as to reflect on questions of finance—trusts, wills, and various insurance options—he did not specifically use the word "marriage" in conversations with Muriel. Nor did he mention the matter to his mother, who would not have been overjoyed at the prospect of his marrying a Catholic, even though strictly speaking Muriel was Catholic on her father's side only and not a practicing one. Mrs. Bartlett had begun by then the long decline that preceded her death, and there was no point in upsetting her unnecessarily.

But if "courted" is not exactly what he and Muriel did, at least there was a long and friendly association, hardly a bitter word spoken between them. There were many meals in her apartment, her mother Doris presiding over the roast, and the occasional visit to his own house, his mother propped up in bed and Lillian sullenly pouring the coffee and serving the date-nut cake. He saw Muriel every day at the bank, of course, where she never presumed on their private relationship, and he was always grateful for her soothing presence at staff parties. One year they had tickets to Symphony. Often they went to museums; they preferred the Fogg and the Busch-Reisinger to the MFA because of the more manageable size. On one memorable July Sunday they went to Fenway Park and ate hot dogs and stood during the seventh-inning stretch. The hot dogs were overpriced and the Red Sox ignominiously trounced, he recalls.

It is true that Muriel was a gentle and agreeable soul, but sexually she was about as easy to maneuver as that giant cactus and all its spines. One difficulty was that there was practically no place they were able to be alone, at least not in the natural course of events: certainly not at his house—after his mother died there was still Lillian—or at Muriel's apartment, or at the bank, or in Symphony Hall. And so far as he could tell, Muriel was quite oblivious to the need. Whenever he organized some plan to land them alone together—a weekend trip to New York City, for example, or a drive to the western part of the state to view the foliage—something inevitably came up. His mother would take a turn for the worse or Muriel herself would catch the flu. One thing about Muriel: she always seemed to be coming down with something or recovering from something, her nostrils red and her acne inflamed, and from time to time she referred obscurely to some chronic ailment he did not inquire into.

When the trip fell through, Muriel would express disappointment but give no indication she understood what the trip was *for.* Is it possible for a woman in her thirties, though almost certainly a virgin, to be so very naïve? Well, she is in her thirties no longer. They did not celebrate her fortieth birthday with what had become the customary restaurant outing; she was too busy with packing and other arrangements connected with the move to Phoenix to spare the time, as she apologetically explained to Ray over the telephone.

The same psychoanalyst who might be coaxed into explicating the significance of Muriel's cactus might also point out to Ray his fatal failure to take control. Yes, he knows all about it. Easier to say in retrospect, though, or about some other person's muddle.

Last February something surprising happened. A woman who lived in her apartment building persuaded Muriel to buy a raffle ticket for some charity, and Muriel, who claimed never to have won so much as a turkey in her life, won the grand prize: a holiday for two on the island of Aruba in the West Indies, eight days and seven nights, all expenses paid.

But Ray, when invited, declined to accompany her. He could not tell her why. He invented a story about confidential merger negotiations coming to a head for which his presence was mandatory. Well, not in fact *mandatory:* Muriel was familiar enough with the inner workings of the bank to realize that might be an overstatement. But prudent, at least, for a bank officer with ambition. And so Muriel flew off to Aruba with her mother, whose arthritis apparently benefited from the change in climate an amazing amount in just one week.

What Ray could not admit to Muriel was that he was unable to swim. Not that Muriel would change her overall opinion of him, he felt confident, if she knew the truth. However, he saw that it could be difficult to get her to trust his masculine expertise in bed if all he did during the day was sit on the beach or wade into the sea up to his ankles. A mistake on his part, perhaps, but what's done is done.

Ray takes the postcard out of his pocket. No doubt Lillian has spent the afternoon digesting it and has stored up many comments on cacti and Arizona and Muriel for delivery over dinner. Well, at least she is too stupid to have caught Muriel's slip. He might as well be grateful for that, he reflects, dropping the card into the wastebasket.

IVORY BRIGHT

. . . .

It is now the end of November, the days short and raw, Union Square well settled into dingy gloom. Ivory, wearing a buttoned-up cardigan worn through at both elbows, is crouched in the display window of her shop. She is sprinkling fake snow onto the crèche she's arranged on a draped white sheet; her hand full of gritty snow, she sees Raymond Bartlett round the corner of Sherman Hardware and wait for the light to cross Somerville Avenue. He is heading for the dry cleaner, maybe, or the Chinese carry-out, but as the light changes he makes a sudden jog and is now moving in the direction of Wallpaper World. He pauses under the striped awning of the toy shop, hands in pockets, and looks into the window.

On the other side of the glass his head is no more than a foot away from Ivory's; she has never been so close to him. Unaware of her, or who she is, at least, he examines the painted wooden crèche figures: wise men, camels, cows, angels. He wears no hat; his delicate ears are pink with the cold.

Ivory waits, scarcely breathing, the snowflakes cupped in her hand, for him to look up and recognize her. He does. His lips part slightly in surprise, but he doesn't smile. Nor does she. Seconds pass. At last he shrugs his neck into his gray woolen scarf and moves away out of her sight, toward Wallpaper World. She opens her hand and lets the shiny flakes drift down on angels and camels.

By afternoon a little real snow has begun to fall, the first of the winter, and when he enters the shop there are oversized irregular crystals stuck to his coat and scarf. "Hello," he says.

"Hello."

He clears his throat. "I noticed, when I balanced my checkbook the other day, that the check I wrote you was still outstanding."

"I guess I haven't got around to cashing it yet," she says, pushing up the sleeves of her old cardigan, too late to hide the holes.

"I thought perhaps you had misplaced it."

"No, I just . . . No."

He is looking around in a confused sort of way, stunned, probably, by the extraordinary profusion of objects jumbled on all sides.

"I didn't know you worked here," he says. "For some reason I never noticed this shop before." He sounds as if the shop has sprung up overnight like an unpleasant variety of mushroom.

"How is your cat?"

"Very well," he says, playing uneasily with the fringe of his scarf. Ivory wonders whether he is uncomfortable because of the way they stared at each other through the glass or whether he is simply eager to make a quick getaway now that he has admonished her about the check. His fingernails are neatly pared and as clean as a surgeon's. It is obvious he has never bitten them, and there are no tobacco stains on his fingers, either. "He seems to have given up wandering," he says.

"Recovered from the gunshot wound?"

"It was an abscess."

An abscess. She doesn't know what he means and decides she'd better not ask. If he's in a hurry to leave he doesn't seem to be able to extricate himself; he's looking at the cover of a jigsaw puzzle box, a simple one for preschoolers.

"If you're into puzzles, I have more complicated ones," she says, brushing her bangs away from her forehead. Because the shop is warm the bangs are damp and stay where she's pushed them.

"I'm not very good at them."

"They *are* kind of a waste of time."

All toys are, he's probably thinking, but he says, "I used to help my mother fit in middle pieces of sky. When she was dying," he adds, as though to explain why she would have needed his help.

So. The woman he lives with is not his mother.

"My mother's dead, too," Ivory says, after a pause. "She died in a Laundromat. Electrocuted by a faulty dryer."

"I'm sorry."

"That's all right. It happened a long time ago."

She knows she has said a stupid thing; Raymond looks more uncomfortable than ever. Respectable people do not die ridiculously in undignified places like Laundromats.

In the street a truck backfires and they both jump. Somehow or other she has to divert the conversation away from sudden death. "I'm not very good at puzzles either, but at one time I was a yo-yo champion."

He smiles, bemused; clearly he's never looped the loop in his life.

"Of course, *that* was a long time ago, too."

"Well, I must be getting back to the salt mines," he says, adjusting his scarf and pulling on a pair of gloves. The gloves are definitely hand-knit, probaby made for him by the woman-who-is-not-his-mother, Ivory thinks dismally. Ivory does not know how to knit.

"Come in again," she says, as he moves toward the door. "Anytime."

"I will," he answers, but he doesn't look back, and she figures she's blown it, once again.

Six

....

RAY IS IN THE YARD raking up pods and leaves and twigs,
and withered little crab apples that have somehow migrated
around the corner from the front of the house, and is stuffing
it all into a black plastic trash bag.

The spooky face of that girl troubles his thoughts. Perhaps
it was the crèche in her shop window, or perhaps the way she
looked with her hair pushed away from her forehead, that
makes him think of the crudely carved wooden statues in the
Busch-Reisinger. It's true: her lopsided face is like the warped
perspective of those faintly disturbing medieval madonnas, and
she has the same smile. He can't quite think of a word for it.
Not cunning, exactly, but not really guileless, either.

Astonishing to discover the strange little toy shop right there
next to Wallpaper World—how is it that he never noticed it?
—but absolutely appropriate to find the girl there.

He remembers a book he was given when he was six or seven.
On the cover was a drawing of the old man Gepetto, his
shoulders hunched, his face grimly determined, taking a knife
to the log that would become Pinocchio. Who would run away
with the bad boys and grow a donkey tail. Ray grew to hate the
book so much that he smuggled it out of the house and threw
it down a storm drain.

What upset him, he thinks now, was the idea that a toy

might have the power to become something else, something uncontrollable. As he rakes, the anxiety he felt then is once again alive for him.

And yet the girl is clearly harmless. A little lonely, a little eccentric. Certainly disorderly: neglecting to deposit his check though she must scarcely earn a penny out of that business. Disorderly . . . and nervous: the bitten fingernails, the squashed butts in the ashtray on her counter. Somebody ought to tell her not to smoke in that firetrap of a shop; all that wood and paper and plastic would go up in seconds. An insurance adjuster's nightmare, and not a very pleasant way to meet one's maker, either.

Electrocuted by a faulty dryer. Extraordinary. Odd people to whom odd things happen. Imagine a mother who would give a daughter such a name. Was a bar of soap the first thing she saw after giving birth? Or was it ivory like the elephant tusk that she had in mind? Or dice, or teeth, or piano keys?

A girl from a patchworky kind of background; a girl with a slangy and mumbling way of speaking, in an accent that isn't local, isn't anything at all he can identify. A yo-yo champion!

Ray stops to free some leaves that have become impaled on the rake. His hands, even in woolen gloves, are frozen, and so are his ears. Winter has crept up on him this year.

Lillian, cranking open the casement window above the kitchen sink, calls out to him, "Do you smell it *now?*"

"Smell what?" he answers, pretending to have no idea what she is talking about. If Lillian were as sensitive to odors as all that, you'd think she would have discovered underarm deodorant. He can't think what is going on in her mind when deodorant commercials come on the television. He supposes she feels they don't apply to her, any more than the ones for sports cars or white wine or credit cards do. Doubtless her mother taught her that good honest Protestant soap is all a person needs in this life, and half a century later she still believes it.

Lillian jerks the window shut, having given up. Now he'll have to endure her pinch-mouthed silences over leftovers. They always have leftovers for Saturday supper, so she can start out fresh with a roast on Sunday. The inevitable Sunday roast, as tough and tasteless as particleboard.

Sometime he wishes he'd made more of an effort to wrest Janeen away from the television repairman. Whatever else might be said about Janeen, at least she could cook. Twisting the wire tie around the neck of the trash bag, he remembers the feel of her plump warm body after a meal of herring salad, stuffed cabbage, and apricot cake in her Staten Island apartment, and the exhilarating ferry ride back to Manhattan in the small hours of the morning. He didn't mind cold so much then. Janeen would be fat now, and most likely a grandmother. If he'd married her and given her babies, he'd be a grandfather. Strange to contemplate.

He drags the bag of dead vegetation around the corner of the house and out to the curb for collection. It depresses him, in an insubstantial, vaguely melancholy way, to think of the Bartletts ending with him. Not a very fertile family, only one or two sons in each generation, and now dwindled down to none.

It strikes him that what he'd like most in the world right now is a hot whiskey and milk. He's chilled to the bone; he deserves it, though it's only four in the afternoon. He goes into the house humming, but it's not long before something reminds him of that Ivory girl again. As he's putting the rake away in the basement he hears his and Lillian's clothes tumbling and turning in the electric dryer.

....

Lillian is aware of it all the time now, and not only in the yard: a gassy, rusty odor that is sometimes like rotting food and sometimes like—she flushes at the thought—blood in a sanitary napkin. She doesn't dare mention it to Raymond anymore; he's made it plain that so far as he is concerned the odor is all in her head, and he doesn't care to be bothered by it further.

It *can't* be in her head; she is not mentally unbalanced. She has never in her life had hallucinations, nor has anyone in her family. The Dunlops were solid, practical, down-to-earth people. Well, except for her cousin Flo, but flighty is not the same thing as crazy.

On her own, when Raymond is at work, she makes investigations. She sniffs at the exposed gas pipes to try to detect a leak. She searches with a flashlight under the range and behind the Frigidaire on the chance that a turnip or apple rolled there and began to decompose. She struggles to move the boxes stored in the basement and garage in case Sammy caught a small animal and abandoned it there to rot. She telephones the gas company to suggest there might be a leak in the main and the police to inquire whether one of the city's industries has been releasing something unusual into the atmosphere.

She even forces herself to face the possibility that something about her own person might be the culprit. She boils her underwear and throws out her slippers and the foam innersoles of her shoes and sends her dresses to the dry cleaner in batches. She bathes with brown soap and uses medicated shampoo on her hair and douches with vinegar.

And still the odor remains.

On account of it other things go wrong. The snowball cookies she makes every December come out this year hard— Raymond says it and she can't blame him—hard as little golf balls; the sauce for her creamed peas curdles; she clean forgets to send Flo the regular postal money order until Flo writes tactfully wondering if it got delayed in the Christmas rush.

She feels she *will* go crazy if she doesn't find a way to get rid of the odor soon, and yet Raymond goes blithely about his own affairs, totally oblivious to her distress.

The odor began the day Sammy came home, but he can't have brought it with him, since she first became aware of it *before* that girl appeared at the door. It was, she remembers, just about the time she received the telephone call. She'd hung up the phone and gone back to the kitchen to finish drying the mixing bowls and saucepans—she always washes them before dinner so she won't have to do them afterward—and when she put the dish towel out to dry, that's when she noticed it. But the smell wasn't so bad then; she'd been merely curious to know where it came from, the way you'd naturally wonder about anything new or odd. How could she have guessed that the smell would come to take over her whole life?

Well, she can connect the onset with the ugly girl's call, but how far does that get her? The girl couldn't have set it off by telephone. She's not a *witch* after all, though she may look like one.

Lillian is stumped. The pain in her left knee is worse and she has a pain in her back now as well, the result of all that crouching to peer under things and moving so many boxes without a scrap of help from Raymond, who is preoccupied with his own thoughts more than ever these days, it seems to her.

As Ivory tears open the cellophane on a fresh pack of Salems she sees, under the dangling stock room light bulb, that sparkles of artificial snow cling to her fingers. Absently she rubs her hand on the bib of her painter's overalls. Now the overalls sparkle, too, and she smiles wryly. Oddball Ivory all dressed up for Christmas, oddball Ivory Snow.

She hasn't always dressed like a freak. Back when she had her first full-time job working at the dry cleaner's she spent a big chunk of her salary in downtown department stores, Jordan's and Filene's, and not always in the basement, either. A lot of good it did her. Necklines that looked all right in the dressing room mirror gaped strangely as soon as she got the blouses home; skirts stretched and sagged and hung limply to her shins. In those days she still imagined that if she kept her mouth shut and wore what everybody else wore, people wouldn't notice she was different. She hardly said a word to customers beyond asking whether they wanted starch in their shirts and did they recall the origin of the stain on the tie and would Monday be satisfactory for the slacks. Of course, none of her efforts had done any good. She overheard remarks about her and saw girls, younger than she, rolling their eyes in her direction and then at each other in a meaningful way. Meaning *get a load of her.* It was a relief when she didn't earn a salary anymore, when she needed to put every cent back into the toy store and had the excuse to dress in secondhands and hand-me-downs.

She drags on a cigarette and looks down at the sparkles on her bib. It was Christmastime the second year she worked at the dry cleaner's when she got into the jam. Roger drove the delivery van. He was big and broad and fair, with a floppy unathletic body and a kindly face. He drove the van all around to different towns, delivering dry cleaning in plastic sacks to the branch stores and returning to the plant in South Boston with the soiled clothes in nylon bags. He didn't seem to mind the job. At first Ivory thought he must be "slow"; how else could he be so cheerful? Maybe he slept in one of those shelters for the mildly retarded and was let out during the day because he was trustworthy and didn't stray out of the delivery area and didn't dent the van or get into disputes with the customers. And then she heard him say he had two children, and she didn't suppose that shelters would put up with *that*, so maybe he wasn't slow after all, just congenitally cheerful.

That Christmas Eve she worked until six, the only clerk in the shop. No point in staying open so late—people were thinking about other things besides laundry—but the management wouldn't have been interested in Ivory's opinion. Just before closing, Roger came in to collect the day's accumulation of dirty clothes. Lifting the two nylon bags, he asked was she hungry. He'd be getting something from the Chinese carry-out next door before making the trip back to South Boston; maybe she'd join him in a bite, just for the company.

While Roger was ordering the food Ivory locked up. The van was parked in Webster Avenue, next to St. Joseph's. They sat in the back with the bags of dirty laundry from all the different towns, the van reeking of carbon tetrachloride. They ate out of the little white cardboard cartons, using fingers because Roger had forgotten to ask for plastic forks: egg rolls, chicken wings, honey-dipped spareribs. They laughed and licked their fingers. When they realized they were thirsty Roger left the van to buy a six-pack of beer. They drank it out of the cans and sang "Joy to the World" and "God Rest Ye Merry, Gentlemen," in the dark. They sat close together for warmth, and when the beer was all gone, he opened her coat and gently made love to her.

On the following Monday she gave in her notice and soon started to work for the watch repairer around the corner. Of course Roger never knew anything about the abortion. Years later, when he came into the toy store to buy a present for one of his kids, she and Roger talked in a casual friendly way. No browser in the shop could have looked at them and guessed: *This man and this woman committed adultery. He took her virginity. She aborted the issue of their sexual act. She has not known a man in the biblical sense since.* Now his kids must be just about grown-up, so he'd have no reason to come into the shop, and besides, she's noticed that somebody else has been driving the van these last couple of years.

Once in a while Ivory wonders what has happened to him, but not very often. She has no regrets—not about Roger, anyway.

Ivory stands at the little swinging gate, waiting for Raymond's secretary to notice her. In the end it is Raymond himself who looks up from the document on his desk and, startled, says, "Ah."

The secretary turns from the copy machine. When she opens her mouth to say, "Yes?" Ivory can see that one of her lower incisors is bluish, as though the nerve is disconnected from the gum. Like a Christmas tree bulb that won't light, Ivory thinks. "Yes?" the secretary says again.

Raymond has half risen from his swivel chair. The secretary glances at him, shrugs, and turns back to the copy machine. Ivory goes through the gate and sits in the vinyl chair next to Raymond's desk. "I'm interested in a life insurance policy," she says.

"Well," Raymond says, smiling a little, "that's what we're here for." Lightly he weaves his fingers together and places them in the center of his blotter. Feathery brown hair grows on his wrists; he's wearing a gold expansion watchband. "At the present time," he begins, "what would you say your situation is, with regard to life insurance?"

She unbuttons her beaver jacket. "I don't have any."

This does not seem to surprise him. "We offer a variety of plans. To meet individual needs."

He has begun to stroke, with a slow circular motion, the back of one hand.

"Individual needs," she repeats, staring at his hands.

"For instance, we have a new plan called the Nonsmoker's Special."

"I smoke. Like a chimney," she says rashly, as if she means to provoke him.

He clears his throat. "If you quit, you would be eligible to apply in only one year."

"I don't know if I could do that," she says, wishing she could light up right now. "Besides, I might be hit by a truck tomorrow."

He pauses, perhaps picturing bits of Ivory stuck to the Bow Street pavement. "Well, there's Straight Life. Or Twenty-Payment Life. Or Life Paid Up at Age Sixty-five. On each of those policies cash and loan values begin in the first year."

Ivory cannot imagine living to age sixty-five, or anywhere near it. Calamities run in her family. Now that she's here, the choices are more complicated, the implications greater, than she'd anticipated. And there is the question, she sees now, whether her life is even worth insuring. "Maybe I should forget the whole thing," she says, starting to button up her jacket.

"I have the impression you don't realize that life insurance can be a form of saving," he says. He picks up a ball-point pen and taps his blotter with the retracted point. "It is none too soon to plan for your future. Have you considered what you will do for income when you retire?"

"I guess I haven't thought that far ahead."

"No. People don't. They live their lives any old way and then find it's too late."

The bitterness in his voice surprises her. Probably he resents all those people walking through Union Square who could be paying premiums to the bank and are instead recklessly spending their money on six-packs of beer or rolls of wallpaper. Or toys.

"You could end up a bag lady if you aren't careful," he goes on, the shells of his delicate ears turning white in his exasperation.

"I already am a bag lady."

He ignores this. "You don't even cash your checks," he says, raising his voice. "That is a lunatic way to organize a life."

"I do so cash checks. Just not yours."

"Just. Not. Mine."

There is a silence. Ivory realizes that Raymond's secretary and several customers standing at the slip-filling-in counter are listening with casual curiosity to this exchange.

"No," Ivory says softly. "I didn't want to."

Of course she cannot tell him that she'd be accepting a reward for an animal she herself had stolen. Or admit that she likes to take the check out of her tin repoussé box and unfold it to look at his handwriting.

"I suppose you thought it would be amusing to keep my checking account unbalanced forever."

She can't tell whether he is making a joke. She decides he probably isn't. "Why don't you stop payment—"

He sighs and tugs at his tie to loosen the knot.

"—since it bothers you so much?"

"I want you to have the money, Ivory." He takes two tens and a five out of his billfold and reaches across the desk for her hand. He puts the money into her hand and closes her fingers around it, crumpling the bills. "Be so kind as to tear up the check," he says, and Ivory feels the sharp edges of the new bills cutting into her palm.

Seven

·················

IT IS NOW THE NEW YEAR, a damp day with a pale sun and a listless wind. There have been a few inches of snow, but they melted in a hard rain after Christmas, so that the sidewalks in Union Square are clear except for rock salt and gravel flung down by the merchants to provide traction and avert suits. Sale signs are up in the store windows now, *Drastically Reduced, Everything Must Go*, contributing to the dismally left-over look of the Christmas decorations. Cardboard Santas and angels have become partly unstuck and hang crooked, the cellophane tape that holds them having loosened in the damp; no one bothers either to fix them or to take them down altogether.

Ivory has not laid eyes on Raymond since the abortive attempt to buy life insurance. She thinks about his hand covering hers, his muscles tensing, shutting the reward money inside. An impulsive and meaningless gesture, she tells herself, or if not meaningless, then what it signified was no more than his eagerness to be rid of her. *I want you to have the money, Ivory.* Her name seemed to come easily to him; he didn't have to struggle to remember it. But it's an oddball name, the kind that sticks in your head, maybe, whether you want it there or not.

Her determination to have him is crumpling, not because he is less desirable to her—the reverse is true—but because she doubts whether she is worth having in return. It isn't a new doubt, but sometimes she is capable of damping it down underneath her hopes. Misbegotten hopes, she's thinking, taping up her own January sale sign.

Misbegotten toys, too, a little shopworn. Doomed to be purchased reluctantly, if at all, because they are bargains at half price.

She laughs out loud to shake herself out of melancholy and blows a wobbly smoke ring. The hell with giving up smoking. The man had a nerve to suggest it; what's it to him if she speeds along her own demise? Let him worry instead about the old bird who knits his gloves. She might as well face it: his wife. Lots of men don't wear wedding rings.

Richie opens the door of the toy shop and bangs it behind him. He's wearing a number of layers of sweaters and jackets, a watch cap with the cuff rolled back so that it sits on his head like a woolen halo or doughnut, and ugly tan boots from an army surplus store. He's thin, like Ivory, though a person could hardly tell it when he's bundled up that way, and his features are like hers—same pointy chin, hazel eyes, same wide mouth —but in his case stuck on straight instead of lopsided. "Hiya, kid," he says. "What's the good word?"

In the six years since Ivory opened the shop this is practically the first time Richie has come in on his own hook, without having been wheedled into moving a heavy crate or doing something to the plumbing. It's such an unusual event that she's immediately worried. "What are you doing in Union Square?" she says.

"They got me on the Christmas tree detail. Hard on the hands, Christmas trees. Needles and tinsel and sap."

"You should wear gloves."

He looks in mock wonder at his raw hands. "Now why didn't I think of that?"

"Is this a social visit, Richie?" she asks, stubbing out her cigarette.

"Not exactly, no." He plucks the cap off his head and sets it on top of the cake-display glass counter. "I have to talk to you."

"What about?"

"Maybe you noticed Roselle's been acting kind of peculiar lately?"

Ivory tries to think back. No more peculiar than usual, but then Ivory's attention has often been elsewhere in the past few months. "She's not sick, is she?"

"Warm."

"Richie. You're not getting a divorce."

He laughs, rather guiltily, she thinks, as though she hasn't quite hit on it, but she's come closer to some sort of truth than he'd be willing to admit. "She's pregnant."

"But I thought—"

"It was an accident."

"Accidents happen."

Richie looks at the ceiling, where three dragon kites are tacked. "So she sent me to talk to you. She says it's my place since I'm your brother."

"I don't understand what I have to do with it."

"Babies take up a lot of room. You remember how it was. Cribs and playpens and high chairs and toidy seats . . ."

"I remember."

"Listen, Ivory, this wasn't my idea," he says, absently punching the crown of the cap so that it collapses into the doughnut roll. "I'm just telling you what she told me to tell you."

"And what *is* that, Richie?"

"She says we need your room for the baby."

"It's kind of drafty for a baby."

"I'm going to fix it up."

"Great."

"Roselle says you'd be better off with a place of your own. More privacy and that."

"She has a point there."

"The thing is, I know you can't afford it."

She squints to examine a ragged cuticle. "I'll manage."

"She says you're invited for dinner every Sunday."

"Thanks, Richie."

"Ivory, I feel like a shithead telling you this."

"Don't be silly. You think I planned to spend the rest of my life on Granite Street?"

"I guess not."

She stands at the door of the toy shop, watching him climb into the orange DPW truck double-parked in front. The open rear of the truck is filled to overflowing with used Christmas trees. The tinsel on the branches, thousands of brilliant spangles, shiver and gleam as he drives off and rounds the corner into Bow Street.

It is very strange: Ray cannot get the girl and her cockeyed madonna face out of his thoughts. These thoughts are accompanied by physical sensations that seem distressingly familiar, though he is certain he has not felt them for a very long time. There is a hollowness in his armpits, a shortness of breath, a kind of numb tingling in various parts of his body, especially the chest and groin.

Suddenly he recalls the circumstances of his previous experience of these feelings: when, as a child, he craved candy. It was cheap, chewy candy, fruit-flavored, the sort that came in nickel boxes, that he longed for. Most of the time his cravings went unfulfilled, since his mother approved only of healthful sweets, tapioca and junket and bread pudding, and he was expected to save up his pocket money to purchase Christmas and birthday gifts. Those nickels went directly from his mother's change purse into the sacrosanct glass piggy bank on his bureau, not held in his palm long enough even to warm them. Whenever he was able to buy the candy he ate it secretly and privately in his room, and that was part of the pleasure. No doubt it would taste repulsively artificial to him now.

He is not so naïve not to realize that his current sensations are to some extent sexual in nature, and yet they are nothing like what he felt in his relationships with Janeen or Muriel or the various other women with whom he's socialized from time to time. He is worried and abashed. He wonders whether he is reverting to infantile behavior, a sign of mental instability or approaching senility. To put it bluntly, he feels he may be losing his grip on things, and that girl is to blame.

He is relieved when days or weeks go by and he does not see her. Unfortunately, because of the eccentric patterns of the streets in Union Square—paved-over cow paths is what they are—his errands bring him inexorably past the toy shop. The crèche in the window is gone now, replaced by a jumble of faded and dusty sale items.

Three days ago eight inches of snow fell on Union Square and more flakes are coming down as Ray picks his way irritably over gravel-strewn ice on his way from the dry cleaner's to the Triple A, a pile of Lillian's dresses in plastic bags over his arm. The girl, he is thinking, suffers from a total deficiency of taste or style. Whatever possesses her to shove all those rejected toys into the window in that unappetizing, higgledy-piggledy way? No wonder no one buys them.

He enters the Triple A and there she is, in the flesh. The wind has battered her hair into an even more disorderly condition than usual, and there are gritty pools of melted snow on the linoleum beneath her counter stool. She hunches over a half-eaten sandwich, wearing that ratty jacket, the fur of which has dried into sharp little peaks. Ray's heart goes *whap*, like a beaver's tail on pond water, but it is too late to back out of the sub shop. The waitress has noticed him and is asking whether he'll have corn or bran this morning, the blueberry's out.

"Corn," he says dazedly. If the girl, Ivory, hears him speak and recognizes his voice she gives no indication; she pushes the plate with the half sandwich away from her and takes a package of cigarettes out of her cloth bag.

He carries his cup of coffee and the muffin with its pat of butter on a plate over to a booth, the dry-cleaned dresses still over his arm, and manages to get everything settled without spillage. Once seated, he helps himself to a paper napkin from the dispenser. From the booth he can see Ivory, but she wouldn't be able to see him unless she took a precipitous notion to swivel around on her stool in an almost 180-degree turn. Anyway, Sally, the counterman, has begun to speak to her. "You didn't finish your sandwich," Sally says reproachfully.

"I don't want to hurt your feelings," Ivory replies, "but it tastes horrible."

"What do you mean, horrible?"

"I don't know." Her voice is weary, and sad, and Ray feels a surprising pain. "Like asphalt shingle," she says.

Sally lifts the top slice of bread off the sandwich and looks inside. "Slate maybe yes. Asphalt no. This is a class establishment."

"Oh, Sally."

"So what's bugging you?"

She inhales on the cigarette and turns her head sideways to blow out the smoke. "They're throwing me out."

"They terminated your lease?"

"No, not the shop. Nobody but me would be stupid enough to rent that hole. It's home they're tossing me out of."

An almost tender look passes across Sally's round, pasty, goateed face. "How come?"

"You know. Accidents of life and all that."

"Right," Sally says, as though he knows what she's talking about, though Ray certainly doesn't. To Ray's annoyance three bookkeepers from the bank sit down in the next booth, chattering about some movie and doing their best to drown out the conversation at the counter. Whatever Ivory and Sally are saying to each other Ray is now shut out of.

After a few more minutes Ivory pulls a red cap over her untidy hair and slides down from the stool. She moves past Ray's booth with a loping stride, jacket unbuttoned and swinging open, rubber boots slapping on the linoleum as if they are sizes too big for her feet. She doesn't notice him sitting there. Carelessly she lets the door slam behind her, and the whole sub shop rattles.

Home? He's never imagined her at home, or at a place of any kind other than the toy shop, to say nothing of being thrown out of such a place.

He presses a bit of butter onto the last of the corn muffin and eases it into his mouth so he won't get crumbs on his tie. Who are the *they* throwing her out? he wonders, wiping his mouth with the paper napkin. And why?

Accidents of life, she said.

Ray walks slowly back to the bank. His own life has had damn few accidents in it, he thinks. He's never even broken a bone, in spite of the slapdash, halfhearted fashion in which sidewalks are cleared in this city. He says a sharp word to Madelyn about a mistake in a policy, then realizes the mistake was his own. He does not apologize.

....

Standing on the kitchen stoop waiting for Sammy to finish his business, Lillian sees that there are a multitude of icicles hanging from the gutter along the eaves of the house. Some of them are strangely asymmetrical and have more than one prong. The icicle on the far corner must be four feet long, at least. With a shudder Lillian imagines it suddenly cracking off as Raymond passes underneath with the garbage, plunging down and piercing his skull.

She shuts the storm door after Sam and goes into the lavatory to comb her hair. The roots need a bit of touching up; she wonders if she dares keep her Tuesday appointment at the hairdresser, with all that snow and ice underfoot.

One thing about the cold snap, however: it has done away with the terrible odor. Perhaps whatever it was has frozen, and come spring will thaw and begin to fester again, but she will worry about that when she has to. In the meantime she thanks God that she is not going crazy on account of a brain tumor, which is what happened recently to one of the characters in her favorite afternoon television drama. Lillian knows that brain tumors occur when actresses want to take other parts or have babies, but they happen in real life, too, and quite likely they sometimes derange the sense of smell.

Just as the eight-day clock on the hall table strikes a note for quarter past five, she hears the front door open and then Raymond's keys clink down next to the clock.

"Oh, Lillian," he says, looking up from his mail. "I picked up your dry cleaning, but I left it in the office. I'm sorry; I'll be sure to bring it tomorrow."

"No rush," Lillian says, actually rather pleased that for once it is Raymond who has had a lapse in memory. He prides

himself on being a trustworthy person and expects the same
behavior of others; though Lillian admires him for it, he does
not leave her much room for absentmindedness. "Raymond,"
she says, "I feel I must warn you about something."

"Oh?" Raymond puts down the telephone bill he has been
studying. Sometimes when he is startled his scalp tightens in
such a way that his ears seem to twitch. "Warn me about
what?"

"Icicles."

"Icicles?"

"You must be careful to keep well away from the sides of
buildings in case one should happen to fall while you are under
it."

"Thank you, Lillian," he says, his face serious. "I'll try to
keep that in mind. It is a treacherous world out there."

"It certainly is."

"A world full of accidents." He has removed the loose
change from his trousers pocket, as is his habit upon returning
from work, and is stacking them on the hall table, nickels on
nickels, dimes on dimes. "And other nasty surprises."

Since it is unlike Raymond to take so much notice of something she has said, Lillian wonders whether he is thinking
about some accident other than icicles. However, she doesn't
like to ask. He does not take kindly to questions like that,
questions that might seem to be prying into his private life, no
matter how sympathetically she intends them. Still, she can
definitely tell that something's bothering him.

"Lillian," he says, lining the stack of dimes up with his
fingertips, "if you had to leave home suddenly, what would you
do?"

"Do?" she asks, not completely sure she's hearing him cor-
rectly.

"If you were the sort of person who has trouble making plans"—he lifts his fingers from the dimes—"and very little money. Where would you go?"

She feels dizzy; the design in the hall rug trembles as though there is a minor earthquake in the vicinity of the dining room.

"Never mind," he says. "I didn't expect you to have an answer. There *is* no good answer, I suppose."

He goes into the lavatory and she hears water rushing into the sink. When it stops she still hears something: a kind of very high-pitched painful whine. At first she thinks it must be a radiator valve, but it's there inside her ear all through dinner, and since Raymond doesn't remark on the sound and in any case seems more than usually preoccupied, she doesn't mention it either.

It's probably a violation of some ordinance or other, Ivory figures, but who's going to catch her? And how much could they do to her if they did?

She is tacking a queen-size cotton bedspread to one of the plank walls of the stock room. The spread came from India, via Filene's basement, and is decorated with orange-gold elephants on a magenta background. The elephants grasp in their mouths the tails of the elephants before them as they march around the border; beside them other elephants march steadfastly in the opposite direction, and so on, row after row, as far as the medallion center of the bedspread. No elephant can stray into another column or switch directions. There is something tidy about that, Ivory thinks, and reassuring, but also rather dull for the elephants.

On another wall, all around the sink and toilet tank and up to the rafters, she has taped dozens of pictures cut out of magazines and newspapers, snapshots, recipes, postcards, and greeting cards. She has papered the third wall, the one between the storeroom and the shop, with rolls of remaindered wallpaper in a minutely figured, vaguely Turkish design in crimson, chocolate, and cream. "Love your notepaper," the clerk at Wallpaper World said when he rang up the sale, feeling safe in his sarcasm just because nobody else in the city had had the imagination to appreciate it. She hasn't yet decided how to decorate the fourth wall. She'd paint it red to tie together the wallpaper with the bedspread, but Richie told her the paint would sink right into that soft, unfinished wood; she could wind up putting ten coats on it and it would still look like hell.

Richie does not approve of her moving in here. "It's uncivilized," he told her. "There aren't any windows."

Lucky baby, she thinks, to be inheriting her view of the systematic trashing of Osgood Park.

"You'll asphyxiate yourself," he said.

"There's a vent."

"Or go blind, like a mole."

"No, no. I'll be just fine," she told him.

She will, too, she thinks, having finished mounting the bedspread and begun to unpack the cooking utensils Roselle graciously spared from Granite Street. She's arranging them in fruit-crate cabinets. Too bad the flea market next to the high school doesn't operate in winter—she could use a cover for the iron frying pan, and a mixing bowl, and a slightly better grade of can opener—but she doesn't imagine she's going to be a gourmet cook on a two-ring hot plate, anyhow. What she'll do is make a big pot of chili and eat out of it for a whole week. Plenty of garlic and hot peppers, the way Roselle and the girls would never eat it. Curry, too.

Maybe, now that she thinks about it, this is not going to be such a hardship, after all. She'll have the satisfaction of making Roselle feel guilty *and* the fun of living her life as she pleases.

She tosses some emptied grocery cartons into a dumpster in the back alley and pauses a moment to look up into the night sky. Three or four snowflakes alight on her face. She can hear traffic in the square, but it seems muffled, either by snow or by the high brick buildings around her. In this secret dark alley, with the snow drifting down, she feels alone but not lonely.

There aren't any windows.

She'll *make* a window.

Leaving most of her possessions unpacked and the mattress on her bed still stripped to the ticking, Ivory puts on her jacket and boots and goes out into the square in search of materials. Since it's after nine the Mid-Nite is practically the only store still open. It sells paperbacks with the covers torn off, Portuguese groceries, cigarettes, odds and ends.

"A *big* piece of paper," she tells the crimped-haired elderly gentleman at the counter. He peers at her between a stack of cigarillo packages and a display of novelty key chains. "And paint. Lots of different colors."

"What you want to paint?" he asks.

"Grass. Trees. Flowers."

He thinks this over. "Birds?"

"Sure, why not?"

"What kind of birds?"

"I don't know. Parrots," she says, reasoning that in the Azores there are probably parrots.

"Okay," he agrees. He hobbles to the rear of the store and pokes around, grunting and shifting things, and comes back with a rolled-up piece of poster board, somewhat dog-eared, and a cardboard box. He blows the dust off the box and opens it. "Paint," he says.

There are five squat jars and a small paintbrush inside. "That's not very many colors," Ivory says.

"You mix. Blue and yellow, presto: green. Red and yellow, presto: orange."

"What about black?"

"What you need black in your picture for?"

She can't think of anything specific, and anyway, he's already adding up the price of the poster paper and the paint and figuring the tax.

She stays up until four in the morning painting buttercups, peonies, and tulips—she has to omit black-eyed Susans—and a many-branched tree with strange creatures among the leaves that may or may not be recognizable as parrots. It's the first picture she has painted since kindergarten. When she's finished she leaves it on the table to dry, rolls herself in her quilt without undressing, and sleeps on the bare mattress: her first night on her own.

Eight

. . . .

"I NEED A CARPET," she tells Fogel. "Desperately."

"You're planning to fly away on it?"

"Not in the near future, no."

Fogel has marvelous fingernails. They are yellowish, tough, scoop-shaped, corrugated; they look like tools made in primitive times out of some unlikely natural material. Camel bone, say, or horseshoe crab shell. He now patiently taps these artifacts on the lid of a circa-1950 portable phonograph.

"On this carpet you were thinking of spending how much?" he asks.

"Not a whole lot."

Fogel smiles. His teeth, unlike his fingernails, are blindingly white. "The carpets in your price range, Miss Bright, are magic carpets."

"Really?"

"Imaginary."

"I don't know, Mr. Fogel." She takes off her cap and stuffs it into her pocket. "I don't think my imagination works well enough to cover my floor."

"No? Then you need maybe a *partly* imaginary carpet." Fogel drags a thin grayish tube tied with twine out from beneath a bureau. He unknots the twine and unrolls the carpet as much as is possible in the path between stacked bureaus and arm-to-arm overstuffed chairs. "This rug is a genuine Kazak," he says. "Made by nomads."

"What made the holes, genuine goats?"

"For the holes you use your imagination."

"Ha, ha."

"Ten dollars," Fogel says, wasting no more words on jokes.

"There isn't ten dollars' worth of thread *around* those holes."

"Seven, then," he says, rerolling the carpet and putting a double knot in the twine. "And that's a gift."

"A real gift would be free."

"Because I presented you a fine antique shawl from the kindness of my heart, you shouldn't conclude I'm running here some kind of charity operation."

"The truth is I don't have seven dollars."

"Aha."

"I don't have any money at all."

"But a carpet you need desperately."

"Yes."

Fogel sighs. "Go ahead. Take it. Only have the goodness you wouldn't bother me anymore for at least a week."

"I promise to pay you the seven dollars," she says, pulling the red cap down over her ears, "as soon as humanly possible."

Long-suffering Fogel opens the door for her and bows as she walks past, the rolled-up carpet on her shoulder. It sticks out four feet both in front and behind, buckling somewhat in the middle.

Last night three inches of snow came down on top of the eight inches that fell a week ago, temporarily obliterating the exhaust grit and dog urine, but also reclogging the sidewalk. The soles of Ivory's boots are bald, like the tires of used cars, and the rug, bouncing slightly on either side of the fulcrum of her shoulder and now and then jostled by gusts of wind, confuses her sense of balance. It is just after five o'clock, and dark.

Suddenly, as she is cutting across the parking lot next to the old brick fire station, she sees Raymond Bartlett heading her way. He seems to be observing, with mild puzzlement, the progress of the carpet through the gloom, without yet realizing that Ivory is attached to it. If only she could avoid him by ducking into the fire station, but what would she say to the firemen: *Excuse me, I fear my carpet's on fire?* Too late, in any case; he's moving toward her with deliberate steps, picking his way between parked cars and over crusted snow.

"Ivory?" he says.

"Yes, it's me."

"Can I help with that?"

"Oh no. I'm managing all right, thank you."

The wind is twitching the end of his gray scarf and also buffeting the carpet.

"Let me help anyway," he says, taking hold of the rear end.

As they move through Union Square in rush hour traffic, stopping for red lights and making way for pedestrians, Ivory has time to reflect gloomily that two people carrying a carpet are an even sillier procession than one person doing so, especially two people as different in general appearance and level of respectability as herself and Raymond; it is amazing they're not collecting a troop of barking dogs and hooting children along the way. It is amazing also that she ever imagined the two of them could be a plausible couple, whether or not on either end of a carpet. And when they reach the toy shop she can tell from his expression that he has regretted his good manners; as she searches in her tote for the key he shoulders the rug with strained courtliness.

Inside she says, "Just drop it anywhere."

Doubtfully he looks for a clear spot amid tricycles, toy stoves, tea sets, dollhouses. "You'll have to move quite a lot of things if you want to put it in here," he points out.

In fact, there's no place to set it down, even in its rolled-up state, and since she can't let him stand there endlessly with the carpet swaying on his shoulder, she opens the door to the stock room.

"Actually, back here is where it goes."

She pulls the light cord. She doesn't dare look at his face, which she knows must register even more astonishment than when he first stepped into the toy shop. "It's just for the time being," she says quickly. "I hope you won't turn me in."

"Turn you in?"

"To the authorities. Living here is probably illegal, immoral, and every other damn thing."

He has set the rug on the floorboards and is gazing at the elephants on the wall, the toilet, the hot plate, the one-armed bandit, the balled-up crazy quilt on the mattress. "No," he says vaguely, "of course I won't." At the table, his hands in his coat pockets, he examines the window painting. He's like a man who has stumbled into a madhouse and is nervously going along with the general delusion that it's an art gallery so as not to agitate the inmates.

"Interesting," he says. "Especially the flowers in the tree."

"Those are parrots."

"Ah, parrots," he says cautiously. Not only is she a lunatic, she may even be violent.

"Like in the Azores."

"I see," he says, stroking his knuckles.

"Azores parrots are a different species from Somerville parrots. That's the reason they look a lot like flowers."

He smiles, really rattled now. Probably he's wondering if she's about to leap at his neck and take a bite out of it.

"Would you care for a cup of tea?" she asks, her hands knotted behind her.

He looks at her intently for a moment but then says, "I'm afraid I mustn't stay."

They walk through the shop, past the glass case of dolls, the shelves of toys and games. At the door she says, "I guess your wife must be expecting you."

"My wife?" He laughs, embarrassed. "Lillian is not my wife. Lillian is the housekeeper."

Ivory nods, as embarrassed as he. What does she know about housekeepers? She's sure that by blurting out her worst fear she's given herself away. Though it doesn't matter, really, whether it's a nut he thinks she is, or a fool. "Well," she says, "thanks for helping with the rug."

"Don't mention it," he says, his hand on the doorknob. She thinks he's about to say something more, but instead he turns the knob and is gone.

Ray dreams about a statue of the Virgin in the Busch-Reisinger. Her coiffed head is perched on her neck at a wry angle; her wooden body bears speckled traces of paint and gilt; her supplicating fingers are broken off at the second joints. As he watches, tears ooze from her wooden eyes and drip into the carved folds of her gown. It is like a miracle one reads about on the front page of a tabloid and dismisses as a hoax or fraud. Except that in his dream Ray cannot dismiss the weeping face; his feet are so heavy he is unable to move away from her. The dream goes on endlessly, without plot or resolution, like the repetitive and hallucinatory dreams he had in childhood fevers, in those days before antibiotics.

When he wakes he tests his forehead with his palm and, finding it to be clammy, wonders if he's coming down with something. His armpits, also, are damp; his groin and head ache dully.

He closes the far window, which has been open only a crack in this six-degree weather, and turns back the blankets and top sheet to air. Against his will his mind shoots to Ivory's bare mattress with the shiny, wildly colored quilt tumbled on it. He knows the dream was about her, and he'd rather not think about what it might mean. It would be best to shut off all thoughts of her and her strange room.

Sitting on his bed to pull on his socks, he's grateful for the comforting familiarity and simplicity of his surroundings: the blue-gray walls and white woodwork, the unbleached muslin curtains—washed so many times they are now like linen—the Constable reproduction, the dried bayberry branches in a jug, the polished maple floor. The smell of brewing coffee, also comforting, begins to drift up from the kitchen.

In the bathroom he takes two aspirin tablets with a swallow of tap water, urinates and flushes, washes his face and neck and genitals, brushes his teeth, and then sets about shaving. From time to time over the years he has used electric razors for brief periods; the electric razor seems to be the sort of gift that people think of when they think of him. Muriel, for instance, gave him a Remington cordless for Christmas last year.

Can it be only a year ago that he and Muriel were still going to concerts and museums together; *less* than a year since she and her mother flew off to Aruba? Ray is astonished. He has hardly given her a thought in many weeks, perhaps not since he received the Audubon Society Christmas card. It was signed *Muriel and Doris Neely*, though Ray never called the old lady by her first name, never felt so inclined. No message, just the signature. He could scarcely blame Muriel for that; he had not written to her, not even to acknowledge her wistful phallic cactus. Her silence is a reproach he hasn't even noticed. In a way he feels guilty and less than pleased with himself, yet it would not have been a kindness to Muriel to encourage her further when he had no intention of marrying her.

Today he does not use an electric razor, Muriel's or anybody else's. He works up a good foamy lather in his shaving mug and begins to apply it to his cheeks. He likes the warmth of the lather and the feel of the bone-handled brush in his palm. He cannot, in fact, figure out what possesses any man to use an electric razor in preference to soap and blade. Of course, a woman wandering around a department store in search of a Christmas gift could not be expected to understand that, even if women do sometimes shave various parts of their bodies, because hair on the face is a special situation. Facial hair has a texture and behavior all its own. Very likely most of the men around the world using electric razors are only doing so to avoid injuring the feelings of some female relation. Ray is relieved he doesn't have any.

He notices, by the time he is cleaning the clot of hair and soap out of the sink strainer, that his aches have nearly disappeared and the dream of the weeping statue faded in memory. It's going to be a sunny day, he thinks, closing his terry-cloth bathrobe in case Lillian should be lurking about in the hall. She's been doing that a good deal lately, poking around in odd corners, her nose working like a rabbit's. Well, he supposes it's a harmless eccentricity, so long as she stays out of his personal belongings.

Not that he has any secrets, particularly. Not since he got rid of the foil package of prophylactics he bought at the beginning of his relationship with Muriel and never had occasion to use once in six years. It's just that he wouldn't like to think of Lillian looking in his drawers or his closet while he's at work, opening his shoe boxes, climbing up to inspect the back of the closet shelf with a flashlight.

There might be some secret from long ago that he's forgotten about, he thinks, and then laughs at himself. What could it be? Empty Jujyfruit boxes under the cobwebs? A copy of *Pinocchio* not down the storm drain at all but returned to haunt him?

He snaps apart the paper band around a clean shirt—he's recently started taking his shirts to the laundry since Lillian's ironing has deteriorated—unfolds the shirt, and slips it on. He chooses a navy tie with a small white diamond pattern on it to go with his gray suit, and as he's knotting it, his eye is caught by the brilliance of the sun striking the icicles on the gutter next door. Lillian's accidents. He resolves to stay well away from overhanging eaves and other treacherous situations.

And yet, on account of the dream, his mind keeps returning to the girl, to Ivory. What he feels when he thinks of her is not entirely unpleasant.

Saturday night Ivory is picking through a pound of kidney beans, removing pebbles and bits of straw, when the telephone begins to ring in the shop. The police, she thinks. Somebody's snitched on her already. Or it could be Richie. Roselle having a miscarriage and begging her to come back. No, she'll say. Never. On the ninth ring she picks up the receiver and says, with a cough meant to disguise or confuse, "Yes?"

She hears static, a bad connection. Whoever is on the other end rattles the hook several times and then shouts, "Is that you?"

"Who?"

"This is Ray. I'm calling from a pay phone. I can't get it to work properly, and I don't have another dime."

"Dial the operator," she shouts. "You don't need a dime for that."

The connection goes dead and she stands with the phone in her hand looking at the skater, the baby doll, and the Harlequin in their glass case. "That was Ray," she tells them. "It seems he has a nickname."

In five minutes the man himself is at the door. "She said she'd give me credit against my account for the dime I lost," he explains. "But she wouldn't put another call through unless it was an emergency. I didn't think it was quite that."

"Oh. Good."

"Is it all right if I come in?"

"Sure," she says, in something of a daze. In the back room she takes his coat and lays it on the bed, which is now made, the quilt spread out neatly. "I'm sorry I only have the one chair," she says, "and it's not very comfortable."

He sits on the edge of the quilt, next to his coat. He's dressed more informally than she's seen him, in somewhat wrinkled chinos and a brown cable-knit pullover, not a new one.

"How about a glass of wine?"

"Yes, all right. Thank you."

As she's unscrewing the cap from the jug she asks, "What do you think of the carpet?"

He stares at it for a moment. "It looks fine."

"A tiny bit threadbare in spots." She pours burgundy into a couple of nonmatching bar glasses. Handing him one, she says, "You find these glasses on the sidewalk on Sunday mornings, and not always broken, either. I guess drunks carry them out of bars at closing time. I soak them in Clorox. You never know what bugs are out there."

"No. You don't."

"Well," she says, sitting sideways in the straight-backed chair, "how are things?"

"Fine. Fine."

She takes a sip from her glass. "Did you come about anything special?"

"As a matter of fact, there's been something on my conscience. Your life insurance . . . I let you get away without properly explaining all the options. I've brought some forms with me. . . ." He searches in an inside coat pocket and brings out some rumpled folded papers.

"I didn't realize you make house calls."

"I don't, usually. It's not necessary to make a final decision tonight, of course."

"I do feel a little tired."

"Ah. The customers?"

"Well, no. To tell you the truth, I didn't sleep too well last night."

"Oh?"

"Probably it's the stuffiness in here. I had a weird dream."

"What . . . sort of dream?"

"I was in a hospital." She brushes her bangs aside. "They were going to amputate my left arm up to the elbow."

He looks somewhat queasy, as if he is visualizing the bloody stump.

"If I was *lucky*, up to the elbow. Otherwise, the whole arm. But that's not what bothered me."

He shifts on the bed, crossing his legs.

"The worst part was the waiting. The dream seemed to go on and on and on."

Raymond puts his hand, the one not holding his wineglass, on the quilt. She knows how the velvet must feel to him: slithery, with the grain of each patch running a definite, separate way. "Your arm—what was wrong with it?"

"I couldn't tell you. If there was a point to the amputation, I didn't know what it was."

"Perhaps you are worried about being cut off from something. Or someone."

"Do you think dreams have meanings, in that way?"

"Sometimes they seem to," he says, almost as if it is painful for him to admit it.

There is a silence now. She sets her glass on the table and goes to the sink to finish picking over the kidney beans. She dumps them from the colander into a kettle and runs water on top to soak them overnight. "These are for chili," she says. "I have a craving for chili, the really hot kind. That's one good thing about living alone: you can put in as many peppers as you like and there's nobody around to complain."

"Who complained?" he asks.

Does he imagine it was a man, a lover? Would he care? Ivory wonders, absently stirring the beans with her fingers in the cold water. "My sister-in-law. There's a baby on the way, which is why they need my room, but it was time for me to get out of there anyhow."

"I wondered where you'd go."

She turns from the sink, startled. "How did you know?"

"I overheard you talking in the Triple A. I wasn't spying on you, Ivory."

"Of course you weren't. I have a big mouth."

No, he would not care if she had ten lovers. A hundred.

"Not so big," he says.

"A huge, hideous, lopsided mouth," she says, turning back to the sink. "It's a well-known fact."

Raymond has got up from the bed. He must be worried that she's about to cry, because he says tentatively, "I think I should go now."

She nods, not trusting herself to speak.

"I'll leave the forms here on the table." It's only six or seven steps from the table to the sink, across the holey carpet. He stands behind her for a moment; her fingers trail listlessly in the bean water. Soon she hears him letting himself out through the front of the shop.

Early on Sunday morning they run into each other on the sidewalk outside St. Joseph's. Parishioners are straggling down the steps after mass.

"You weren't in the shop," he says. "I knocked on the front door. Then I went around and knocked on the back door."

"How did you find it?"

"Not easily."

"I went out to the deli." She lets him look inside the brown paper bag she's carrying. "See? Eggs."

"Ivory, it came to me in the middle of the night. You don't need to worry about your dream. Whatever you were afraid of losing, or being cut off from, you can survive it. Because it was your *left* arm they were going to amputate. Do you understand what I'm trying to tell you?"

Ivory is bundled up like a mummy; only a little of her face shows between the red cap and a ragged shawl that is wound twice around her neck and fastened with a safety pin. She squints at Ray in the sunlight. "But I'm left-handed," she says.

The air is too cold for Ray to take a deep breath.

"It runs in the family," she says. "We're all of us left-handed. Except for Roselle."

Ray's gloved hand is on the sleeve of her beaver jacket. "I was so sure I had it figured out."

"Don't be upset. Please," she says, clasping the grocery bag against her coat as though to keep the eggs from freezing. "It was only a dream."

"I didn't want to leave you last night," he says. A spindly old lady makes her halting way around them, thumping the rubber tip of her cane on the pavement, and starts slowly up the church steps. "But I was afraid to stay, because . . ."

Ivory waits, listening closely, cradling the eggs.

"Because I wanted to"—his voice is strangled—"hold you and I didn't want you to think . . ."

"That it was only to comfort me for losing an arm?" she suggests, after a long pause.

He smiles wanly. "Well, something like that."

"Could you eat some breakfast?"

He considers. "I think so. Yes."

He takes her elbow and helps her across Washington Street as if she is as fragile as the old lady or the eggs, although he feels that actually it's some part of himself that is in imminent danger of breaking. Between a funeral home and a shoe store they enter a narrow alley partly blocked with vats of refuse. By the rear door of the toy shop they see great fresh holes in the crusted snow where a short while ago he stood fruitlessly pounding.

Inside the back room, he unpins the shawl and gently unwinds it from her neck.

"But it's all okay, since I have both my arms," she says. "Legs, too."

He touches her icy cheek with his palm. "You do," he says.

Nine

....

FINALLY, OVERNIGHT, a thaw. This morning the sky is overcast and the mounds of snow have visibly shrunk. While waiting in the podiatrist's office recently, Lillian read a magazine article about a condition called osteoporosis; old people, it said, grow shorter because the bones in their spines become hollow and brittle and gradually collapse, one into the next. That is how the snow piles look to her, as though they are collapsing inward.

Lillian shakes some cleanser into the lavatory sink and rubs at the slimy yellowish deposit under the hot water tap. Raymond spent practically the whole day out yesterday. He telephoned at noon to tell her not to put the roast in the oven. She already had, of course, so she took it out again. It now sits on a plate in the Frigidaire, pale brown, with small white dabs of fat clinging to it. Then, when he did come in, he wouldn't eat anything, went straight into his study. Of course it would have been too much to expect for him to tell her where he'd been and what was so very important it prevented him from eating his Sunday dinner. But he might have chatted a little, suggested they watch TV together in the living room later on. Instead, she made herself a cheese sandwich and carried the tray up the two flights to her own room. When she switched on her portable television she found that the whole evening's schedule had been cast to the winds on account of some football game.

Lillian lets a trickle of water mix with the cleanser and scum. She wrings out the sponge.

She has not mentioned the sound to Raymond. He would tell her it was wax. She knows it isn't wax. She made a special trip to the drugstore to buy a preparation for earwax control and squeezed it into both ears twice a day for four days, and the siren sound is still there. He would say she's like a dog and can hear sounds that are too high-pitched for ordinary human beings. But that can't be true, either, or why wouldn't she have heard them before now?

She is convinced the disorder is in the heating system, not something to do with her at all, and that Raymond is too stubborn or preoccupied to admit that he hears it. Well, she can wait just as long as he can. Until one of the radiators explodes, if necessary. *Then* he'll have to take notice, she thinks, poking the toilet brush down into the depths of the bowl and jiggling it so that the bristles scrape the bottom.

If you had to leave home suddenly, what would you do? Those were his exact words. Nobody could blame her for being shocked and for thinking, at first, he was talking about her. There's as much chance of knowing what goes on in Raymond's head as inside a boiler or pipe or furnace.

But the more she ponders it, the more she feels it must be Muriel Neely that he meant. A *person who has trouble making plans,* he said. Well, that would certainly fit poor Muriel, who hadn't been able to catch him, or even to lay a halfway workable trap, so far as Lillian could tell, in six years of trying.

Lillian lifts a rag from the shutoff valve under the toilet tank and runs it along the wainscot molding. Terrible the way dust collects. Ashes to ashes and dust to dust, most of it landing inside this house, it seems.

Well, suppose for a moment Lillian *did* leave. Stopped scrubbing and dusting and polishing his house. Never again wiped away those springy little hairs from the underside of the toilet seat or loaded his damp towels and underwear into the washing machine or took a Brillo to an oatmeal pan. He assumes it's a total joy for her to do those things. He might just have an unpleasant surprise if she were to up and leave, move in with Cousin Flo in Wisconsin, say. He might find it wasn't such a joy to clean up after himself. He might, indeed, actually miss her and begin to appreciate what she's done for him.

Suddenly, as she's mulling over these thoughts, a mass of snow the size of a sofa loses its hold on the roof, slides past the lavatory window, and crashes onto the barberry hedge. Though her heart thumps, in a strange way the unexpected commotion makes her glad. Raymond may think he controls things, but Raymond had better watch out.

As he passes the watch repairer's shop Ray notices a faded cardboard valentine, in dreadful taste, propped amid the displays of cheap lockets and watchbands. Ridiculously, his heart swells with love; what he feels in his crowded rib cage is almost pain.

He enters the alley next to the funeral home, hurries past four foul-smelling rubbish containers, and rounds the corner to the rear entrance of Ivory's shop. In this dank and hidden spot the snow melts not from the sun but from the restaurant exhaust fans; the holes where he broke the surface of the snow are hardly visible. High above him a pigeon on a sill flaps its wings; looking up, he sees that various sills and ledges are strung with barbed wire. One of the dusty windows on the top floor of Wallpaper World is lit, dimly. Ray wonders whether a person up there would be able to see him or hear him pound, and he's glad that today he has Ivory's key. She was shy about offering it, as though uncertain whether he'd come back. As though she thought he might want her only that one time. Purposefully, smiling a little, he fits the key into the lock and presses his shoulder against the heavy metal door.

She is at the hot plate in the corner by the sink, turning over a chop with a fork. "Hello," she says.

He removes his rubbers and hangs his coat on a nail next to her beaver jacket. He stands behind her at the hotplate and covers her breasts with his hands. She is wearing loose white painter's overalls and a pink blouse, badly pressed, with absurd puffed sleeves. Her breasts, low on her chest, are the size of apples.

"I hope you like pork chops," she says, looking into the pan.

He undoes two blouse buttons and slips his hand inside, under the bib; her nipple feels like a small round stone.

"Oh," she says. The fat in the pan sputters.

His left hand moves over her belly; it is rounded, as though she is in an early month of pregnancy. His hand goes into the pocket of her overalls, past a crumpled tissue and a pencil, so far that he can reach her crotch and grasp it through a thickness of rough cotton.

He licks the back of her neck. It is warm and salty. Like a pretzel, he thinks. Through the cloth he feels the parting in her crotch. It is wet. She makes a small sound, like a mew; her hard little breast pushes against his hand as she breathes.

Her body shudders. He has brought her to orgasm, just as easily as that. She still holds the fork. Droplets of bloody juice are appearing on the surface of the chops.

He takes the fork from her hand and switches off the heat under the pan. By her shoulders he turns her around to face him; he sees that her hazel eyes are glistening. "Are you crying?" he asks.

She brushes her bangs aside and shakes her head. His odd little madonna. He unhooks the straps of her overalls, and pulls them down, and opens the pink blouse. There are raw-looking blotches on her bony chest.

He wants the next part to happen very slowly, not like yesterday. He unknots his tie and lays it across the seat of the ladder-back chair, unbuttons one shirt cuff and then the other, unbuckles his belt, unties his shoelaces.

She is in the bed, waiting for him, under the wildly colored crazy quilt. She's watching him fold his clothes and arrange them carefully on the chair. He knows she can see how hairy his body is, and yet how downy and fine the hairs are. His own nipples are like pebbles, too. As he folds his trousers along the crease he thinks about how his small, neat buttocks will feel to her, under her hands. Her stubby little hands, with bitten and maimed fingernails and yellow stains. The arteries in his penis pulsate.

He lifts the quilt and moves in under it. His knees press against her hipbones, shutting her inside his legs. Crouching, he lays his penis on her low mound of belly, and she covers it tenderly with her hand. "Ah," he says, closing his eyes. "You can take me now."

Tuesday. As Ivory pours wine into her glass Ray places a small object on the table in front of her. It's a gold plastic charm, a four-leaf clover.

"I got it from the gum ball machine at the bank," he tells her, threading his scarf into his sleeve before hanging the coat on a nail.

She looks at him and laughs. "I can't imagine you putting pennies in a gum ball machine."

"These days it's nickels," he says.

"Can I keep it?"

"If you like."

She sets her glass on the shelf above the sink and stirs the chili with a long wooden spoon. "Do you believe in luck?" she asks.

"If luck is what happens to you whether you deserve it or not, then I believe in it."

"But it's just an accident, then."

"Except that sometimes it's good."

She thinks about this. "That must be what the charm is for."

"Well," Ray says, sitting in the straight chair and removing his shoe, "I wouldn't put too much faith in a plastic four-leaf clover if I were you."

She licks the spoon. "I think I'll keep it anyway."

"I see your sale sign is down," Ray remarks, taking a paring knife to the shoe. He's prying bits of gravel out of the sole and dropping them into a paper grocery bag. "And the window is empty."

"I finally gave up on those old toys," she says.

"What did you do with them?"

"Put them in a box and took them over to St. Joseph's."

Ray pauses in the gravel-removal operation. "Are you Catholic, Ivory?"

"No. St. Joseph's is handy, that's all," she says, tapping the spoon on the edge of the dented old kettle. "Would you care if I was?"

After a moment's thought he says, "Religion is sometimes a quagmire."

"What do you mean, exactly?"

"People's minds are already set on certain issues. Moral issues."

"I'm not a Catholic, or anything else." She unscrews the cap from a container of dried oregano. "Any particular moral issue you have in mind?"

This afternoon she went to the family clinic at the hospital and had an intrauterine device inserted; *that* issue is in her mind, if not in his. But she's decided against mentioning it to Ray. He might feel she's taking too much for granted. Making long-range plans, counting on a future. And, rather superstitiously, she feels she is in fact doing those things, tempting fate in a dangerous way. The main thing is, though, she could never go through another abortion.

"No," he says, wiping the paring knife with a paper napkin. "Nothing special."

Though his voice is casual, she feels embarrassed and shaky; she hopes it doesn't show. She looks into the kettle and gives the beans another stir. Her womb has begun to cramp on account of the IUD, pains not so different from the ones after the abortion. He'd be horrified, revolted, if he knew. Sex on a nylon bag of dirty clothes. Both of the major calamities of her life have had to do with dirty clothes, she thinks, not for the first time. It must be something about her.

He is looking quietly into his wineglass, thinking much more blameless thoughts than her own, she feels sure.

The cramping has killed her appetite, but out of nervousness she heaps a mound of mushy beans into her bowl anyway. She sits on the rickety little stepladder she uses to retrieve games from the top shelves; her left hand collides awkwardly with Ray's right as they reach for their wineglasses.

"There was a storm in the house this morning," Ray says. "Over the Sunday roast."

"You never ate it."

"You know I didn't, unless I ate it for breakfast."

"She's angry?"

Ray spoons some beans into his mouth and chews. "She claims it's decaying in the refrigerator, seven dollars and fifty cents' worth."

"She could eat it herself."

"Ah. You don't know Lillian."

"No."

"She's a difficult woman sometimes," Ray says.

Woman? The word alarms her. It's too serious. It implies complexities of personality, experience . . . *shared* experience. Attachments. She wonders if Ray's "moral issue" has something to do with Lillian. "Tell me about her," Ivory says, laying her spoon on the table.

"Oh, I don't know that there's a great deal to tell."

He says that with such offhandedness she feels he must be concealing something. Only fair; she's not beyond secrets herself.

"Is *she* Catholic, Ray?"

He laughs. "She'd drop dead if she heard you. She's Ulster Irish, as Protestant as they come."

"I guess she's worked for you a long time."

"Forever. I was fifteen when she arrived with her cardboard suitcase. Of course, it was my mother she came to work for."

"Cleaning? Cooking?"

"Oh, not cooking, not in those days. My mother was a great cook."

"Cleaning, though. Laundry. Bedmaking."

"Yes," he says in a puzzled way. "All of that."

It has begun to occur to her that perhaps Lillian is the reason he never married, never needed to. This *woman*, furious over the roast, suspecting betrayal. Not young anymore, but not entirely beyond it, either.

"You aren't eating," he says. There's still a mound of chili left in her bowl.

"I've had all I want."

"Your eyes were bigger than your stomach, as my mother used to say."

"That happens to me, I guess."

"Perhaps by now you've had all you want of me, too."

She knows from his look he doesn't mean it. It's a tease, a way to provoke and stir her. He takes her on top of the quilt; his urgency is so sudden, he seems astonished by it himself. Afterward, while he washes, she pulls on her overalls and a long-underwear top and sits at the table to smoke. One bare foot is up on the edge of the chair. She can feel some of his semen still inside her. Picking up the clover charm, she thinks: Good luck. Why the hell not, for a change?

"Who is he?" Roselle asks, lifting her cigarette out of a peanut butter jar top and taking a drag. One of the things she and Ivory have in common is nicotine addiction.

"Who's who?"

"Come on. The guy you're sleeping with."

Ivory sets the bakery box on the dinette table and unbuttons her jacket. "I don't know what you mean," she says carefully.

"*Your sister-in-law finally get married?*" Roselle mimics. "*I seen her up the hospital. Coming outa the family planning clinic.*"

"Holy Moses. You can't make a move in this town without activating an army of secret agents."

"No wonder you were in such an all-fired rush to get out of here," Roselle says, dropping chicken quarters into a bag of Shake 'n' Bake.

Ivory laughs. "If you remember, that was your idea."

"You know, Ivory," she says, giving the bag a violent shake, "you could get yourself in big trouble."

"I appreciate your concern, Roselle."

"Maybe you already are in big trouble."

"I promise you, I'm not."

Roselle crams the coated chicken parts into a baking pan, skin side up, and makes an effort to smack the protuberant wings into submission. "I suppose he's married, on top of everything else."

"You're jumping to an awful lot of conclusions."

"Well, don't expect him to give up his wife for you. Men have their little adventures, but divorce is a very expensive proposition. Alimony and child support and paying for two households and that. Once they have that pointed out to them, they run like maniacs in the opposite direction."

Dry snowflakes are sprinkling past the curtained kitchen windows.

"Does Richie?" Ivory asks.

"Does Richie what?" Roselle puts the pan into the oven and lets the door bang shut.

"Have little adventures."

"Now you're the one jumping to conclusions." She picks her smoldering Winston out of the butts and gets one more drag out of it. She's beginning to show already, but the bulge is probably more pastry than baby."

"I was only asking."

"He'd probably tell you before he'd tell me, anyhow."

Ivory plucks the string on the bakery box; it makes a flat twang, like a toy banjo. "He doesn't tell me anything," she says.

"I don't believe it. He's always been a lot closer to you than to me."

"I doubt that he talks to anybody very much."

"The two of you are just the same with your secrets," Roselle says, disgruntled. "I don't know where you get it from. Your dad wasn't like that."

"My mother, I guess."

Ivory thinks about Frances Bright, quietly packing and un-packing, traipsing from state to state after her husband, doing little things to fix up each new place. Lining the kitchen draw-ers with grocery bags cut to fit, sprouting orange seeds into houseplants. Ivory suspects her mother didn't get much plea-sure out of living on the wrong side of the poverty line; it wasn't a game of wits for her, the way it is for Ivory. But her mother kept her thoughts to herself, and now Ivory has no way of finding out.

"Strange her dying like that," Roselle says, sitting heavily in a dinette chair, as though her pregnancy were a matter of months instead of weeks.

"It was a unique way to go, all right."

"Such a shock to you and Rich."

"For her, too."

Roselle sighs. "Can I bum a ciggie?"

"You hate Salems."

"Any port in a storm. I'm out."

Ivory slides the pack across the Formica.

"Why won't you tell me about him?" Roselle asks, making a face at the menthol.

"Who?"

"You give people such a hard time, Ivory. People who want to be your friend, and you won't let them. The whole reason a person has a sister-in-law is to give them advice."

"You already gave me a good bit of advice, Roselle."

Roselle drops her voice. "Do you do it back in the stock room? Rich said he helped move your bed in there."

Ivory knows there's a red patch spreading on the side of her neck. It does sound sordid, spoken in Roselle's mouth, per-verted almost. She can tell Roselle is getting a sexual kick out of the sordidness, and she wonders whether Ray does, too—if that's the attraction for him. Casually she toys with a matchbook, leaning on her elbow, hand on her neck to cover the flush. "Not so long ago," she says, "Arlene asked me if you and Richie still do it."

Roselle freezes. "What did you tell her?"

"I said I thought you do it quite a lot. Now she knows I was right."

"You didn't have to say *quite a lot.*"

"Only enough to make a baby?"

Inside the oven the chicken quarters are beginning to sizzle.

"I really don't think I need you discussing my sex life with Arlene."

"Why don't we make a pact not to discuss anybody's sex life with anybody?"

"You give me a gigantic pain, Ivory."

"Sorry."

"What kind of pie did you buy?"

"Chocolate mocha chiffon."

"Well, that's something, anyhow."

Ray finds her sitting on the rug, her red challis skirt draped around her, unpacking a carton stamped *Taiwan;* it is full of small plastic toys with windup mechanisms: alligators, helicopters, porpoises.

"The sky tonight reminds me of a smoked haddock," he tells her, peeling off his rubbers.

"Good God. I'm *glad* I don't have a window."

She doesn't even have a fake window; in the end, the undecorated wall became so covered with clothing hanging from nails and boxes stacked against it that there was no room for her painting. The poster board is in a corner, rolled up, a string tied around it.

He laughs and kisses the back of her neck. "That was supposed to be a metaphor."

"I'm glad you told me." Though she pretends otherwise,
she's charmed by what he said.

"It's streaked in rows, yellow and gray, like haddock flesh."

"You are a poet," she says. "How was the roast?"

"Edible. Barely."

"I don't guess she was very mollified to have you there for
the one meal."

He sits next to her on the rug and picks a sliver of excelsior
out of her hair. "It doesn't matter, Ivory."

"Oh, I don't know. Hurting people matters."

"Her nose is out of joint. She'll get over it."

"I guess."

He winds the knob on the back of a yellow alligator; it
skitters drunkenly across the rug, wagging its tail. "She's not
my wife, after all."

"No."

"I missed you," he says, talking into her shoulder. His mouth
is so close she can feel the warm humidity of his breath through
her jersey.

"I was thinking about you, too."

"Nice thoughts?"

Without answering she moves away from him, stuffing excelsior back into the carton and putting it out in the alley. She
leaves the heap of toys on the rug and begins to take groceries
out of a bag. She runs water into the big kettle and sets it on
the hot plate.

"Good thoughts?" he asks again.

She thinks about her conversation with Roselle, and Roselle's prurient curiosity. He wouldn't like to know he was the
object of it. Or would he? She glances at him; he's playing
absently with a toy lizard, waiting for her to speak.

It's not only his ears that are neatly delicate; his straight, thin nose is, too, and his well-formed, careful mouth. The very modesty of his features arouses her. She feels very much like flinging herself down on him, right there on the holey, raggedy rug, but forces herself to carry on with the supper preparations. At bottom, she's scared of scaring him off.

"Ivory?"

"Yes, nice thoughts," she says, hoping her voice doesn't betray her arousal. She makes a false bustle, organizing.

"Is your mind somewhere else?"

"Just on tuna spaghetti."

"I was growing addicted to chili."

Laughing, she says, " 'Addicted' is a strong word."

"Habituated, then."

She's chopping a bunch of scallions. "Stick around, kid, and you're bound to run into my chili again. I only know how to make three or four dishes."

"What about all these recipes on the wall?" He's gotten up and is reading off the names. "Pumpkin curry. Greek spinach pie. Señor Pico chicken."

"Those are to trick people into thinking I can cook, just like ordinary respectable ladies."

"Who is this?" he asks. The dim snapshot is taped between Señor Pico and a picture postcard of Niagara Falls: a thin, dark-haired woman holding the handle of a baby carriage.

"My ma." She moves next to him and points to the carriage with the scallion-chopping knife. "That's me, in the buggy. You can't see my face. It busts cameras."

"I don't like it when you say things like that."

"Sorry," she says quietly, startled by the sharpness in his voice.

"I want you the way you are."

She notices that the stress is on the word *want*. He doesn't deny that she's ugly. Even in the heat of passion, he wouldn't go that far. He wants her in spite of it.

He is lifting her skirt; she feels his hand on her hipbone, his thumb in the softness of her belly. "Come to bed with me," he says.

She leaves the knife on the table and undresses. She hears his shoelace snap, his belt buckle rattle against the table leg. They have to step over the toys. In bed he sucks on a breast until she comes. He says, in little gasps, "I'm going to put a baby in you." His body presses her down.

"And then what?" she whispers.

"I'll take care of you."

Ten

....

TUESDAY MORNING RAY AWAKES with a throat so sore that
the torment seems to reach all the way into his ears, which
crackle dismayingly when he swallows. Though it is not his
habit to take sick days, and he rather scorns those who do—
for anything less than major operations—he feels that this
malaise may be a signal that he has overreached himself. Even
his penis is slightly abraded. Fifty-three is not twenty-three. It
will do no one any good if he wears himself out, and he has his
family's medical history to consider, too; his own father died
of a stroke when still in his forties. The man did not by any
measure lead a prudent life, but arteries are delicate things, and
it might not take much to burst one. Especially if a person had
inherited the tendency. All too easily Ray can visualize thin
pale fluid leaking into his own brain cells and inundating them.

"I'm not well," he announces to Lillian in the kitchen.

"Oh dear," she says from the enamel table, where she is
drinking coffee. She has a shrimp-colored scarf around her
head, made of some flimsy material through which he can see
flashes of metal and repulsive tumor-like lumps. This morning
he has not shaved or dressed, but come down directly in his
bathrobe, surprising her in her hair contraptions. The sight of
her head done up that way embarrasses him, and it does nothing to alleviate his physical discomfort.

"Don't get up; I don't believe it's fatal," he says, beginning to rummage among various boxes on a cabinet shelf. He settles on a trial-size box of Maypo that came one day in the mail and he rejected on first tasting. Fortunately, Lillian failed to dispose of the remainder, because it's exactly what he wants this morning: smooth, hot, and sweet. He squints to read the tiny cooking instructions on the back of the box. One of these days he'll have to break down and get a prescription for reading glasses, though he's prided himself all his life on his excellent eyesight. Another sign of age creeping up on him, he thinks sourly, as though he needed one.

"I'll make it," Lillian says, seizing the box out of his hands.

Ray pours himself a cup of coffee and brushes aside Lillian's residue—grocery lists, errand lists, appointment cards (hair, teeth, feet)—to make a place for the cup on the table. He does not ordinarily eat breakfast, or any other meal, in the kitchen, but now that he's here he might as well sit down. Doubtless the dining room is chilly this morning.

"Do you have a pain?" Lillian asks from the gas range, hesitantly, as though he might be rabid and turn on her.

"Sore throat."

She nods with a pinched mouth but does not comment. Probably thinking it serves him right, out at peculiar hours of the day and night, getting his feet wet and up to heaven only knows what. Ray smiles inwardly. He almost wishes he could tell her what he's been up to. In fact, it's right there on his tongue: *I'm sleeping with the girl with the queer cockeyed face. You remember, the girl who found Sam. In the back room of her toy shop. It's not only my throat that feels sore.* He feels it stir against his leg, inside his pajamas. Of course, he does not say those things to Lillian. She would crash right down to the linoleum, saucepan of Maypo and all.

She's spooning the cooked cereal into a bowl, not one of the shallow bone china soup bowls from the set in the dining room, but a striped plastic object that looks like it came free for a coupon out of the dried cat food sack. A further punishment, beyond her reproachful silences, Ray thinks. He can at least be grateful the bowl doesn't say *Kitty* on the side.

The Maypo feels good going down; his throat seems a little less sore. Perhaps he'll feel well enough by afternoon to start filling in his tax forms. He lingers over a second cup of coffee and the *Globe,* exactly what Lillian would be doing, he suspects, if he had gone to work as usual. Instead, he hears her upstairs, moving from room to room in her maddeningly slow and inefficient way, making beds or whatever. He reads the paper thoroughly, including an article about a winner of the Megabucks lottery, Ann Landers, the movie schedules, and the extended meteorological report. It is fifty-four degrees and drizzling in Taipei, he notes.

A few minutes past nine he goes into the hall to telephone the bank. After he has given Madelyn enough busy work to last out the day and set the receiver back in its cradle, he listens up the stairwell for sounds of Lillian. Since he hears water running in the bathroom, he dials again. He counts fourteen rings before she answers.

"Where were you?" he croaks into the receiver.

"What? Hello?"

"Ivory, it's me. Were you out somewhere?"

"No, I was busy doing things. I didn't guess it was you."

He decides not to strain his throat and waste these moments of privacy by telling her she should always answer her telephone, whether he is on the other end or not. "I'm afraid I can't see you today," he says.

There is a pause and then she says, "Oh."

"I'm not feeling very well."

In the bathroom Lillian has turned off the tap.

"What's wrong, Ray?"

"It's just a sore throat, but I decided to humor it." He laughs weakly.

"I could visit you. Bring you some soup or something."

"I'd like that, Ivory. You know I would. But I don't think it's a good idea." He hears the bathroom door open and Lillian's heavy though indecisive tread in the upstairs hall.

"Because of *her?*"

"That's right." From the sound of the footsteps, he figures that Lillian is now approaching the top of the staircase.

"You said she didn't matter, didn't you?"

"It's too complicated to go into over the telephone," he says, raising his voice a little as Lillian's legs appear between the balusters. "We'll talk about it tomorrow.

"Madelyn," he explains to Lillian, hanging up the phone. "The girl is incapable of following simple directions. She has a mind of mush."

He has not forgotten what he said to Ivory last night about giving her a baby. Back in bed, it occurs to him that she may have concluded from his call that he regrets his words and wishes to step back a little. It pains him to think he might be causing her pain, but something—perhaps Lillian's difficult omnipresence, perhaps merely the lassitude of illness—keeps him from calling her again to reassure her.

Ivory unplugs the phone. Between her teeth she tests several fingernails in case one of them has grown enough during the night to be bitten off. She eats half a stale doughnut. After some thought she makes a decision to cut her bangs. Digging through a carton trying to locate her sewing scissors, she comes upon a small sculpture somebody gave Roselle one Thanksgiving. It's a turkey, constructed out of part of a lobster claw, two scallop shells, two twigs, and a pinecone, mounted on a block of wood. Ivory finds a ball-point pen and prints *Raymond B.*, since that's all she has room for, on the block.

While she's cutting her bangs in the mirror over the toilet tank, the toilet paper roll suddenly unwinds on its own initiative and deposits two yards of toilet paper in laps on the floor. She starts, and a little jag of unevenness in the bangs results. All sorts of evil influences she has released. Poltergeists. Hexes. Bats out of hell.

She holds a clipped hank of hair to her upper lip and does her Hitler imitation. *Sieg heil.* When she's done with the bangs she flushes the hair down the toilet, willing the plumbing system not to protest.

By now it's almost ten. Carrying a mug of tea out to the shop, she unlocks the door and cranks open the awning. Across the street Sherman Hardware is having a sale on wooden clothes-drying racks, she notices. She wonders what the rack, as in medieval torture, actually *did* to the bodies of people accused of treason, heresy, and other forms of treachery. Pulled their bones right out of their sockets, she expects.

She will not cry, she will not.

She foresaw it, of course. It's what you get when you tease fate, count your chickens before they're hatched. In this case it was killing the eggs before they were laid, but the consequence was the same. Though she would like to hurt him, she doesn't blame him. She just wishes his loving had been less . . . addictive. That's the word he used about her chili, though maybe he was kidding, maybe he was really relieved when it was all gone.

She drinks the rest of her tepid tea in a couple of swallows. She sells a box of birthday candles and a connect-the-dot book to a woman who remarks, "One thing you got to give February: it's short." She dusts some boxes of puzzles, thinks about orga-

nizing her bills and receipts, watches some feathery snowflakes
float past the window. It's gradually turning into an ordinary
day, and at noon she walks over to the Triple A and orders the
egg and baloney special with extra onions, and—an inspiration
—a slice of cheese melted over the whole thing.

"You look different," Ray says.

There are untidy piles of invoices and canceled checks on
her table, no sign of anything being cooked. Ivory, at the table,
stares at him.

"Did you get your hair cut?"

"I cut it myself."

"I won't kiss you," Ray says, going to the sink to wash his
hands. "You might catch what I've got."

He finds several mugs, plates, and forks in the sink; one of
the forks has egg yolk between the tines. The bar of soap has
bits of hair stuck to its surface, and a limp morsel of lettuce
partly plugs the drain.

"I tried to call you from the bank this morning," Ray says,
lathering his hands in a clear corner of the sink. "Evidently you
were out."

He hears Ivory strike a match and smells the whiff of sulfur.

"—or not answering the phone."

"Maybe I didn't hear it ring."

He sees now, on the crowded shelf above the sink, the
lobster claw–scallop shell sculpture. "What's this, Ivory?" he
asks.

"It's a turkey."

"A turkey named Raymond B.?"

"That's right."

He dries his hands on the damp towel hanging by the sink.
"I don't think that's very funny."

"You weren't meant to see it."

"You just happened to leave it on the shelf."

"I thought you wouldn't be back here."

"What made you think that? Ivory?"

She's wearing that absurdly childish pink blouse with the button that doesn't match the others; below the puffed sleeves her arms, thin and straight as stop-sign poles, are mottled with cold. She doesn't know enough to put a sweater on in a chilly room. He sees a sweat shirt, half inside-out, on her unmade bed and brings it to her. Obediently she pulls it over her head but doesn't bother to right the sleeve, so that she is now one-armed, as in her dream. She hasn't answered his question.

He opens the small stepladder and sets it up near her chair; he settles himself somewhat precariously on the top step. "Am I going to have to do all the talking tonight, Ivory? I'm the one with the sore throat."

"How *is* your throat, Ray?"

"Better. But you could put out that cigarette if you wanted to please me."

With her free hand she thrusts the tip abruptly down into the dish so that the paper slits. Threads of tobacco poke out of the halves.

"Did you really think I was breaking off with you, over the telephone? You must have realized Lillian was listening to every word I said."

"It baffles me why you're so scared of her."

"I'm not scared of her." The stepladder teeters as he speaks. "You said yourself that hurting people matters. She's used to the household operating in a certain way; naturally a change is going to upset her."

"What kind of change are we talking about?"

"My not being there." He pauses. "Or your being there."

"With a pot of soup, even?"

He pictures Ivory's scorched and dented kettle on the white porcelain range in Lillian's kitchen. "Especially with a pot of soup."

Thinking, Ivory rubs the sweat shirt material on her trapped arm. "Is what you're saying: there aren't ever going to *be* any changes?"

Ray doesn't know precisely what he means. He's imagined Ivory's belly growing big right here in this room, in this— burrow—but he sees what she's getting at: sooner or later there would have to be a household that included her and her child, if not on Westwood Road, then somewhere else. This is a strange and unnerving situation for him to be in, calculations coming on the heels of feelings, rather than the reverse. Even when he ate Janeen's stuffed cabbage and apricot cake, it was with a clear head and an ample supply of prophylactics in his trousers pockets.

"Changes could have begun already," he says at last.

She understands him; she lays her nail-bitten hand on her belly. "Maybe," she says.

"I love you, my little urchin."

"I hope so, Ray."

He tugs her up out of her chair and wraps his arms around her in her sweat shirt, the one arm caught inside. "Do you love me?"

"Yes."

"Even if I *am* a turkey?"

"Yes," she whispers.

For three days it rained, leaving only a few low piles of snow, stiff with exhaust soot and gravel, along the curb and in shady places near the house. There's practically a swamp down by the garage. Today, since the clouds have parted and there's some thin sunshine, Lillian decides she'd better take advantage of the light to wash and wax the kitchen linoleum. She finds that if she does it on a gloomy day, patches of unwashed or unwaxed linoleum inevitably appear after she has finished. Holidays, her father the house painter called them, but to Lillian doing the floors has nothing at all to do with holidays.

She gets out the plastic bucket from the pantry, the sponges, scrub brush, ammonia, and soap powder from the cabinet under the sink. Somehow, doing even that much stooping and carrying seems to take all her strength. Her troubles are wearing her out. The sound she hears is not, she now knows, the heating system; it was so unseasonably warm on Saturday that the furnace scarcely switched on and the radiators stayed cool, yet she still heard the hiss. The only other explanation she can think of is something in the airwaves, something electronic shot out of a transmitter or beamed down from one of those communications satellites.

The mysterious thing, though, is that apparently nobody else hears it; there's nothing about it in the *Globe*, and it's not mentioned on the talk shows or the local news reports. Or maybe it has been, and she missed it. She doesn't feel that her mind is any less acute than it used to be, yet the external evidence is otherwise: she does miss things. Either that, or there's a general agreement to keep certain pieces of information from her.

Lillian pours a small heap of soap powder into the bucket and adds a splash of ammonia. Well, if there were a pact like that, Raymond would be the first in line to join. What he doesn't realize is that she knows more about him than he thinks she does. Always has.

She runs hot water into the bucket and sniffles as the ammonia fumes rise.

From the beginning, she knew he watched her as she moved

about the house at her work. He'd pretend to be reading a book or cleaning under his fingernails with a fork or some other tool that was handy, but really be looking at her out of the corner of his eye. Looking at her body. She'd open the bathroom door and there he'd be standing, right outside, hoping to see her bathrobe open a little. "Oh, sorry," he'd say, pretending to be surprised. Once she heard a step up on the top floor, outside her room. She knew it was the boy: there was no reason for anybody else to be up there, certainly not Mrs. Bartlett. Luckily, Lillian's door was closed, or at that moment he would have seen as much as he wanted.

Of course, he'd never have been bold enough to turn the doorknob. She'd have screamed bloody murder, and then he'd have gotten it from Mrs. Bartlett. The truth is, he was scared of his mother. Strange thing, too, because Mrs. Bartlett was a reserved person, never raised her voice once in all the years Lillian knew her. Though she certainly had her opinions, if you didn't know her you'd think she was downright shy.

Lillian, on her knees with her housedress hitched up around her thighs, starts to scrub in the corner between the gas range and the sink.

The boy was not as innocent as he wanted his mother to think. Lillian knew about the stickiness in his underwear and sheets, and she knew how they got that way.

He was a handsome enough boy then—still had all his hair. But it didn't surprise Lillian that he had no girlfriends, in spite of his good looks. He was timid. Or possibly proud, rather than timid, is closer to the truth; he wouldn't have risked humiliation, just as he wouldn't open her door. And maybe he was a little too pretty to interest Somerville girls.

She wrings the sponge, and gray scummy water streams into the bucket. Her bad knee creaks, reminding her to give it a bit of a rest. As she sits at the kitchen table and eases her feet out of her shoes she admires the square yard of clean linoleum next to the range. It's always best to start with the hardest part in any undertaking, she's found.

Naturally, when Raymond came back from New York City with his banking diploma he was too high and mighty to go creeping around after Lillian anymore. He went out on dates now and then, but there weren't any women he was serious about, or were serious about him, for years and years. Not until Muriel Neely. Moreover, Lillian would be willing to bet that Muriel never let Raymond get very close to her. You could tell by the way she sat on the edge of her chair those times she came to the house that she was ready to spring out of it like a rabbit if he so much as said boo. Some women are that way. They want a husband, all right, but don't want to meet a wife's obligations.

Well, now some woman has got her hands on Raymond who *does* like to do those things, or makes a good show of liking it anyway. He thinks Lillian's too dumb to realize something's going on, but there he's mistaken. And he's going to land himself in serious trouble if he hasn't already. What kind of woman would want him now—fifty-three years old and practically no hair left? Worse: set in his ways, fussy and short-tempered, and bossy, as well. A woman who would put up with that is a woman not worth having, in Lillian's opinion. She must be a desperate old maid, or a gold digger, or a crazy person.

Lillian sighs and gets up to refill the bucket. She wouldn't mind so much Raymond getting himself in a fix—you might say he deserves it—if it didn't mean that she, Lillian, is going to be dragged into the fix with him. She can see it coming with the naked eye.

Eleven

· · · · · · · · · · · · · · · · ·

THE WEDDING IS ARRANGED in such haste that a normal person would think a baby is already on the way. In fact, that is exactly what Lillian does think. Raymond gave her no details, no warning, no opportunity even to buy a new outfit for the occasion. "I'm going to be married on Tuesday, and I'd like you to be a witness. No need to dress up, the ceremony will be very private." That's all he said, period.

Private! Lillian thinks, hooking her brassiere. Secret, is more like it. A very good thing his mother is dead and in her grave. Lillian came close to declining to witness such a travesty, but then decided that without a single family member present the ceremony would be even more disgraceful. For the moment Lillian forgets that she is not, strictly speaking, a member of Raymond's family.

Stepping into the skirt of her navy blue double-knit suit, Lillian wonders whether Raymond realizes that his wedding day is also Valentine's Day. It is just the sort of tasteless, sentimental idea that would occur to this woman, whoever she is. Lillian does not know her name, or any other vital statistic, but does not need to. It is all over for Raymond, and for herself, as well.

Nevertheless, she will do her best to put a good face on things. It's how she was brought up, and what Mrs. Bartlett would have expected of her. She opens her quilted satin jewelry box and selects an ornament for her suit jacket, a filigree butterfly. It was Raymond's Christmas gift to her one year, before his mother had her last illness, before Muriel Neely. It seems ages ago, now. Even though she knows that Mrs. Bartlett purchased the butterfly for Raymond to give to her, as she pins it to her breast tears come into her eyes. She takes a fresh hankie out of the Louis Sherry box she keeps them in and dabs at the tears. It is more like dressing for a funeral than a wedding, she thinks, tucking the slightly damp hankie into her sleeve. One thing, anyway: the hiss in her ears has departed, just as suddenly as it came. It's just as well she never mentioned it to Raymond.

Two stories below in the driveway the Oldsmobile coughs and grumbles as its engine warms. The car isn't new, but since Raymond uses it on Saturday mornings only, it's in very good condition. Every spring Raymond backs it out of the garage and gives it a thorough waxing with Turtle Wax.

Lillian's mind travels back to the pet turtle Raymond had in his room the year she came to live on Westwood Road. Kind of a cute little thing. She remembers how when she'd be making Raymond's bed in the morning the cat—not Sam, this was several cats before Sam—would sneak into the room and reach his paw into the turtle's glass tank. The cat was only being playful but the turtle never understood that. Quickly it would pull its head and legs and arms into its shell and squeeze its eyes shut, pretending to be dead, waiting for the cat to grow bored and go away. If only it were always so easy to get unpleasant things to go away, Lillian thinks sadly. If only . . .

Raymond is calling up the two flights and asking whether she is ready. She runs a comb through her curls and takes her church coat out of the closet. Four years old, but, like the car, in good condition because it's not much used these days; it is

too treacherous to walk all the way to church over ice and snow.
She wonders whether she is on her way to a church now. In
this city it could easily be a Catholic church, she suddenly
thinks, with something like horror.

She settles her navy hat on top of her curls and adjusts the
veil, taking less time about it than she would like, but she
knows that Raymond is at the bottom of the stairs rattling the
change in his pocket and pushing back his coat sleeve to look
at his watch. She takes a last look at her peaceful, cosy room,
almost as though *she* is the bride. But her life will change as
drastically as any bride's.

Raymond doesn't seem as tense as she expected; he even
hums a little as he helps her into the passenger side of the
Oldsmobile and walks briskly around to the driver's side. As he
reverses the car out of the driveway, he lays his arm along the
seat back, just touching her church coat, and looks out the back
window. She remembers when he used to pick her up after
choir practice. Oh, *that* was a long time ago. Her hands, in
imitation leather gloves, are clasped in her lap. They are good
gloves, quite expensive. The only way a person could tell they
are not real leather would be by smelling them. The matching
handbag is on the seat between her and Raymond.

He's turning the car onto Central Street, heading south,
both hands on the wheel. It's a misty day with a flannelly cloud
cover; there's no snow left on the ground, but no sign of spring,
either. The grass in front of the Home for the Aged looks as
though it will never come back to life. There are beer cans on
the lawn and fast food wrappers in the hedge, but Lillian does
not have much time to reflect on time and tides and so on,
because he's now on Church Street, apparently headed for
Union Square.

She is determined to ask no questions; he'll only sidestep
them, and she doesn't want to give him the satisfaction of

seeing her curiosity. In the square, people are going about their business just as though it is an ordinary day, sitting under hair dryers, eating pizza, waiting on the corner for the bus. Lillian does not go into Union Square very often; she prefers the shops up on Winter Hill, which have, she feels, a slightly better class of clientele. Raymond told her once that mobsters live on Winter Hill, but she's never seen any sinister men in dark glasses; she thinks he must have been pulling her leg.

He's double-parking in front of a toy store and telling her to wait. "What if the person parked in that space wants me to move the car?" she asks as he's getting out. But he doesn't reply, just shuts the door. He goes under a faded green-and-white-striped awning and inside the shop. She expects him to return with a teddy bear or a stuffed giraffe. Nothing he could do now would surprise her, she thinks, but in only a moment she is forced to eat her words because she *is* surprised—astounded—by what he brings out of the shop: that odd homely girl who came to the house with Sam in her arms. She's wearing a ruffled dress with the hem dangling unevenly to her ankles and the same ratty fur jacket. The *bride*, Lillian thinks, appalled. Never in her wildest dreams did she imagine it could be *her*, and yet now that she knows, there is something sickeningly believable about it. Right from the start she'd had a hunch the girl was up to something. But, oh Lord, not this.

They walk—skip, practically—around to the driver's side of the car, and now the girl is sliding past the steering wheel; she's going to sit between them, crammed right up against Lillian. The fur coat smells alive. Lillian moves her handbag to her lap and grips the handle; she looks straight ahead at lines of cars and trucks bullying their way past blinking lights through Union Square.

"You remember Ivory, Lillian," he is saying.

The girl turns toward Lillian, but if Lillian turned too, their noses would be only inches apart. She is entirely unprepared for such intimacy. "How do you do?" she says, knowing full well how foolish this sounds, but what could she have said in this preposterous situation that would not sound foolish? Never mind; neither of them is paying the slightest attention to her.

Where to now? Lillian wonders. Perhaps they have chosen Stone Zoo to be married in, or Wonderland Dog Track. He's turning the corner onto Bow Street, passing the bank. Lillian thinks of Muriel Neely out in Arizona with the giant cactuses, sweet Muriel, who may have had an unfortunate complexion but at least would have known what is appropriate and dignified attire for a wedding, especially a hasty wedding under a cloud. But if Muriel were the bride it wouldn't *be* under a cloud, Lillian thinks, a little rattled by the girl's body, so close to hers, and the smell of the old fur, and by the twists and turns in her own reflections.

Raymond has turned up Walnut and is now heading out Highland, past the high school and City Hall, and the girl is pointing out the thrift shop where she buys most of her clothes. Imagine *saying* such a thing, even if it's true; but it explains a good deal. She sees with dismay that the girl's coat has begun to shed onto hers.

Beyond the hospital Raymond turns into a side street and pulls up in front of an unremarkable gray shingled house. Lillian is relieved to see that there is no plaster Virgin Mary in the small fenced yard, where two or three snowdrops have pushed their way up through the pebbles. A sign of spring after all, Lillian thinks, though she's unwilling to admit the possibility that it might be a good omen. As they wait on the steps for someone to come to the door Lillian brushes the left side of her coat, not too surreptitiously.

Right away Lillian recognizes the woman who answers Raymond's ring: years ago she was a member of Mrs. Bartlett's literary circle, a minister's wife. Behind her back Mrs. Bartlett used to say she looked like a sheep, and so she still does, but a quite kindly and respectable sheep. Chatting pleasantly, the minister's wife leads them into a chilly room crowded with an upright piano and great quantities of old-fashioned furniture. Raymond trips over a mushroom-shaped footstool and laughs, which is unlike him. He must be nervous, Lillian concludes. And no wonder.

The bride, now relieved of the balding fur coat, looks more ridiculous than ever, especially in contrast to the minister's wife in her plain wool dress and Lillian in her suit. The neckline of the ruffled dress is so low you'd be able to see a good bit of her bosom, if she had any, and she's wearing a necklace with only six pearls on it, and her bare arms are goose-bumpy and thin as broomsticks below the flouncy sleeves. The dress dips and pulls strangely over the area of her stomach. Lillian tries not to look there but can't help herself; definitely something is amiss, either with the cut of the dress or with the condition of the person inside it. Taking the hankie from her sleeve, Lillian blows her nose, more out of discretion than need. Better to have something, anything, to do other than look at the girl's questionable midsection.

As his wife plays "Here Comes the Bride" on the upright the minister is shaking hands and muttering inaudible half-sentences and fumbling in his prayer book to find the marriage service. The three of them—Lillian, Raymond, and the girl—bunch awkwardly in front of him, trying to avoid floor lamps and end tables. *Dearly beloved,* the old minister mumbles suddenly, *we are gathered together here in the sight of God . . .* and then, before Lillian can quite catch her breath, the thing is done.

When it is her turn to sign the marriage document under *Witness* her hand is firm, but Lillian feels as though she has been forced to participate in some bewildering party game the point of which she missed when it was being explained; her only hope now is to get through it as decently and with as much dignity as possible.

Back on Westwood Road, Raymond uncorks a bottle of champagne. They stand in the dining room, the three of them, as he pours the wine into his mother's tulip glasses, last used God only knows when. Lillian cannot bring herself to offer a toast, But Raymond does not seem to notice. After a few sips Lillian excuses herself and goes upstairs to her room. No plans have been revealed to her. She turns on her television set and is amazed to find that the same characters are involved in the same situation as yesterday. Soap opera is not like real life at all.

"We buried my mother at sea," Ivory tells him. She is sitting in a chair next to his bedroom window, smoking, wearing one of his undershirts and the add-a-pearl necklace she inherited from her mother. "Richie and my father and I. Well, not exactly at sea. We tossed her ashes into Boston Harbor."

They've drunk a whole bottle of champagne, made love, slept, and it is now seven in the evening of their wedding day.

Ray, from the rumpled bed, asks why they chose Boston Harbor.

"It's what she wanted, a sea burial. But we didn't know where to go to find it, just off the bus. We asked people in the street where the sea was; of course we didn't tell them why we wanted to know. 'Follow your nose and you'll fall right in,' a man said. He thought we were crazy, looking for the sea in February. We stood on a dock near some battleships and opened the box."

The cigarette smoke drifts toward the window, which is

open just a crack. Outside, it's dark and drizzling. "Go on," Ray says.

"There were small pieces of bone that hadn't been completely burned. 'Cut-rate funeral parlor,' my father said. He didn't pay for it, the Laundromat did, after getting my father to sign a paper saying he wouldn't sue."

"He should have sued."

Ivory shrugs. "He didn't trust lawyers. He was afraid of them. Anybody who knew more than he did about any particular subject made him very nervous. He would have been afraid of you, for instance."

Ray laughs self-consciously. "He wouldn't have approved of me as a husband for you?" He's picked up his watch from the bedside table and is expanding and contracting the band.

"I didn't say that." Ivory presses the end of the cigarette into a heavy green glass ashtray. There are already three filters there. "He would have been impressed, though he wouldn't have said so." Rain trickles on the window glass.

"After we emptied the box," she says, "he found a bar. Richie and I went into a luncheonette across the street. They called soda pop 'tonic' there. Richie thought that was very funny, like we were in a foreign country. He noticed that some of Ma's ashes had blown onto my coat sleeve. 'Wipe it off,' he told me, giving me a paper napkin out of the dispenser, but I wouldn't. When my father came out of the bar he said he'd been talking to a man who was going to help him get a construction job on a housing project. So we moved to Somerville. But it turned out you had to be in the union, and he couldn't get in, and he never did find the man who said he'd help him. Maybe he dreamed it. He worked as a night watchman in an envelope factory instead. But it was just as well, because he found out he had diabetes, and he wasn't fit to do construction work anymore."

"What did you do about . . . your coat sleeve?"

"The ash just wore off, I guess."

She feels she's told him too much about her family; besides, there are more important things to talk about. Opening the catch of her mother's necklace, she says, "Aren't there some things we have to decide?"

"Like what?"

"Where we're going to live, and so on."

He smiles. "Now that you're a married lady, you think you ought to start being practical, is that it?"

"Well," she says, "that's one way to put it."

"I thought we'd just stay here. For the time being, anyway."

Ivory jiggles the necklace lightly in her hand but doesn't say anything.

"From time to time I've considered selling the house, but there's the problem of what to do about Lillian. It's not only that she doesn't have money of her own, but this has been her home for nearly forty years. She doesn't have much of anybody else. It's a question of responsibility."

"I understand all that."

"I was sure you would."

"The thing is, I get the idea she doesn't like me a whole lot."

"Nonsense."

"*I* wouldn't like me, if I was her."

He smiles. "She's harmless, you know."

"I suppose."

Her chin on a knee, she studies his room: white curtains, so old they are fraying at the hems; sticks with hard grayish berries on them in an oyster-colored vase; a framed picture of trees in a grove; a tall oak bureau with a cross-stitched dresser scarf. Though she wouldn't have chosen any of these things, she finds them beautiful; she wonders, however, whether she isn't an intruder among them, and whether Ray won't soon feel so himself. She shakes the last cigarette out of the pack and puts the filter between her lips.

"There's something I've been wondering about, Ivory," Ray says, returning the watch to the bedside table.

Oh God, here it comes, Ivory thinks. *How did you lose your virginity? Who was the man, your lover?* She strikes a match, her fingers shaking a little; the flame wavers in the window draft.

"How did you get your name?"

She laughs in relief. "My mother couldn't decide on a name. It was time to go home from the hospital and there was still a blank space on my birth certificate and it looked like I'd be nameless forever. So my father grabbed a Gideon Bible out of the cabinet by her bed and said, 'Stick a pin in it. Anywhere.' She took a diaper pin and shut her eyes and stuck a verse about ships bringing gold and ivory and apes and peacocks to King Solomon, and that was that."

"They might have named you peacock."

"Oh no. My mother was much too romantic to do a thing like that."

"I love you, Ivory."

"You know what? I think it's time to go foraging in Lillian's refrigerator."

He gets out of bed and tosses his bathrobe to her. "Make yourself decent," he says.

In the morning Ray is up and dressed and off to the bank before Ivory is even half-awake. It is a dull day with an aluminum-colored sky, and the air feels strangely warm for February. She pads down the hall to the bathroom in bare feet. Nobody has thought to supply her with washcloth and towel, and she has no toothbrush. She makes a soapy lather in her hands and washes her face and crotch with her fingers.

Inside the mirrored cabinet are an assortment of personal items, some plainly Lillian's, some Ray's, all unsegregated. A shaving brush with the bristles worn down almost to the nub, foot powder, an earwax softener, several lipstick tubes, various bottles of capsules and tablets with prescription labels, and so on. There'd be no room on one of the shelves for anything Ivory might want to store. She dries her hands with a length of toilet paper, not wanting to be caught using anybody else's towel; since they are white, the least soiling would be obvious.

Back in Ray's bedroom, she realizes that the only clothing she has with her is her wedding dress; not even Ivory Bright, ordinarily oblivious to the stares of passersby, can go clomping around town in that. Anyway, she's no longer Ivory Bright. Bartlett is a much more serious and noticeable sort of name. It surprises her now that she did not think beyond the wedding, not even so far as to put a toothbrush in her beaded clutch bag. *And so the prince and princess were married and lived happily ever after.* Of course, the only experience of weddings she's had was Roselle's, and at the time Ivory was grieving too much for Richie to pay any attention to Roselle's plans and preparations.

Feeling a little like a burglar, she slides open the top drawer of Ray's oak bureau and selects a pair of socks, dark blue, with clocks. In another drawer she finds a stack of shirts, all professionally laundered, with blue strips of paper around them. He doesn't seem to own a single jersey or turtleneck. She unbuttons one of the dress shirts, narrow gray and white stripes, and slips it on. The starched front feels cool and stiff against her breasts; the sleeves are too long, so she folds them back and is reminded of the feathery hairiness of Ray's forearms.

Suddenly she is giddy with sexual desire. She imagines walking into the bank, past the swinging gate, past the secretary with the frizzy perm, and seducing Ray at his desk. Perhaps he'd go on checking figures on a computer printout while she unzipped his trousers, go on clicking the tip of his ball-point while she worked her hand inside his underpants, continue to sort through the in/out box while she made him come.

She opens the closet door and considers a row of slacks clamped neatly by their cuffs to wooden hangers; she finds a pair of chinos, probably the ones he was wearing the night he came to the shop to insure her life, or whatever it was he thought he was up to.

The chinos are much too big, even though Ray is a compactly built man. She rolls them up at the cuffs and, since she can't find a belt, pinches them together at her waist with the cord from Ray's bathrobe threaded through the loops. Not the most respectable outfit for the new Mrs. Bartlett, but not so terrible, either. Shoes are the hard part. Finally she folds under the toes of the socks and puts on a pair of yellowed sneakers that look like they could date from his teenage years, perhaps pre-Lillian. They'd clearly gotten wet at some point and shrunk, canvas tugging the rubber, so that though they're too big for her, they are not absurdly so. She wonders what wetness he walked through in them. Dewy grass? The surf at some beach? Maybe so in love with a girl he wasn't noticing his sneakers shrinking on his feet. She finds that she's jealous of that girl, although she herself wouldn't even have been born yet, by quite a number of years. It makes her uneasy to think that Ray might have his own secrets.

In the kitchen she finds Lillian at the table polishing silver; there's a smell of tarnish and ammonia mingled with reheated coffee and gardenia bath powder. "Good morning," Ivory says, while Lillian, sucking her teeth, takes in her outfit. "Will I be in your way if I make myself some breakfast?"

"Tell me what you want," Lillian says, beginning to hoist her substantial body out of her chair.

"You don't have to wait on me," Ivory says, more sharply

than she should have; the woman looks wounded, or insulted. "I'm not used to it," she tries to explain.

"Suit yourself," Lillian says, picking up an old toothbrush and working thick pink polish into the monogram in the center of a tray.

It's no accident, Ivory knows, that Lillian chose to bring out the family silver on this particular morning. Put the little stray in her place. She opens the refrigerator and takes out a carton of milk. She'll just have dry cereal. Some other time, when Lillian is not around, she'll investigate the whereabouts of skillet, spatula, can opener, butter knife. After opening and closing two or three cupboards, while Lillian pointedly ignores her, she finds the boxes of cereal. Cheerios. She remembers Arlene and Diane as babies, inserting Cheerios into their mouths with fat, careful fingers.

"Does Ray like Cheerios?" she asks, pouring some into a striped plastic bowl.

"Raymond likes Maypo," Lillian says. She takes in hand a rag, a discarded undershirt; she rubs the tray vigorously and the flesh of her upper arm waggles like a rooster's dewlaps.

"Maypo," Ivory repeats, mildly puzzled.

"There's hot coffee in the pot."

"Thank you; I won't have any this morning." Should she explain she only drinks tea? Will that seem like eccentric fussiness, putting everybody to more trouble? She'll have to remember to bring back a handful of tea bags along with her clothes. She sits at the table and sets the cereal bowl down in a small space that is not covered with silver polishing equipment or scraps of lists and cents-off coupons.

"Raymond usually has breakfast in the dining room," Lillian observes.

"Well, just for today, I'd like to eat here. Maybe you and I could have a talk."

"That's up to you," Lillian says, pushing her glasses up to the bridge of her nose.

"This marriage must have seemed to you a little sudden," Ivory says. "You must have been surprised."

"It's Raymond's business, not mine."

"I know, but . . . I don't want you to think it was done on impulse." Though of course it was, on his part, at least. "Or carelessly."

Lillian attacks the tray once more with the toothbrush. "People do what they have to do," she says.

Though the comment is ambiguous, Ivory decides to take it as a kind of blessing, if a grudging one. "I intend to be a good wife to him."

Lillian, scrubbing at the tray, doesn't reply.

Twelve

. . . .

BY THE TIME Ray reaches the bank it has begun again to
drizzle. Strange, he thinks, how the painfully joyous fullness
in his heart contrasts with the glum February weather, the
grubbiness of the carpet, the overheated stuffiness of his office, the pimple on the back of Madelyn's neck. Since Monday the pimple has come to a head and he has become a
married man.

Of course he will have to tell them, but he has no idea how.
Yesterday he took a "personal day" off; he was required to give
no explanation and he gave none. He has always hated to be
the subject of gossip, that was the worst part of his association
with Muriel, and he knows that now the tellers and bookkeepers and secretaries will have a field day. For the first time he
wishes he had a close friend among the bank employees, a
person who could make the announcement for him, tactfully
low-key and phrased in such a way as to defuse speculation. But
he has no such friend. From the beginning he has been careful
to keep his relationships with the staff coolly professional, with
the possible exception of Muriel. Though in retrospect, and
compared to his passion for Ivory, that relationship was cool
enough. Besides, there is no staff member subtle and tactful
enough to carry out such a mission, even if Ray *had* been more
forthcoming. No one other than Muriel, that is, and he could

hardly ask Muriel, even if she were not thousands of miles away.

He thinks about the girl he left in his bed on Westwood Road. Very strange to be sitting here at this steel desk, with his blotter and stamp tree and push-button telephone and box of ball-point pens with *Union Square Savings Bank* printed on them, thinking about his wife's naked body, still flushed with sleep and lovemaking, still filled with his seed. He senses that she'd let him do anything he wanted with her, and though he would never hurt her or act improperly, the power her trust implies is acutely exciting to him. It's a feeling he's never quite had before.

Madelyn turns from the copy machine to answer the telephone. On the line is one of his more difficult clients, a widow in late middle age who is both timid and stubborn, a combination that reminds him of Lillian. The widow's chief interest in life, so it seems to him, is tinkering endlessly and pointlessly with her policies. This morning Ray handles her in a sort of daze; after he has finally hung up he could not have reconstructed any of the conversation. On his memo pad he pens a notation that is more of a doodle than anything else, clips the page to one of her policies, and returns her folder to the file cabinet himself. There are several calls he is obliged to make, follow-ups to policy applications that came in yesterday's mail, and he puts those through in a similarly dazed state. He finds it remarkable that his mouth and ears will do things automatically while his brain is occupied with other matters; it is a revelation to him and, in a way, a frightening one.

By quarter to ten there is a lull in the busy work, and Madelyn, fingering the pimple on her neck, swivels her chair around to face him. "I heard a rumor," she says slyly.

Ray gapes at her. He cannot imagine how she could have got the news so soon; it is impossible that the feeble old minister and his wife are part of an information network that would reach Madelyn in less than twenty-four hours. Not only is Madelyn Catholic, she lives in Medford. Lillian, he thinks. Meddlesome Lillian on the phone already, deliberately setting out to haunt and mortify him.

"You may as well hear it from me, then, Madelyn," he says. "Yes, it's true. I was married yesterday."

Now it is Madelyn's turn to gape. "You were?"

"Isn't that the rumor you heard?"

"No-o." Her mouth makes a foolish lipsticked zero, revealing her discolored lower incisor. "It was about Miss Neely."

"What about Miss Neely?"

"Janice Fell—you know, one of the bookkeepers—got a letter from her. She hinted she'd . . . found somebody. But I certainly didn't know about *you*, Mr. Bartlett."

Ray picks up a stray paper clip that must have fallen out of a file, but, uncertain what to do with it, puts it down in another spot on his blotter. "Well," he says, "now you know."

"I guess it wasn't Miss Neely you married."

"It was not."

"Well, now you've gone and done it, I hope you'll be very happy. You and Mrs. Bartlett."

"Thank you, Madelyn."

Madelyn takes her break early, a few minutes before the hour. Though he keeps himself busy with various odds and ends, he can't help being aware that there's a certain low level of commotion behind the tellers' glass partition and at some of the desks on the other side of the floor, a certain number of covert or overt glances directed toward the Life Insurance Department. Hooks the loan officer gives Ray a decidedly inane grin on his way to his inner office. The cat's out of the bag now, Ray tells himself with resignation. At the same time, however, he feels a sort of secret pleasure in their knowing. Yes, he's gone and done it, and now they can say what they like about him.

Roselle is doing her nails in front of a rerun of "Love Boat" when Ivory appears, in Ray's clothes, dripping with rainwater. "That's the damnedest getup I ever saw," Roselle says. "Even for you."

Ivory switches off the set.

"Hey." Roselle's face is bland and shiny; she is like a darning egg with pin curls.

"We interrupt this program to bring you a special news bulletin."

Roselle blows on four rose-pearl fingernails. "The store burned down with all your clothes in it?"

"Pay attention, Roselle. I got married yesterday."

"Congratulations."

"I have the feeling you don't believe me."

"What makes you think that?"

Ivory removes a movie magazine, a nylon jacket, and an empty Sprite can from a chair and sits down. Blotting the rainwater from her hair with a section of paper towel, she says, "How come you're so ready to believe I'm sleeping with somebody but not that I'm married?"

Roselle takes a long look at Ivory's left hand, where there is now a thin red-gold ring. "I thought he was already married."

"He wasn't."

Roselle lays a stripe of polish along her thumbnail cuticle. "Thanks a lot for inviting us to the wedding."

"We didn't have a wedding, just a two-minute ceremony in a minister's living room." It has taken Roselle well *under* two minutes to deflate her.

"I didn't know you knew any ministers."

Ivory lights a cigarette. "He's not exactly a buddy."

"Well, who's the lucky groom?"

"His name is Ray Bartlett. He works in a bank."

"That sounds prosperous. Did he knock you up, or what?"

"Not yet."

"Then why the big rush to the altar?"

Ivory retrieves the Sprite can and taps her cigarette ash into the pop-top hole. "We just wanted to, that's all."

"You know, there's a five-cent deposit on that can," Roselle says.

"They still give you your five cents even if there's ash in the can."

"It's supposed to be *clean*."

"Since when did you start being such a responsible citizen?"

"I hate hassles in the supermarket." Roselle starts in on the pinkie of her right hand. "You could have had your wedding here. I could have worn the green dress I bought to be in my cousin Sheila's wedding and haven't had one single solitary reason to wear since. And now she's divorced, for God's sake."

"Maybe she'll get married again."

"It was a miracle she found one man to marry her. Lightning doesn't strike twice."

"You couldn't squeeze into that green dress now."

Roselle looks down at her softly spreading belly and sighs. "I would have tried." She screws the cap on the nail polish bottle and picks a pack of Winstons out of the clutter on the coffee table.

"You shouldn't be smoking, Roselle."

"You're a fine one to talk."

"As soon as I get pregnant I'm going to quit."

"So this guy wants kids, does he?"

The way Roselle puts it sounds strange to Ivory. A baby is one thing, but it's hard to imagine two or three kids running around the house on Westwood Road. In fact, she now recalls the night she first laid eyes on Ray's house; then she dismissed as out of the question that the gaps in Ray's hedge could have been made by any kids of his.

"Funny," Roselle continues. "Most men loathe the whole idea."

"Richie is a good father."

"I'm not saying he isn't. But he wasn't so wild about the prospect."

"He was very young."

"Not too young to make them," Roselle says sourly, kicking out of her flip-flops and putting her bare feet on a pile of magazines on the coffee table. "He was all gung ho for that part. How old is this Ray, anyhow?"

Ivory blows a smoke ring and watches it waver out of shape and slowly disintegrate before she replies. "Fifty-three."

"Good God. Are you sure he's not too *old* to make them?"

"Everything seems to be in working order."

Roselle's browless eyes narrow. "Has the man ever been married before, Ivory?"

"No."

"It probably didn't cross your mind to wonder why not."

"He never fell in love before."

"Ho, ha."

"Okay, what's your explanation?"

Roselle takes a bobby pin out of her hair, rewinds the curl under it, opens the pin with her teeth, and pokes it back in place. "Could be any number of things. One: there's something seriously wrong with him that you overlooked in your hurry to nab him. In other words, he's remaindered goods, and nobody but you would touch him with a barge pole. Two: he's queer. Three—"

"Oh, come on, Roselle."

"I mean it. Lots of times queers get married just to have some poor cluck take care of them in their old age."

"He already has somebody to take care of him."

"Wonderful. Now he's got himself a harem."

"Why do you always see things in the most disgusting possible way? She's just a housekeeper, an old bat."

"And you're moving in with him and the old bat?"

"For the time being."

"Good luck to you, Ivory."

"Thank you."

Roselle looks sadly at the chipped polish on her toes. "You know what? I always planned to be married on Valentine's Day myself, but it didn't work out that way."

"We did it by accident." Ivory finds a spot for the Sprite can on the corner of the coffee table and gets up to go. "Tell all your spies who saw me back at the clinic this morning," she says, "he made an honest woman of me."

For years it has been Ray's and Lillian's habit to be at the Winter Hill Star Market on Saturdays when the door opens at 8 A.M., and this Saturday is no different. From Ray's bed Ivory can just see the Oldsmobile idling in the driveway by the kitchen door, puffs of its exhaust mingling with the general fog. Then a door slams and the car, its dark green surface slick with rain, slips backward out of her sight.

Rain has been falling off and on for five straight days, ever since her wedding day. Early this morning she began to bleed, her period brought on early by sexual activity, perhaps, or the removal of the IUD, or some derangement of the hormones due to love. Tears come to her eyes, but this is one of those times when indulging in emotion is delicious. She finds it poignant, in an admittedly lunatic way, that she may not bleed again for nearly a year.

She lets the curtain fall and climbs out of the twisted bed-clothes. The house feels damp and chilly, no heat yet in the radiators, though she hears a certain amount of banging in far-off internal pipes. She washes quickly, pulls on her painter's overalls and a red long-john top, and, standing in the middle of the kitchen, eats a bowl of Cheerios.

Opening the dishwasher door, she sees that Lillian has al-ready emptied it of the clean dishes; she adds the cereal bowl to the saucers and cups from their evidently Spartan breakfast. She's never lived in a house with a dishwasher before and doesn't know how to work one. The dials look capable of transporting the dishes to the moon. Maybe the dishes are actually scrubbed by moonpersons in overalls, little urchins like herself, and then zapped back to Westwood Road at the end of the cycle. Would Ray think that's funny? Too infantile a joke, probably, for his taste.

She guesses she has an hour and a quarter, maybe a bit more, before they return laden with grocery bags. Lillian moves slowly, and Ray with care and precision. She can readily imag-ine him studying lists of ingredients, comparing price-per-unit volume numbers; she smiles fondly at the thought.

The first room she investigates is the kitchen. Opening the drawers below the counter, she finds more utensils than Roselle ever owned, though it's true Roselle is not the most ambitious cook there ever was. Ivory can't figure out what some of the gadgets might be used for, for instance, a stiff graduated spring on a metal handle. A cap belonging to a moonperson, she decides, left by mistake in the dishwasher and stowed away by Lillian in case it might someday come in handy. Inside the lower cupboards Ivory discovers an extensive assortment of saucepans, skillets, muffin tins, baking sheets, and the like. There's a cast-iron pan with small depressions shaped like ears of corn, and a waffle iron so old it has no electric cord.

Ivory hears a mew at the kitchen door; she lets Sam in and affectionately tweaks his ear. He pays no attention to her rummaging reconnaissance; idly he licks a paw and then wanders away to take a nap somewhere.

She finds in the upper cupboards four different kinds of loose tea, one of them chamomile; a box of horehound drops; some dainty cans of deviled ham and liver paste. There are a great many other cans and bottles and jars filled with food, both here and inside the pantry. The three of them could survive for months, years even, in the event of a nuclear catastrophe. Assuming Somerville were not reduced to a cinder pile in the blast—an improbable hope given its location and Ivory's own luckless tendencies, but you never know.

Next she walks through the dining room, a rather gloomy room with a bare-branched spiky tree growing smack up against the outside of the window, doing its best to cut off any light that might filter through the fog. There's a long table of some polished dark wood; clumsy chairs with embroidered upholstery the color of milky tea; a cabinet full of bone china; and a sideboard with cut glass, silver, and a strange pink vase.

She and Ray and Lillian have eaten dinner here on the previous three nights. Wednesday night Lillian said she'd prefer to eat in the kitchen, but Ray said no, she was to eat in the dining room as usual. Since there was not much conversation, Ivory had time to examine the various pieces of furniture and the pictures on the wall. Afterward Ray told Ivory privately he had no intention of letting Lillian play the martyr. But Lillian sat in her place purse-lipped and silent, picking invisible things off her dress. Ivory felt that her resentment at being deprived of martyrdom was possibly more painful to her than martyrdom would have been. She didn't tell Ray what she thought; she sensed it wouldn't go down well.

In the living room Ivory pauses and takes her cigarettes out of her pocket, the pocket Ray reached into to give her that weird unexpected orgasm. How did he know how to do that? she wonders, striking a match. Whose pocket did he practice in?

This is another gloomy room, the furniture arrangement and complicated drapery fixtures dating from Ray's mother's time, Ivory has no doubt. In front of the fireplace is a massive television console, clearly selected to harmonize with the other furnishings, but top-heavy and slightly silly on its splayed bow legs. Ivory turns the knob and after half a minute some wise-ass cartoon crows come into snowy focus in black and white. On another channel there are dancing cows with polka-dot skirts and false eyelashes.

She taps a quarter inch of ash into a plain glass ashtray, the only object on the coffee table. The table also has splayed legs, and she notices that there are tiny nicks in them. The slipcovers on the sofa and chairs are worn, too, not quite to the point of shabbiness, but dowdier than she would have expected. Money was not flung carelessly about in this house. The slipcovers are brown, with large salmon-colored flowers, and made of some material that would be itchy to bare skin.

The eight-day clock on the hall table strikes a single metallic note marking the half hour. She leaves the bit of ash in the ashtray—it occurs to her she's like a small dog leaving its sign on a snowbank—and walks across the hall to Ray's study. Here the furniture is more delicate in proportion, and also sparser. On the sills of the uncurtained bay window is his cactus collection: a dozen or more plants in miniature clay pots. Some of them, he told her, are not strictly speaking cactuses. All cacti, he said, are succulents, but not all succulents are cacti. Succulents conserve moisture because their natural habitat is the desert. One has the appearance of a cleft gray stone, but Ray assured her it's alive, and now she gently touches its fleshy surface, which proves his point by not being stonelike at all. The plant is simply pretending to be a stone, in case some hungry goat or camel comes along.

She looks around for an ashtray and, finding none, lifts the pot containing the succulent stone and deposits a worm of ash in the saucer under the pot. There's a fireplace here, as well as in the living room, but the opening is covered by a panel of wood painted to match the pale olive-green walls. The only place to sit in this room, except for the straight chair in front of the secretary, is a cracked leather armchair. Well, a person could sit on the rug, though it is nearly as threadbare as the one she got from Fogel.

On both sides of the fireplace are built-in bookcases that go all the way up to the ceiling. The books are mostly jacketless, with faded bindings in dull colors. No paperbacks. There are records, though, and a turntable with a clear plastic cover and an FM receiver. She pulls a couple of albums out from the row to read the titles: *F. Couperin Les Nations Vol. II; Mozart Five Divertimenti in B Flat Major.* What is the man doing with a wife who doesn't know one thing about this kind of music? She feels anxiety like a faint wave of indigestion or a minor cramp. No, the cramp is real. But so is the anxiety.

She turns the brass key in the secretary door and carefully lets the door down while sliding out the wood supports as she saw Ray do months ago. Here are his checkbook, a pocket calculator, a fountain pen, a letter opener, paid bill stubs from Bostongas and New England Telephone. No personal letters. Inside one of the arched cubbies, though, is a color snapshot: two women, shot from the waist up, with a dusty-looking palm tree. The elderly woman on the left has gray hair cut short and an alert, beady expression; the other woman is fortyish and quite pretty, in spite of acne scars and twenty or so extra pounds. Both wear pastel sundresses and have white cardigans around their shoulders clipped to chains at the neck. Nothing is written on the back of the snapshot except the developer's date stamp: *February 1983.* Exactly a year ago.

Could Ray have been along on this trip, indeed have been the photographer? The idea distresses her, not only because of her uneasiness about the nature of his relationship to these unknown women, but because she is so ignorant of the details of the fifty-three years of his life before she entered it. Up to her wedding day she'd assumed that Lillian was the only person with any sort of hold on him. The truth, she realizes, might be very different and a great deal more dangerous.

She slips the snapshot back into the cubby and locks the secretary. Her watch reads almost quarter to nine. She's spent too much time pondering the snapshot, which may have no meaning at all. In the lavatory she flushes away the cigarette butt and rapidly climbs the stairs, running her hand along the smooth oak banister.

The front bedroom, at the top of the stairs, was old Mrs. Bartlett's until her death. As she's passed the open door these five days Ivory has had the sense that some part of Mrs. Bartlett still inhabits the room, though Ray apparently makes no shrine out of it. Under the tufted bedspread on the big double bed Ivory finds plain mattress ticking, and the closet is empty except for some bare wire hangers, a desiccated sachet dangling from the pole, and a dust ball or two.

The drawers of the dressing table have been similarly cleared; no ornaments or personal articles sit on the bureau's linen runner. And yet there's a hint of perfume—in the patterned maroon carpet or clinging to the ball-fringe curtains—and possibly her body odor, though it may be only the mustiness of the unaired mattress. On the walls are murky landscapes in dark wood frames, under glass, and a framed photograph of a young, delicately constructed male child. The brownish photograph looks so old that quite likely it is not Ray but some ancestor Ray favors. There's nothing more to find here, Ivory decides, no more clues to Ray.

The only other room on this floor, except for the bathroom and Ray's bedroom, is at the back of the house, overlooking the garage and the small soggy yard. Though the back room was once meant for guests, Ivory supposes, it is now obviously where Lillian does the ironing, and stores the Hoover, and hangs her hand washing on a rack to dry. Inside the closet door a large red enema bag bobbles from a hook. Ivory shudders and shuts the door. This will be the baby's room. Lillian will just have to change some of her habits.

The eight-day clock downstairs is now tinnily striking nine. If she's going to do it, she'd better get cracking. At the foot of the enclosed stairwell leading to the attic she hesitates for a couple of seconds and then starts up the steps. These treads are narrower than those below, with grooved metal strips along the edges; instead of a banister there's a painted bar attached very close to the plaster.

Halfway up she pauses to listen for sounds of a car pulling into the driveway, but she hears instead something overhead: a dull thump and then the whine of a floorboard. Ivory gasps. Lillian has not gone to Star Market after all. It is a plot to trap her, with Ray the knowing or unknowing accomplice. Or perhaps it was Ray who wanted to find out what she'd do the first time she was left alone in his house.

A fat mottled face pops out of the shadows at the top of the stairwell.

"Hoo, you wretched animal. You scared me half out of my wits."

Sam, unabashed, flops past her on some business of his own, his toenails clicking and scrabbling on the metal strips. Ivory goes down to make Ray's bed and to accomplish one or two other housewifely chores before his return.

Thirteen

....

RAY PICKS UP a Phillips screwdriver, squints, inserts the tool into a screw in one corner of the upended toaster. Ivory, across the kitchen table, feels such a surge of physical love for him that it's almost painful for her to restrain herself from embracing him. But she doesn't want to spoil his concentration; she doesn't want to put herself in a situation where she might be shrugged off. She spreads peanut butter on a slice of bread that the toaster has refused to toast.

Ray removes the fourth screw, places it with the others inside a teacup so he won't lose track of it, and pries up the piece of metal concealing the toaster's innards. "What seems to be the trouble?" he asks the toaster, peering into its arrangement of wires and coils. Crumbs sprinkle onto the table.

Ivory smiles. She herself often has conversations with inanimate objects, but in her case it's just lunacy. Or loneliness. Ray does it with dry humor and with an air of quiet mastery over the balky appliance.

It is the middle of the night, and they have come down from their lovemaking for a snack. For Ivory to have a snack, more precisely. Ray seldom eats after 8 P.M. It isn't that he wouldn't like to, Ray assures her, but the snack might not like him. Experimentally he pokes a coil, prods a wire. "Hm," he says.

"We used to have a toaster that never sent the toast up. You had to lift the knob yourself. If you forgot, that toaster just held on to the bread and burned it to a cinder," she says, putting a layer of apricot jam on top of the peanut butter.

Ray picks up another screwdriver, not the Phillips this time, and gives something a firm quarter turn.

"My father got it free for opening an account at a bank," Ivory goes on. "Why doesn't your bank give out toasters?"

"Toasters never work properly," Ray says, fitting the metal plate back over the toaster's internal organs.

"Or table lamps? Or clock radios or food processors?"

"I can't say I've given it any thought. I suppose the management in its wisdom feels that interest earned is sufficient reward."

"Aren't you part of the management?"

Ray laughs. "I don't make that sort of policy, Ivory."

He has answered her gently, but almost as though she is a child, and she feels slightly hurt. She watches him fit the four screws into their holes and tighten them with the Phillips.

"Some banks give you free trips," she says. "If you open a big enough account. To Florida, say."

Ray plugs the toaster cord into the wall socket behind him and drops a test slice of bread into one of the slots.

"Have you ever been to Florida, Ray?"

"Never," he says, lowering the bread into the machine.

Ivory pictures the snapshot in the cubbyhole in Ray's secretary. She thinks about the two ladies in their pastel summery dresses under a dusty palm tree. It wouldn't have to be Florida. There are probably hundreds of places you could go on a vacation where they have palm trees. *Have you ever been to Bermuda, Ray? Puerto Rico? Tobago? Tahiti? L.A.?* Obviously she can't ask him one by one about every tropical spot on the face of the earth. And anyway, what would it prove if he said yes? He wasn't necessarily there with *them*.

The toaster makes a small urgent sound and then the toast appears, daintily tanned. "Bravo," Ray says, praising the toaster.

"February is a good time of year to go somewhere warm," Ivory says. "Especially if you happen to live in Somerville."

"Ivory, we've already discussed this, remember? I can't simply abandon my work whenever I might happen to feel like it. Vacations have to be planned for."

"I know that. I was talking in general."

"Why don't you eat this piece of toast, now that I've made it?"

Obediently she takes the toast but doesn't spread anything on it, just takes a bite out of a corner. Also she lights a cigarette. "You know. Just in general what a good idea a February vacation is. Most people take them in the summer, when it's nice where they already are."

"Probably they have children in school, or other responsibilities that limit their options," Ray says, gathering the spilled crumbs into his cupped hand and rubbing them off into the trash bin.

Children. Of course. Maybe the person in the sundress, the pretty fortyish one, got to be too old to have a baby and he decided he wanted to be a father more than he wanted her. Momentarily Ivory feels sorry for her, but she also feels worried for herself. Maybe he still thinks about that person. Maybe sometimes he wishes things had turned out differently, that he didn't have to take for his wife a messy ugly oddball just because she's of childbearing age.

Ray's hand is lightly on Ivory's hair. "Finish your cigarette and come to bed," he says.

Although in the past Lillian has done her shopping almost exclusively in the stores on Highland Avenue and up on Broadway, something now pulls her toward Union Square—in spite of trucks cutting through the square to get to the expressway and not caring whether they knock a local person down on the way; and retarded people from the shelter wandering the streets in straggly packs; and huddled teenagers up to sinister things in doorways and alleys; and refugees looking half-frozen in secondhand coats and speaking mysterious languages.

She is pulled, undeniably, to the toy store.

It's a shabby enough little establishment, with its tattered awning and carelessly decorated window. The window has nothing in it but a teddy bear, not a new one, dressed in a kelly-green polo shirt. *That's* the girl's idea of a display in honor of St. Patrick's Day. Lillian is not one of those people who pretend to be Irish on St. Patrick's Day. She *is* Irish, thank you very much, but not thank God southern Irish, and she wouldn't be caught dead in green on the seventeenth of March. If it were Lillian's shop she'd think of something more cheerful to put in the window than that sad and scrawny teddy bear.

The first week after Raymond married her the girl hardly went to the shop at all; she lazed around the house half-dressed, getting in Lillian's way and asking endless questions. She wanted to know where the thermostat was, as though Raymond would put up with anybody but himself monkeying with it, and what day the garbage is collected, and a hundred other things that aren't particularly her business. No more sense than a clothespin. In a way, you have to feel a little sorry for her. In over her head, maybe.

After that week the girl pulled herself together and went back to work. Probably Raymond had a word with her after Lillian mentioned to him she was having a hard time getting the housework done on account of all the interruptions. It must have been very annoying for people to go to the shop, planning on buying a birthday present, only to find the place locked up with no explanation. Serve the girl right if new customers took their business to the malls and never came back, although Lillian would not want the shop to fail altogether. Then the girl would be in the house and underfoot permanently.

At least there's no baby on the way. Lillian saw those cardboard tubes in the bathroom wastebasket. She wonders whether Raymond wasn't somehow fooled, or perhaps the silly girl was fooling herself.

From inside Sherman Hardware—she's pretending to be examining the packets of vegetable seeds on a revolving wire rack, then she's trying on different sizes and styles of stapled-together gardening gloves—she keeps an eye on the shop. *Toyland* it says in cracked painted letters on the awning.

One person goes in, but comes out with only a small bag, and the next makes no purchase at all. After twenty minutes or so the girl herself suddenly appears at the door and yanks it shut behind her—Lillian can almost hear it slam—and in her red hat shambles across Somerville Avenue, against the light and nearly getting run down by a taxi, and vanishes around the corner. She can't be going to have lunch with Raymond. It's just past noon, and Lillian knows that Raymond never eats his lunch before one.

Lillian hangs the gloves back on the rack and walks through Sherman Hardware with calm dignity, as though she has given the gardening wares her best attention and found them wanting. Not one of the clerks shows any sign of paying her the least notice; for once the indifference and rudeness of clerks is a blessing. Out on the sidewalk she just catches sight of the red hat, well past the bank, bobbing down Washington Avenue in the direction of the fire station. Lillian pushes the pedestrian button at the traffic light and as the sign flashes *walk* she sees the hat enter the Triple A Sub Shop.

Without any particular plan Lillian heads toward the sub

shop, the sort of place she almost never sets foot in. She does not believe in eating food prepared by strangers, except in decent sit-down restaurants, and it's rare enough she goes to those. Even if she wanted to spend the money, she would not like to sit at a table alone and be speculated on by the other diners and perhaps ignored by the waitress. Last year for her birthday Raymond took her out to a famous seafood restaurant down by the waterfront in Boston, but the occasion was not a success. They had difficulty in locating a legal parking spot among all those docks and piers, and before they were seated they had to wait in a long line full of tourists, and Lillian's scrod was undercooked, and Raymond thought the waiter made a mistake in the bill. It turned out the waiter hadn't; the fresh broccoli did not come with the dinner as Raymond naturally assumed, and they charged him extra for it. Lillian will be fifty-nine on the nineteenth of August. This year Raymond will probably not remember to buy a card, even, never mind treating her to Sunday lunch in a restaurant.

She walks right past the sub shop, not looking in the window. She can certainly smell the food, however, and the penetrating hot greasiness of it makes her feel nauseated and light-headed with hunger at the same time. She hurries on to the post office to buy a money order for Flo. Also, before leaving the window she purchases some penny postcards, although she has no special person in mind to send a postcard to, and nowadays they sell for thirteen cents apiece.

"What's that strange shiny yellow stuff outside?"

"Sunshine, I believe it is called," Fogel says. There's a definite suspicious quality to his gaze. "So what can I do for you this afternoon, Miss Bright?"

She decides not to correct him, since that would involve

going into more explanations than she's in the mood for at the moment. "I want to buy a sofa."

Fogel taps his relic-like fingernails on a Victorian plant stand. "Indeed."

"Not just any sofa. I have a certain one in mind."

"Oh yes?"

"The brass daybed. Of course, it's not in mint condition, but it could have possibilities."

"A nice piece," Fogel agrees. "It's maybe, from your price range, a little out."

"I wouldn't necessarily say that."

"The charity season, I'm sorry, is finished."

"Well, can I at least have a look?"

Fogel sighs, placing a hand over his ulcer. He moves several floor lamps and a set of rusty ice cream chairs. Delicately he lifts a plaster knight in armor holding an ashtray. The daybed gradually emerges. Fogel folds back the bedsheet dust cover, solemnly, like an officer of the law exhibiting a corpse to the next of kin.

"The brass is tarnished," Ivory observes.

"You'll use Brasso, it'll polish up beautiful."

"I didn't remember that the velvet on the cushions was so worn." She sits in the center of the daybed and bounces. "Not much in the way of springs."

"Miss Bright, if you are thinking you'll drop in, you'll while away the idle hour insulting my merchandise, let me inform you that idle hours I haven't got."

"What's your best price, Mr. Fogel?"

"That depends."

"On what?"

"On whether this is a buy-now-pay-never operation, or you have maybe cash in hand."

"Hard cash, Mr. Fogel."

Fogel, skeptical, looks again at the daybed. He says, "My best and final price is one hundred and seventy-nine dollars."

Ivory runs her hand along the brass rail between knobs and joints, imagining the brass polished and shining, almost like gold. "Okay," she says. She takes her wallet out of her cloth tote and begins to count out the bills.

Fogel is stunned. "You've taken up robbing banks?"

"In a way." She hesitates. "One more thing."

"Yes?"

"How soon can you deliver it?"

"Friday."

"I was counting on having it today."

"Delivery day is Friday," Fogel says firmly. "And for that it's ten dollars extra."

"In that case, could I use your phone?"

"Certainly. You'll kindly restrain yourself: don't call Vladivostok."

She dials City Hall, is transferred to Public Works, and after eight or nine minutes gets Richie on the line.

"Richie, you know those nice orange trucks the DPW uses for hauling Christmas trees and defunct hot water heaters?"

There is a brief silence. "What about them?"

"Do you think you could borrow one?"

"No."

"It would only be for a half hour, I promise."

Another silence. "Roselle tells me you got married."

She hears the resentment in his voice but is not sure how to acknowledge it. "It all happened kind of fast."

"A banker, Roselle says."

"He's not exactly a . . . Listen, Richie, about the truck."

"I could get canned for misappropriating public property. I could get arrested and thrown in the slammer."

"Who's going to know the article I need hauled isn't trash on its way to the landfill?"

Fogel snorts.

"Please, Richie."

"Oh, what the hell. I got enough troubles, what's one more?"

"I'm at the junk store across from the fire station," she says, hanging up fast before he has a chance to change his mind.

"A junk store this is not," Fogel says huffily.

"I just told him that so he wouldn't have any trouble finding it."

A few minutes after five Richie pulls up in front of Fogel's. In the meantime Ivory has rewrapped the daybed, tying the sheet on with lengths of fraying clothesline crisscrossed over and around it, threaded through the tarnished frame, and secured here and there with improvised knots not out of any scout manual. "Reminds me of the way Ma used to wrap parcels," Richie says.

"The talent must run in the family."

"What the hell is it?"

"You'll see when we get there," Ivory says, as she and Fogel are maneuvering the daybed around assorted obstacles toward the door. Once it's loaded onto the back of the truck Ivory climbs into the cab, rolls the window down, and leans out to wave to Fogel. He returns it with a wave of a lit cigar, his celebration of the cash in hand.

"So where are we going with this mystery item?"

"Westwood Road. I'll direct you."

Richie lets in the clutch. "I know where it is." He doesn't add: The reason I know is I'm there every Wednesday picking up the street's garbage.

"I appreciate this, Richie."

"You can call it a wedding present," Richie says shortly.

She glances at him; he's wearing his watch cap low on his forehead like a frown. "You act like it was some kind of sin to get married," she says.

"No, it's *you* acting like it's a sin, the sneaky way you did it."

She scratches her knee, unproductively, with chewed-off fingernails. "It didn't feel sneaky," she says in a small voice.

"Roselle is mad as a wet hen."

"I know. She didn't get to wear her matron of honor dress."

"It's not that. She figures you're ashamed of us, now you're a grand lady living in a house on Westwood Road."

"That's crazy, Richie. Nobody in the world is frumpier than me."

"All I'm telling you is how she feels."

They are at the end of Summer Street now, passing the old people's home. A man with oriental features is picking up cans and bottles and dropping them into a sack that drags behind him over the ragged brown lawn like a deflated balloon. Idly Ivory wonders whether the man is an employee of the home or whether he makes his living combing Somerville for stray containers and turning them in for the deposit.

"And I'm the one she takes it out on," Richie continues.

"I don't know how to explain so you'll understand."

Richie shrugs.

"I didn't want him to feel ganged up on," she says, after some thought. "So soon. It's hard enough for him to get used to having me."

Richie goes on by Westwood Road, since it's one way the wrong way, and turns into Cambria Street.

"I'm sorry, Richie. I didn't know Roselle cared what I did."

They are silent until he turns the corner. "The stucco house," she says, "with the green trim."

"Trim could use a coat of paint." He brakes and turns the key in the ignition.

She'd hoped to get the daybed into the house before Ray returned from work—he'd mentioned something about getting a haircut—but she sees by the stacks of coins on the hall table that he's already here. She adjusts the gadget on the storm door so it will stay open and goes back to the truck to help Richie unload. The daybed is heavier than one might expect, and as they are struggling up the porch steps, Lillian's bulky form in orchid polyester materializes in the doorway. "Goodness gracious," she cries, whether referring to the advent of this gigantic inscrutable parcel, or to Richie's disreputable attire, or to the orange DPW truck at the curb, Ivory can't be sure. Probably all three. Sam, alarmed, breaks for the door and plunges into a bush next to the porch.

"This is my brother Richie," Ivory pants, backing into the hallway with her end of the daybed. Ray emerges from the lavatory; he and Lillian stare at the strange procession as it passes by and edges around the corner into Ray's study. Lillian, eyes bulging, and Ray, with the small lavatory towel between his hands, follow along behind. Ivory sets down her end. "Richie, this is Ray," she says, breathless. "My husband." The men reach across the mummified object to shake hands.

"Well, I have to be going," Richie says.

"No, wait," Ivory says, frantically beginning to untie knots. "You haven't seen it yet." After a bemused moment the others approach the knots, and eventually the brass daybed with its ruby red velvet cushions is freed of its bindings.

Nobody says a word. In the setting of Ray's calm, spare study it looks as out of place as a furnishing for a whorehouse, which is no doubt exactly what it is, Ivory suddenly realizes. She never dreamed the cushions would glare so in the light of day; even the cactuses seem to cringe into their pots.

"Won't you stay and have a drink?" Ray asks Richie, recovering sufficiently to acknowledge this only dimly imagined brother-in-law, now unexpectedly here in the flesh, complete with down vest and baggy khakis stained with heaven knows what.

"Thanks, but I gotta get the truck back before they notice it's gone. Some other time."

Lillian lets him out, and Ray closes the study door so that only he and Ivory, and the daybed, remain.

"We needed a place to sit," Ivory says. "For the two of us."

Ray's palm is flat on his tie.

"We can sit there together and drink sherry."

"I don't really care for sherry," he says after clearing his throat.

"Or whatever."

He begins tentatively, "I may need some time . . ."

". . . to get used to it." She nods and begins to pick up odd lengths of clothesline from the carpet.

Ivory turns the hot water faucet on full force. She makes a row of objects along the edge of the tub: throwaway plastic razor, shampoo tube, washcloth, hair conditioner bottle. In this house they use a kind of imported glycerine soap that is the color of amber, and through which you can actually see light when the bar has worn down to a silver. It has a slightly caustic, medicinal smell: *Ray's* smell. It's what she was aware of when she first held him in her arms, his fine-haired head between her little breasts, but she didn't know it then. Now, as she sits in the nearly scalding water and rubs the soap over her body, she feels herself becoming lazily, sweetly aroused.

Since only yesterday her breasts have swollen. That happened the first time she was pregnant, too, the first sign that something strange was going on inside her body. Gently she soaps the softly convex belly, petting it, though she knows what's in there can so far be nothing more than a tiny clutch of cells in a nest of blood, barely visible to the naked eye.

She takes the razor and shaves in her armpits and then along the lengths of her legs between knees knobby as baseballs and Ping-Pong-ball ankles. Above an ankle a tiny cut appears; a little blood runs pink into the bathwater. Type AB positive, on the rare side, another peculiarity that runs in her family. Once after an explosion and fire in a meat-packing factory in East Cambridge they asked over the radio for type AB donors and she went to a strange Catholic hospital on the bus, but the nun would only take half a pint out of her because she was so skinny, and the way the nun clucked, Ivory was worried *she* was the one going to be prayed over instead of the burn victim. Ivory wonders whether this child will inherit her blood type, her left-handedness, her scrawniness, her fidgets and cravings, her general nuttiness. No, she decides, it will be Ray's child, a Bartlett, O positive and calmly confident.

He won't be back for quite a while; this morning, after Star Market, he and Lillian are going to K-Mart out at a mall to take advantage of the Washington's Birthday Sale. The other day Lillian, sitting at the kitchen table, made *x*'s in the sale flyer next to the items she planned to stock up on, and when she went upstairs Ivory paged through the flyer, putting together a sort of profile of Lillian the housekeeper, Lillian the woman. Brillo pads; ironing board cover; toothpaste; adhesive shelf liner; dress shields; calcium tablets; Listerine antiseptic; Dr. Scholl's cushion innersoles. Except for toothpaste, Ivory cannot remember having purchased a single one of these items in all her thirty-one years. There's much more to life than she ever thought.

She pulls the rubber plug and steps out of the tub as the

water begins to drain reluctantly into the pipes. Drano, that's what they need. Ivory has certainly bought Drano enough times.

Drying herself with a clean white towel, she's aware of a possible darkening of the nipples. That's another sign, she once heard Roselle remark grimly. Roselle resented every change in her body, more or less the way you'd resent a vandal marking up your house with graffiti. Ivory will not be like that. She'll be glad of the changes, streaks in her belly and bulging vessels in her calves and all. She towels her hair, brushes the damp bushiness into something like order, pulls on a pair of jeans— once Richie's but Roselle washed them in hot water and they shrank—and a jersey striped horizontally as if for a sailor or a prisoner.

Halfway down the stairs she sees that the mail has been thrust through the slot in the door and is now lying untidily on the little rag foot-wiping rug. Though she doesn't expect to find anything for her, she gathers it up and glances through the various envelopes and advertising flyers. One piece jumps out: a picture postcard showing a huge natural tunnel in a cliff of dun-colored rock. You can tell the hole is huge because of the fruit fly–size person standing inside it. *"Ear of the Wind,"* Monument Valley, Arizona, the caption reads. *Monument Valley is internationally famed for its picturesque buttes and pinnacles.* The message, handwritten, says: "Can the rumors I hear be true? As ever, Muriel."

Ivory imagines that the fruit fly is this Muriel. She imagines the rock suddenly caving in and crushing her.

Fourteen

....

IT IS THE LAST day of February in this leap year. A troubling sort of day, Ray thinks, since it wouldn't exist save for the awkward fact that the solar year divides into days unevenly. The "leap" is rather like juggling figures in a ledger; it offends Ray's sense of order. Moreover, it's a puddly day with treacherous-looking clouds and a raw wind. Removing his rubbers in the bank doorway, Ray notes that the maintenance man has once again failed to unroll the strips of vinyl that are supposed to protect the heavily trafficked areas of carpet in inclement weather. However, Ray doesn't say anything. Let the trustees worry about the carpet.

He feels confused and a little jittery this morning; his breakfast coffee is an acrid irritant in his throat. The last several days have not gone particularly well. He spent most of Saturday escorting Lillian from mall to sordid mall in pursuit of advertised specials. That evening Ivory insisted on their sitting on her brass daybed and listening to music on the phonograph; he didn't want to admit to her that his back was sore from lugging parcels and he would have much preferred to read the newspaper in his own comfortable armchair. They did not make love that night—he didn't really feel up to it—and all day Sunday she seemed troubled by something but didn't say what. Well, he does not in fact wish to hear about women's hormones and other internal difficulties; such things faintly disturb him.

By Monday evening Ivory seemed in somewhat better humor, but Lillian spent the entire dinner hour complaining about her numerous physicians: how long they make her wait to see them and what short shrift they give her ailments. Perhaps he should have let her take her meals in the kitchen after all. Last evening Ivory was again out of sorts. After dinner she brought the bottle of Christmas Scotch into the study after dinner and in his opinion drank more of it than she should have. He remembers her jiggling foot in its orange and green argyle sock, moving not to the rhythm of the harpsichord concerto on the phonograph but to some irritable meter of its own. They have not made love in five days. Neither put the other off; for some reason it just didn't come about.

Absently he turns his small metal pencil sharpener around the end of a pencil and blows the shavings into his wastebasket. The truth is he feels his household has an unsettled air to it, and though he knew living with Ivory would not be a placid experience, he did not foresee this uneasy sense of . . . waiting for something. Perhaps what bothers him is nothing more than the sight of the boxes of Ivory's possessions, half-unpacked, cluttering his mother's bedroom.

He supposes the sensible thing would be for the two of them to move in there. But for some reason he is uncomfortable at the idea, and Ivory, as if sharing his reluctance, does not suggest it. Eventually, though, they'll have to arrange something more practical and permanent, especially when she begins to have a big belly. As it is she seems to have dozens of sharp angles and protuberances on her body that nudge him into wakefulness a number of times every night.

He must have sighed out loud without realizing it, because Madelyn turns from her typewriter. An indecipherable look crosses her rather stupid face and she says under her breath, "You've heard, then?"

"Heard what?" he asks, thinking randomly of chemical spills, presidential assassinations, declarations of war.

"About Miss Neely."

"What about her?" Married, probably, to some unsuitable person. On the rebound, he believes they call it. Foolish woman; she could even have mailed that picture postcard of some Arizona tourist trap while on her honeymoon.

"She's dead," Madelyn says, shivering, as though a body were laid out in this very room.

"What are you talking about?"

"They're asking everybody to contribute to a wreath."

"A wreath." Appalled, Ray stares at her.

"Heart failure. She had a bad heart, you know."

"No." Ray pulls at his tie knot, gazes at the liver spots on his hand. "No, I didn't know."

"When she was a kid she had a disease that damaged it, some kind of fever. I'm surprised she didn't tell you. At one time you and Miss Neely were pretty thick, weren't you?"

Thick. What an inane way to describe whatever it was he and Muriel were.

"A lot of people around here knew. Funny you didn't."

Ray rises out of his swivel chair, but there's nowhere in this office to go. Five paces to the file cabinet, five to the copy machine, five to the wall behind him with its painting of a galleon in full sail on a garishly moonlit sea. He feels the glances of the tellers fix on him as he moves fretfully in this circumscribed little spot.

"Well, if you have to die it's a good way to go," Madelyn is saying. "Quick. Not like cancer or one of those diseases that eat you up a little at a time."

"Do you know when it happened?" Ray asks, thinking that when he picked up the postcard from the hall table she might already have been dead.

Madelyn shrugs. "Over the weekend, I heard. She was on a vacation trip someplace, and it took quite a while for the police to notify her mother and for her mother to notify her friends."

Tactfully, Madelyn does not point out that he, having received no such call, was not numbered among Muriel's friends at the last. He supposes Doris Neely must feel bitter toward him for letting Muriel down. Indeed, it now occurs to him, she may actually blame him for bringing on Muriel's death with his own marriage. *Can the rumors I hear be true? As ever, Muriel. As ever . . .*

Ray sits at his desk. The odium is going to stick to him, he sees that. Muriel had many friends in the bank; they will all be on her side against him, in spite of the fact that he never mentioned the word "marriage" to her, and it was she who pulled up stakes and went to live in the desert, excoriating herself like some sort of female St. Simeon. All his life Ray has been afflicted by martyrs. First his sainted widowed mother, then Lillian, and now Muriel. He does not believe he deserves it.

An unfortunate coincidence is all it was. It cannot be true that a heart literally breaks.

"Can I help?"

Scowling, Lillian turns the hot water tap hard. "Needs a new washer," she says. "But *I'm* not going to tell him. Not the mood he's in."

"I mean with dinner."

"Raymond has his moods," Lillian says darkly, ignoring the

offer. "I could tell you a good deal about Raymond's moods, believe me."

Ivory is not eager to imagine what Lillian knows about Ray's inner self. Nonchalantly she leans against the refrigerator and takes a yo-yo from the pocket of her overalls. "I didn't notice anything different," she says untruthfully. She lets the yo-yo spin out as far as the gas range and then reels it in with a jerk of her wrist.

"Didn't you?" Lillian eyes the yo-yo. Her expression is the same as if the yo-yo were some unreliable small breed of dog, apt to make a mess in her clean kitchen. Sucking in her teeth, she goes back to paring carrots in the sink.

"He didn't say much at all." The yo-yo snaps to the edge of the counter and returns to Ivory's hand.

"That's how you can tell. When he comes home from the bank quiet like that." Lillian's knife blade makes harsh scraping sounds against the carrot.

Ivory unwinds the cord from the yo-yo and slowly winds it around her wrist.

"He goes inside himself," Lillian says. "He might as well be a million miles away or on the moon."

Or in a desert, Ivory thinks. A desert with picturesque buttes and pinnacles.

"Well, you'll find out for yourself."

Unwinding the cord, Ivory sees that she's made white furrows in her wrist. Her hand throbs.

"People do, sooner or later," Lillian says, beginning to slice the carrot into rounds.

People. Meaning this Muriel, familiar with Ray's moods. Maybe less content than Ivory to put up with them. Maybe it was Muriel who broke off with Ray, and not the other way around. And now she's sorry she was so rash and wants him back again.

Ivory is frightened that in any serious contest she'd be the one to lose, wedding ring or no wedding ring. Hand in her pocket, she touches her belly, willing there to be a baby inside.

"Sooner or later," Lillian repeats.

"Please can't I help with dinner?"

"Nothing left to do," Lillian says briskly, running water onto the carrots and lighting a fire under the pan.

"Sneeze on a Wednesday, sneeze for a letter," Lillian says to herself, wiping her nose, though she wonders whether sneezing as a result of laundry detergent counts. God knows it's not often she gets a letter, except for self-serving billy-doos from local politicians wanting you to vote for them or give them money, and the monthly church bulletin, and once in a while a depressing letter from Flo.

Lillian's cousin Flo is one of those people who suffer more than their share of life's misfortunes: major surgery, widowhood, floods, automobile crashes in vehicles on which the insurance has just lapsed. Lillian feels sad about Flo, though she can't help suspecting that certain people, including Flo, bring their troubles on themselves in some mysterious way. The cousins have not laid eyes on one another in more than forty years, ever since Flo eloped with a sailor she met in a Hayes-Bickford cafeteria and ended up in Beulah, Wisconsin. That's when the calamities started. By now Flo must have more stitches in her than Mrs. Bartlett's dining room chairs, especially after the last operation, when she had both breasts removed. Lillian feels more than a little queasy just thinking about it, even though Flo never had much bosom to speak of.

She turns out the pockets of Ivory's overalls, finding a crumpled tissue and a matchbook; the girl doesn't know enough to empty her pockets before she drops her clothes in the hamper.

Lillian stuffs the overalls into the machine along with a couple of pairs of socks and the rag rug from the hall. She supposes that Ivory will not notice if the overalls pick up a little lint from the rug. In any case, Ivory certainly can't expect Lillian to run the machine through all its cycles just for one or two articles of clothing, and it's not as though the girl is what you could call fastidious. Badly brought up. Not brought up at *all.* Even Muriel Neely, who was not exactly a fashion plate, did not appear in public looking like a sewer worker.

Lillian frets to think of Muriel. She couldn't help seeing that postcard when she emptied the wastebasket under the hall table. *Can the rumors I hear be true?* she wrote to Raymond. Well really, she might have taken Lillian's word for it; Lillian is not in the habit of sending falsehoods through the U.S. mail. Muriel had every right to know what Raymond had done, and since Raymond was not likely to have the graciousness to enlighten her himself, Lillian felt it was up to her to do so. It's terrible to let somebody go on hoping and praying, even in one little corner of the mind, for something that isn't going to happen. So although some might label it butting-in and busy-bodyness, Lillian is satisfied she did the right thing. It's lucky she rescued Muriel's Christmas card envelope from the wastebasket; she must have had a foreboding that someday she was going to need the address.

Lillian pulls the knob to start the fill cycle and settles herself in a canvas deck chair to await the moment to add the bleach. It's lonely and humid down here in the basement. Sometimes it seems to her that her whole life has been nothing but a string of these empty snatches of time, too short to do anything else in, but long enough to bore a person to death. However, she has no intention of whining about it. A person just has to make the best of things in this life, though God knows it would not be the easiest thing in the world to carry on with both breasts cut off like poor Flo. Reflexively Lillian's hand lifts to her bosom. It might be better to let the cancer spread where it would.

She watches the cold water rise behind the circle of glass, soaking into the rag rug and the overalls. Once Flo wrote that after a big storm the lake overflowed and flooded the first floor of her house. Warped the piano, embedded the living room in silt, nearly drowned the parakeet in its cage. Of course, a person could say that if you live on a lake you ought to be prepared for calamities like that; nobody forced Flo to buy that particular house. Still, nobody forced Lillian to come to Westwood Road, either; yet here she is, nearly forty years later, cooking the girl's meals, scrubbing the bathtub after her, emptying her ashtrays, washing her grimy overalls.

Lillian's thoughts wander back to her innocent childhood, when she and Flo rode on a tire swing and squeezed lemons for lemonade, and even though the stock market had crashed in faraway New York City, the Depression hadn't yet touched any of the Dunlops. When the machine screeches to a stop at the end of the last cycle, Lillian discovers she has forgotten to add the powdered bleach. Well, probably the girl won't notice the difference. As she's transferring the heavy damp laundry to the dryer, one of Ivory's silly green and orange socks drops by mistake to the concrete floor. Lillian stoops to retrieve it. Something comes over her then, and instead of popping it into the dryer, she tucks the damp sock into her apron pocket.

Ivory, smoking, gazes at a cobweb woven in the far corner of Ray's study, just under the ceiling. "What would happen," she asks, "if I went to the pantry and got the broom and poked that cobweb down? Would Lillian try to grab the broom from my hands and do it herself?"

Ray holds a record delicately between his palms, taking care not to touch the grooves, and reads the label. He takes a breath. "Lillian is upstairs," he says, making a show of patience.

"Suppose she came down for a cup of Ovaltine and caught me in the hall with her broom?"

Deftly Ray flips the record and places it on the turntable. With a small motion of his fingertip he moves the arm, lowering the needle to the first groove. "Ivory, the time has come to tell me what's bothering you," he says.

Violins begin to make what Ivory sees in her mind as jagged pinnacles. Strange that he should accuse *her* of being bothered, when it is *he* who has retreated into a mood, as Lillian called it. Thinking, she studies the filter of her cigarette. It's a Kool; in an intermediary stage to quitting she has switched brands.

"Lillian is doing her best to adjust," Ray says. "It isn't easy for her."

She watches as he slips a record into its sleeve and jacket, reaches to insert it into its proper place on the shelf. The back of his neck is dear to her. The nape is defenselessly slim, tapering rather sharply from the fine muscles behind his ears. At last, when he turns to face her, she asks, "Ray, who is Muriel?"

His look of guilty surprise is so brief, before he composes his perfect features, that she might have missed it if she hadn't been watching him so carefully. "Has Lillian been talking to you about Muriel?" he asks, frowning.

"No."

"Who has, then?"

"Nobody, Ray. I happened to see the postcard she sent you."

He sits next to her on the daybed. "Put out the cigarette, Ivory." When she's squashed it into the glass ashtray, he takes her left hand and looks at the chewed nails and cuticles, the tobacco stain on the index finger. "She's a woman who used to work in the bank," he says, turning Ivory's hand over and staring into the palm. "We were friends, quite good friends." Gently he traces the creases in her palm with a fingertip; she feels herself becoming aroused, in spite of herself.

"Did you love her?"

He pauses. "I was very fond of her."

"You aren't answering the question."

"I believe it accurately describes how I felt."

She pulls her hand away and clasps it with the other. "But she went away to Arizona," she says, her voice tight with wretchedness, "and then you settled for me."

"You don't need to be jealous of Muriel, Ivory."

"That's easy to say. How would you feel if I was bombarded with mail from old lovers?"

"There won't be any more mail from Muriel. Muriel is dead."

Ivory closes her eyes. She sees again the rock collapsing, crushing the tiny woman in the tunnel, breaking every bone to splinters.

"She died of heart disease," Ray is saying. "She had a weak heart, some childhood illness. It just gave way on her, that's all."

Ivory's knuckles are white on the cold brass arm rail. "When?" she whispers.

"I'm not sure. Sometime over the weekend."

"How queer," she says, in a hoarse, cramped voice. A heart attack could feel to the victim like a rib cage crushed by falling stones.

"Yes, I know. The postcard arriving when it did. Posthumously, I suppose, is the word."

Let him think that's what she meant. She begins to shake, terrified of what she has wreaked with her evil thoughts. But his hands are on her now, reaching under her jersey, fumbling for her breasts. "Don't think about Muriel anymore," he says into her ear. It is a strange, dry, hard lovemaking, there in the room with the cactuses; she feels that only by swallowing him whole, alive, could she be completely satisfied.

Fifteen

....

"SOMEBODY KNOCKED DOWN the tree in the island in front of the hardware store," Arlene says, shaking sleet out of her stringy yellow hair.

"I saw."

"They must have done it with a Mack truck. All that's left is a stump." She drops soggy mittens on the top of the glass counter, takes a stick of gum out of the pocket of her ski parka, and unwraps it. "Want a piece?"

"Not right now," Ivory says.

"Some people are crazy," Arlene observes, crumpling her gum wrapper into a small ball and dropping it into the kite basket. "They go knocking down trees just for the fun of it."

"Maybe they were angry for some reason and took it out on the tree."

"Some excuse."

"I didn't say it was an excuse, just an explanation."

Arlene shrugs and winds the key in the back of a shaggy mechanical monkey.

"Any special reason you aren't in school?"

The monkey claps a pair of tinny metal cymbals together with half a dozen spastic jerks of its arms and Arlene laughs. "It's a holiday."

"What holiday? Nobody told me about any holiday."

"Arlene Bright Day."

"That's called truancy, Arlene. You want to grow up not knowing the products of the state of Iowa?"

Her smooth high brow wrinkles as she thinks. "Pigs and corn."

"Amazing."

"I won't be able to finish this term anyhow," she says, shifting her gum to the other side of her jaw.

"You're planning on setting fire to the school?"

"No, but I'm not supposed to tell."

"What exactly is going on, Arlene?"

Arlene takes a swing at a ball attached to its paddle with a piece of elastic, and misses. "Don't tell Mom I said. We're moving."

"Oh really? Where are you moving to?"

"Billerica. Diane's mad because she'll have to leave all her friends. I'm not so wild about it either."

"When did all this get decided?"

"Who knows? Mom told us a couple of days ago," she says, taking another swing at the ball and narrowly missing a stuffed owl. "Half our stuff is packed already, and nobody can find anything. I think she packed my language arts book."

"Were they going to leave just like that, without even telling me?"

"You got married without even telling us."

"That's not the same thing."

"Mom says it is. Mom says, next time Ivory wants us for something, let her find us gone." She pulls the ball hard away from the paddle and lets the elastic snap. "Everything bad has been happening since you left, Ivory," she says resentfully. "Diane never does her turn on the dishes, and Mom's varicose veins hurt so all she cooks is hot dogs."

"I suppose all that is my fault."

"I miss you." She swallows her gum. "Besides, I always wanted to be a flower girl."

"You're too tall to be a flower girl."

"And now I never will be," she says mournfully.

"You'll like Billerica. They probably don't knock trees down with Mack trucks in Billerica."

"Maybe *I'll* knock them down."

"No you won't."

Arlene picks up a toy eggbeater and thoughtfully turns the crank. "Is your husband rich?"

"Not particularly."

"Mom says he must be. Everybody on Westwood Road is rich, and besides, he works in a bank."

"That's ridiculous."

"Mom says he's real old, too. When he kicks the bucket you'll be a rich widow."

"He's not all that old."

"I wouldn't want to marry somebody old," Arlene says, losing interest in the eggbeater. "Even if he was rich." She looks into a kaleidoscope, squinching the other eye shut. "I took one of these apart once. All that's inside is mirrors and little colored pebbles."

"That's where nosiness gets you."

"It was a scientific experiment."

"Some things you should just leave be."

"Ivory, is he a nice man, at least?"

"Yes. I think so. Let's go over to the Triple A; I feel a great hunger coming on. How about an egg and baloney special?"

"Anything but a hot dog," Arlene says, picking up her soggy mittens from the counter and stuffing them into her pocket.

. . . .

Lillian, watching from her spot between the seed rack and a roll of galvanized fencing, sees Ivory and a young girl in a two-tone hooded jacket leave the toy store. Lillian also notices that the girl lets the door fall shut behind her but does not pull it tight. That's how youngsters are these days: careless. At the counter Lillian purchases one packet of Scarlet Gleam Improved nasturtium seeds for the outrageous sum of seventy-five cents. Plus tax. "Have a good day," the clerk says, although outside sleet is falling and right in front of his own store what used to be a maple sapling, recently planted by the city, is now nothing but splinters. Opening her handbag to slip in the seeds, Lillian shakes her head in mild wonderment. Often it seems to her that nobody but she is aware of the dismal condition the world has got into, and if they don't even notice, they certainly aren't going to do anything to change it. She's glad, after all, she never had children. It would be dreadful to think she'd be leaving her own flesh and blood behind to cope with a world filled with violent maniacs.

In the window of the toy shop the teddy bear now has on its head a top hat made of shiny green cardboard with *Erin Go Bragh* printed on the hatband. If the bear had been wearing no clothes at all a person wouldn't have thought twice about it, but since it has a shirt and hat on, the lower parts look funny. Naked in fact. Is it possible that Ivory did it deliberately? Not long ago Lillian read in the *Journal* about a bakery in Union Square that advertised "adult" cakes and stirred up a great storm among the aldermen. She doesn't like to imagine what could be "adult" about a cake.

Lillian was right: the door is open just enough so that the bolt, although sprung, did not catch in the doorframe. Anybody could walk right in and help themselves to whatever they pleased. Naturally Lillian has no such intention; she only wants to look.

Just as she expected: the place is utter chaos. In a room not big enough to swing a cat there are hundreds of toys of every kind jammed together any old way, without order or organization, from floor to ceiling. Including *on* the ceiling, Lillian realizes; three dragon kites glare down on her in a menacing way.

Soon she notices, with surprise, the dolls in a glass case at the back of the shop. They look expensive: not at all the sort of thing a person in their right mind would give a child to play with, and not the sort of thing Lillian would expect Ivory to possess, either. The smocking on the baby doll's gown could well have been done by hand. The doll's head is lightly squashed, the way those of newborns are; it is quite homely, in fact, and realistic in a way that makes Lillian uncomfortable.

Behind the glass case is a door with an official-looking sign that says *Exit* in large red letters, perhaps a requirement of the fire department. So as not to leave fingerprints, she turns the knob with a gloved hand and gropes gingerly in the murky half-light for the light cord. What she sees, when the overhead bulb goes on, surprises and confuses her. Why, the girl must have been *living* in this back room before Raymond married her and brought her to Westwood Road. Lillian sees a sink filled with dented saucepans, a bed with a ragged quilt on it. The place reeks of tobacco smoke and other things, which Lillian would as soon not try to identify.

Lillian does not want to be discovered here, and yet for some reason she doesn't want to leave the place exactly as she found it, either. On the table she sees a little plastic charm, the kind of trinket that comes in a Cracker Jack box. She drops it into her handbag and hurries out of the shop as fast as her bad knee will allow.

· · · · · · · ·

Ivory's hints to Lillian that one day the little back bedroom will need to be cleared have been met only with uncomprehending silences; Ivory feels that to speak the word "nursery" would be somehow unlucky, and Lillian does not seem to get the point. So Ivory has taken it upon herself to move the ironing board, vacuum cleaner, and drying rack into the hall. The rubber enema bag she places on the bottom step of Lillian's staircase, along with a girdle and a size 42D bra with boned cups that she found draped over the rack. No longer does Ivory have any curiosity about Lillian's room; for some reason that ended with Muriel's death. There are some things that should not be looked into or even thought about. Anyway, she feels she already knows all she cares to about Lillian's personal habits and opinions and tastes.

Ivory is not so reckless as to decorate the room to receive a baby; that would be the surest way to encourage a stillbirth or a hydrocephalic. Instead she drags a wicker armchair up from the living room and places it by a window overlooking the backyard. From the boxes stacked in Mrs. Bartlett's bedroom she unpacks a few of her possessions—the armless one-armed bandit, the tin repoussé box with the gold eyeglasses inside— and arranges them in the sparsely furnished room.

She sits in the wicker chair and looks out at the yard, where there are now some fragile signs that spring may be on its way. She doesn't smoke on account of the baby she is carrying; she doesn't read because it's hard now to concentrate on made-up lives; she doesn't think too much, although some images are difficult to escape: the vandalized sapling near the toy shop, the apartment on Granite Street where she lived for so many years.

She pictures the apartment completely empty except for dust balls and scraps of things exposed by the clearing out of furniture. An odd sock or flip-flop, maybe, or a part of some long-since-discarded game, or a yellowed newspaper clipping fallen behind a dresser, the reason for saving it forgotten. She grieves for the abandoned apartment, or rather in behalf of it; the emptiness is how she felt when her mother died.

And she sees—she can't not see—the snapshot of innocent doomed Muriel in an aquamarine sundress, and the falling rock.

"What are you doing up here all by yourself?" Ray asks, standing at the door of the back bedroom. He has a new pair of reading glasses with yellowish brown plastic frames; these he holds in his hand, having been reading the Sunday papers. "It's not like you to brood."

He thinks he knows what she'd be likely to do and what she wouldn't, and it pleases her that he's given her that much thought, but he'd never guess the truth in a million years. "Just watching spring come," she answers.

He laughs, behind the wicker chair now. He puts a hand on her shoulder and kneads the muscle several times before releasing it. At times his touch is surprisingly painful, though Ivory is sure he doesn't know he hurts her.

"Wild garlic, or maybe it's scallions," she says, "shooting up by the garage."

"Can you see scallions from here?" he asks, his fingers stroking her neck.

"I know they're there."

"Oh, I see. Well, there used to be flowers out there in the spring."

"What kind?"

"Jonquils, I think. I suppose the squirrels have dug up all the bulbs and eaten them by now. I remember my mother so furious at squirrels she'd squirt the garden hose at them. Of course, that didn't discourage them one bit."

"Did your mother care so much about jonquils?"

"I doubt it. She wanted to control things, and whenever she couldn't, she'd feel aggrieved."

"Everybody wants things to go their own way."

His fingers stroke under her hair. "Most people, though, have a more realistic idea of the limitations of their power."

She chews a cuticle. "What if a person has too *much* power?"

"Certain local elected officials we might mention," he says, smiling.

"No, I don't mean them. An ordinary person who can make something happen just by thinking of it."

"Any particular person you have in mind?"

She wants to tell him about Muriel—what Ivory has done to her—but can't. "Not really."

"I wouldn't let such things worry you, Ivory." His indulgent laugh puts an end to the conversation, and they go downstairs to eat what Ray calls Lillian's particleboard roast.

On Thursday, after Raymond and Ivory have left for work, Lillian rescues the *Journal* from under the crab apple tree, where the dunce of a paper boy has thrown it, and carries it out to the kitchen. According to the headline one of the aldermen has been arrested in connection with some local skulduggery the FBI is investigating. A good many chickens coming home to roost lately, Lillian thinks, taking a jelly doughnut from the bread box and placing it on a saucer. A good many skeletons falling out of closets. It makes you wonder why people do wicked things, when sooner or later they are going to get caught. She refills her coffee cup and settles herself at the kitchen table. Taking small bites out of the doughnut, she reads about a ribbon-cutting at a new Chinese restaurant, the spotting by a jogger of an unidentified elderly man's body in the Mystic River, a forthcoming St. Pat's Day dance sponsored by the Shamrock Social and Charitable Society.

As is her habit she scans the names on the obituary page, but if it weren't for having to lick the jelly from her fingers before turning the page, she would have missed the four-line item at the end of one column:

MURIEL   BEATRICE   NEELY
formerly of Teele Avenue
died unexpectedly February
25 in Kayenta, Arizona.

Lillian's hand flies to her breast. She shuts her eyes, feels dizzy, opens them. She reads the item again, on the chance that she could have missed some detail, some shred of explanation, but there is none. *Unexpectedly.* That could mean anything. A car crash, a drowning, a fall from a great height. Murder even. Or suicide.

Lillian cannot help but remember the postcard she sent Muriel and the postcard that came here in return. *Can the rumors I hear be true?* Muriel knew very well they were true, because Lillian had told her so. And possibly, quite likely, Lillian caused Muriel to take her own life. Why, in a way Lillian *murdered* Muriel Neely.

Dazed, she turns the newspaper back to the front page and stares at the picture of the poor incarcerated alderman, who only moments ago looked sinister and now looks wretched. And all this man is accused of is intimidating a government witness. Nothing even approaching murder. Lillian imagines her own photograph on the front page of the *Journal.* Maybe they'd use the one that appeared in the *Journal* the year she was chairlady of the Holiday Craft booth at the church bazaar, blowing her own face up and cutting off the other chairladies. *Lillian A. Dunlop of Westwood Road,* the caption would say, *held without bail in Middlesex County Jail.* In that photograph she'd had an aghast expression on her face, startled by the flashbulb. Oh, she'd look guilty, all right. *Incriminating postcard signed by suspect found among personal effects of victim.*

Preposterous, she tells herself. People do not get arrested for sending postcards. Besides, her intentions had been all for Muriel's good, trying to spare her the pain of hoping and dreaming in a lost cause. How was Lillian to know Muriel would take the news so badly? Anyway, perhaps Muriel is better off dead, after all. At least Raymond Bartlett can't hurt her anymore.

Sixteen

....

SATURDAY MORNING, St. Patrick's Day, Ivory begins to bleed. It's not a miscarriage or a hemorrhage, just a perfectly ordinary menstrual period, timed, as usual, to the phases of the moon. The pregnancy was all in her head; whatever swelling she noticed in her breasts must have been the result of the normal hormone shift at ovulation. Everybody knows that a pregnancy does not automatically go with a wedding like a gizzard with a goose; often these things take time. And yet, flushing away the bloody toilet paper, Ivory feels something like dread. It was so simple with Roger the delivery man; one cosy beery fuck on a sack of laundry and a baby was made. If she can't do it now, with her husband, it must mean something's gone horribly wrong.

The house is quiet and empty. In the downstairs hall she looks up the number of the family planning clinic in the telephone book and dials. "Is a doctor on duty this morning?" she asks the receptionist. "I need to talk to a doctor."

"Is this an emergency, dear?"

She remembers when Ray called her at the shop, and lost his last dime, and could not bring himself to tell the operator that it was an emergency.

"No, not really."

"If you'll hold, I'll see if the doctor can speak with you."

The one telephone in the house is a wall phone, between the lavatory and Ray's study. There is no chair in the hall; members of this household have not been in the habit of having long telephone conversations. While she waits, Ivory paces the small area defined by the length of the cord. The eight-day clock pings nine times. Ray and Lillian may be back any minute, bustling into the kitchen with their grocery bags.

Abruptly a voice says, "Dr. Chan." For a moment Ivory can't think how to begin. "Is somebody there?" the voice asks. It is rapid, nasal, the words run together.

Afraid the doctor will press another extension button, Ivory says, "Please, could you tell me, if a person has trouble getting pregnant, might an abortion cause that?"

There's a rustling in the background, as if the doctor is looking through some other patient's lab results while taking the telephone call. "Did you have an abortion, Mrs. . . . ?"

"A long time ago."

"An illegal abortion?"

"There wasn't any other kind then," Ivory says, feeling her heart thump unpleasantly.

"I'm only trying to establish the facts," the doctor says. "I'm not making a moral judgment."

"Yes, all right."

"What I'm going to say is pure speculation. I can't diagnose over the telephone, you understand."

"Yes."

"If there was postabortal sepsis—that's an infection—there could be a problem with tubal patency. In other words, the tubes could be blocked with scar tissue. The sperm can't get through to the egg," he says, a little more kindly, "and the egg can't get through to the sperm. See?"

"I think so."

"Did you run a fever after this abortion?"

"For a while I felt sweaty at work. I thought it was nerves."

The doctor makes a sound that is part sigh, part grunt. "Like I say, I can't diagnose over the phone. I can't diagnose at all; we don't have the equipment here. What you need is a Rubin test. You got that?"

Ivory can hear the Oldsmobile chugging in the driveway, restrained by its hand brake, while groceries are unloaded and carried into the kitchen. "Yes," she says quickly.

"The receptionist will send you a list of gynecologists," the doctor says. "Hold on and I'll transfer you."

"Thanks, but I'm in a hurry right now," Ivory says, hanging up. There is a nearly full soft pack of Kools in the drawer of the hall table, untouched for ten days. Ray, setting a grocery bag on the counter, watches her lean over the range and light one of the stale cigarettes in a burner flame. It's a signal to him that something is wrong, and she knows he realizes it, but Lillian is chattering about a bargain on a rolled roast of veal, and Ray doesn't ask any questions. Before he comes back from parking the car in the garage Ivory has decided that she can't tell him after all; whatever happens, she can't let him know about the abortion. She buries the Kool in coffee grounds in the garbage can and pretends she never lit up.

"Here's something interesting," Ivory says, reading out loud from the newspaper. " 'You can tell whether the moon is waxing or waning by remembering that when it's shaped like the letter *D* it is waxing and when it's shaped like a *C* it is waning.' "

With an eyedropper Ray squirts a minute amount of water around one of the succulents in its clay pot. " 'The cold fruitless moon,' " he says.

"What?"

"Shakespeare, I think."

"Isn't the moon sideways sometimes? On its back or its belly?"

"That's the trouble with rules of thumb," he says, moving on to a grayish lithops whose cleft is just starting to open. It appears to be thinking of blooming, so Ray gives it an encouraging trickle. "You're not always sure how to apply them."

"Anyway," she says resentfully, "I haven't seen the moon in weeks. All we get is snow or sleet or rain or fog."

He drops the eyedropper into the cup of water and sets it on the mantel. "Is that what's depressing you?" he asks in a tentative tone of voice. He decides he shouldn't say anything about her menstrual period. His mother was very private about such things, and so was Muriel; perhaps that is the way women are.

"No, not only the weather." Ivory folds the newspaper untidily and drops it on the carpet. She pours the last of the Christmas Scotch into her glass.

"Maybe it's giving up smoking?"

"Maybe."

"Or your family moving away."

"You are my family, Ray," she says, but it seems to him that her voice has a hint of uncertainty in it.

"For better or worse?" he asks lightly.

She sips the Scotch, obviously mulling something over. "Ray, some odd things have been happening."

He supposes she means Muriel's death. Well yes. But so far as Ivory is concerned, the only strange thing is the bad luck of the postcard arriving the very day Muriel died; there's no reason for her to suspect that Ray could have been responsible in any way for her death. So he sits in the leather chair and waits for Ivory to continue. In a way, her jealousy excites him; he's not sure he wants to calm her doubts completely.

"I've been missing things," Ivory says finally.

"I don't understand."

"Things of mine keep disappearing."

"What kinds of things?"

"An argyle sock. A cheap comb I carried in my tote bag for years. A fake pearl earring my niece gave me for Christmas. The little plastic charm from the gum ball machine."

"Must be the notorious Westwood Road sock burglar."

"I know it sounds idiotic. I know none of those things has any value, and I don't really expect you to take this seriously. You'll think I've just mislaid all these odds and ends, or the washing machine ate them up."

"They *are* the kinds of objects a person tends to mislay."

"Yes, but not all at once. I'm not as disorganized as some people like to think."

Feeling slightly irritated at what he takes to be a rebuke, he says, "It sounds to me as though you have some explanation already cooked up."

"To tell you the truth, for a while I thought Lillian was doing it."

"What would she want with odd socks and earrings?"

"To get at me."

"Aren't you becoming a little paranoid about Lillian?" he asks slowly, manipulating one knuckle after another on his left hand until they crack.

"Yes, you're right. She could easily have lifted any of the other things, but not the four-leaf clover. It was on the table in the stock room. I'm sure of it, because I'd look at it when I'd be having a cup of tea," she says, flushing a little. "And then one afternoon it was simply gone. Vanished into thin air. Lillian can't have taken that—she's never been in the shop in her life—and so what *is* the explanation? Am I going nuts, or what?"

She looks very vulnerable to him, the way she sits in the corner of the daybed, right up against the brass railing. He wants to be on top of her, making love to her. "Let's not think about combs and socks. Let's go upstairs instead."

"I'm bloody." Her hair is lowered over the glass of Scotch so that he can't read her expression. "You know what that means, Ray? It means I'm not pregnant," she says.

He crouches in front of her and gently butts his head between her denim-covered thighs; he smells the meaty fetidness of her crotch, imagines the warm pool of blood inside.

Vacuuming, Lillian is thinking about when she and Flo were young. Before Flo's dates with sailors and jitterbugging around her living room to big bands on the radio, long before Flo's surgical scars, and impacted molars, and debts growing as chaotically as her tumors. When they were children Flo was so much smaller and skinnier, strangers never guessed the two girls were the same age, born in the same month. Flo had a heart-shaped freckled face, and pale hair the sun would bleach, and perfect small teeth, white as baby teeth. In spite of their mismatched sizes the girls were close, closer than sisters. Until they were twelve or thirteen they went everywhere together.

One place they weren't allowed to go was down by the falls, in case they tumbled into the river, or in case the men who worked cutting and stitching shoes might call nasty things out the factory windows. But Flo wanted to, so they went anyway. They'd throw bits of rubble into the dirty water to watch them hurtle over the falls, and listen to the shoe machinery whining and pecking inside the factory, and giggle about things. Exactly what, Lillian can no longer bring to mind.

Unplugging the old Hoover, Lillian remembers one of the last days the girls sat together on the riverbank. There were dead leaves, Lillian thinks, so it must have been fall, but the sun was warm and made her feel lazy and happy. She reached over to hug cute little Flo in her quilted jacket—Flo, her dearest and only friend—but when she put her arm around Flo's shoulder, Flo drew away and picked up a sharp stick and began to clean her nails with it. It was Flo's expression, fastidious and faintly disgusted, that made Lillian realize Flo thought she had done something dreadful. She felt big and clumsy and stupid, and sinful somehow.

But she knows she couldn't have helped having those feelings. To this day she does not believe they were bad feelings.

She winds the cord around the Hoover's handle, panting a little from the exertion of vacuuming, and wheels the machine into the hall. Later on, Raymond will have to carry it upstairs so she can do the second floor.

As she climbs the stairs she hears water gurgling noisily down into the pipes. The girl, Ivory, has been bathing. And has scuffed up the hall rug, she sees. As she kneels to straighten it the bathroom door opens and the girl stands before her. Ivory's hair is wet, dripping; her feet are bare. Smiling uncertainly, almost shyly, Ivory tightens Raymond's bathrobe around her slim body and brushes past Lillian, leaving damp footprints on the floorboards.

All at once Lillian wants to hug the girl and take care of her and protect her, although from what, she would not be able to say.

It's a mild day with a gray woolly sky, wet underfoot from melting snow. Before opening the shop Ivory stops in at Sherman Hardware to buy light bulbs. As the clerk punches the keys on his adding machine with sausagey fingers he says, "They call you to testify before the grand jury yet?"

She sees the rock falling, crushing the woman.

"The what?"

"Don't you read the papers? Half the pols in town having heart attacks waiting for the indictments to come down."

"I'm not a pol," she says.

The clerk has broken vessels in his nose and freckles like splashes of effluent on his bald head. This is the man who likes to give Shirley McWeeny in the Triple A a hard time. "Shut your gob, Carnahan," Shirley says when she's fed up, and Carnahan says, "Anything you say, McWeeny," snickering over her name as if it were an obscenity.

"You may not be a pol, but you got the FBI on your tail," Carnahan says.

"How much do I owe you?" Ivory says, digging down into her tote bag for her wallet.

"One-oh-nine, with the tax. I got to admit she's kinda peculiar-looking, as undercover agents go. The FBI must be scraping the bottom of the barrel."

"I'm in a hurry, so just give me the punch line," she says, laying two dollar bills on the counter.

"In old J. Edgar Hoover's day agents didn't wear hats with veils. Could be a disguise, of course. Maybe she's really a man with great big rubber boobs and a submachine gun under her coat."

"Could I have my change, please?"

"You hear what I'm telling you? There's an old girl in here two, three times a week standing right there behind that seed rack, watching your shop. Maybe you should think about why."

"Thanks for the advice," Ivory says, taking her paper bag from the counter.

"Have a nice day," Carnahan says and laughs in a sinister way.

As she's screwing a light bulb into the overhead socket in the stock room, Ivory can't avoid wondering about what Carnahan said. Not that anybody in their right mind ought to take the man seriously. Shut your gob, Carnahan, she should have said, the way Shirley McWeeny does. He probably made the whole thing up just to get under her skin. Still, the detail of the seed rack bothers her. Carnahan might have invented a secret agent, even a secret agent in drag, but would he have had the creative imagination to position her behind an actual real-live seed rack?

Ivory thinks about the row of paper cups on the sill in the kitchen. Nasturtium seeds in those cups, Lillian explained, for planting in the iron urn on the front porch. They always had geranium plants from a garden shop in the urn in the past, Ray remarked. She happened to see some nasturtium seeds and the spirit moved her to try something different this year, Lillian told Ray. It was a sudden whim, an inspiration.

Ivory switches on the hot plate and puts a saucepan of water on to boil.

Great big rubber boobs, Carnahan said.

Size 42D, Ivory thinks.

No. Stupid even to speculate on such a thing. Ray says she's becoming paranoid about Lillian and she agrees with him. Anyway, what would be the point of watching the shop? Hoping to catch Ivory with another man? If that's what she hoped, she'd be in for a big disappointment.

Ivory finds it impossible to visualize Lillian making her slow plodding way over ice and snow all the way down Summer Street, boldly crossing Bow Street at the crosswalk where the cars and trucks barrel right through the blinking red light, entering Sherman Hardware—not at all her kind of store—and establishing a stakeout behind the seed rack.

No, she thinks, pouring boiling water on top of her tea bag. Never.

And yet she can believe that Lillian would be curious about her. It was not so long ago that Ivory herself was tempted to climb the narrow staircase to Lillian's room and to look secretly at her mementos, her personal treasures, her mail and photographs and underwear. She knows now that if she'd done it, it would have been not only to satisfy curiosity but as a form of sneak attack. Yes, she recognizes the impulse: knowing about something weakens its power. Lillian could be tracking her to diminish her. And pilfering her possessions one by one as a sort of magical way to steal her soul. With so much to gain, Lillian would not mind the walk and the wait, would hardly even notice it.

Ivory shudders. She sees herself once again on Lillian's narrow staircase, pausing on a step, listening. Lillian emerges from the shadows at the top of the stairs. The two women stare at each other. Gradually Lillian begins to perceive that she is not only the watcher but the watched. She is afraid. Giddily she grabs for the rail but cannot get hold of it in time. She's cut by the metal strip on each step as she falls.

Lillian ties her shoelaces, knotting the bows, adjusts the veil of her navy felt hat, pulls on her gloves. Outside, the day is cool and misty, with a wind that cuts right through the wool of her coat and tries to lift the hat from her head as she crosses Central Street. A stooped and wavering old lady is making her way resolutely along the driveway of the Home for the Aged, her morning constitutional. As old as the lady is, Lillian guesses, she hasn't given up yearning for love. People don't.

There are still clots of snow here and there on the sidewalk and in the gutter, and yet Lillian is happy as she walks along Summer Street. Spring is somehow in the air in spite of the chill. It occurs to her that she might do something different with her hair when she goes to the hairdresser this week. She could ask Wanda's advice about a new and more flattering cut or a livelier tint, perhaps even the touch more of red that Wanda has been urging. With her fair complexion, Wanda says, she can get away with it. Wanda is the professional, after all; she ought to know.

Today, Lillian decides, she will not go into Sherman Hardware. She doesn't care for the way a certain clerk grins when she makes whatever small purchase she has settled on, the way he presses her change into her hand with cold gray fingers. Why, she'll just go around to the rear of the toy shop where the clerk can't see her, and then everything will be all right. Ivory will smile shyly when she opens the door and politely invite Lillian into her private room, and the two of them will have a cosy talk. She'll tell Ivory all sorts of things she could never tell Raymond, because Raymond wouldn't want to listen, or wouldn't understand if he did. Lillian will clean up for her, and after a while fix something for the two of them to eat.

She walks along the broken sidewalk of Hawkins Street, which borders the rear of the wedge of commercial buildings that face Somerville Avenue and Washington Street. To her bewilderment, the single alley off Hawkins ends smack at the loading platform of Wallpaper World. Yet she knows there must be a back entrance to Ivory's shop somewhere.

The third time around the block she notices a gate that somehow escaped her attention before. It's between a funeral home and a disheveled-looking shoe store on Washington Street, a stockade gate that sags so much from its hinges it can't be latched. She pauses and looks around her. A few truants and layabouts are lounging blasphemously on the steps of St. Joseph's across the street, but they don't seem to be paying her any attention, nor do the two boat people waiting for the Central Square bus.

Cautiously she pushes the gate open wide enough to pass into the alley. Here are four huge rubbish bins, all filled to the brim, higher than her hat, with refuse. Bones and eggshells and cabbage leaves litter the narrow passage between the bins and a brick wall. She's certain she hears a rustling sound in one of the bins. Mice. Or rats, even. It is terrible to be in this filthy place, but Lillian plunges stubbornly onward, past the bins, to the far turning in the alley.

Around the corner, in a dark cramped space smelling of urine and rotting food, are the rear entrances. It's like a slum, Lillian thinks, horrified. It *is* a slum. Unnerved, she can't guess how to tell which of the half-dozen metal doors might be Ivory's. The doors have bad words scrawled on them, and they have no windows—or knobs.

Can it be that the doors have no knobs, or is she going blind?

She feels dizzy and sick. Leaning against a fire escape railing, her shoes sunk in soggy, gritty snow, she longs for Ivory's private room, shut away from her. But now she remembers the bed there. She remembers its bare mattress ticking, and the snarled shiny quilt slopping over the edge of the mattress and dragging on the floor. Quite against her will she sees Ivory lying there. She is naked. She's opening her body for him. She's winding her stringy limbs around him; she isn't shy at all. He hurts her, but she doesn't care. She doesn't *care*.

Lillian hurries out of the alley, not noticing now whether she steps on a bone or an orange rind, and through the broken gate. In spite of her bad knee she's almost running now, past the shoe store and the dry cleaner, around the corner past an Indian restaurant and a Chinese take-out. The only place she wants to be is home. If only she can get across Somerville

Avenue without Ivory or the hardware clerk seeing her. She thinks she can just make it across in a lull in the traffic, but her heel slips on something—an invisible patch of ice, perhaps, or a bit of garbage her shoe picked up in the alley—and her knee buckles. The delivery van brakes, not quite in time.

Seventeen

....

"*ARE NOT TWO SPARROWS SOLD* for a farthing?" the minister is saying, "*and one of them shall not fall on the ground without your Father.*"

Lillian suffered fractures of the breastbone, pelvis, and seventeen of her ribs; multiple lacerations and contusions; a punctured lung; a ruptured spleen.

"*But the very hairs of your head are all numbered.*"

Ray is tapping his folded reading glasses on the cover of a hymnal. After the accident Lillian's hair continued to grow, so that when she died, after eight days, gray roots were plainly visible near her scalp.

"*Fear ye not therefore, ye are of more value than many sparrows. Whosoever therefore shall confess me before men, him will I confess also before my Father which is in heaven.*"

In those eight days Lillian did not regain consciousness. Lillian's only known blood relation, her cousin Florence, was unable to attend the service because she herself is convalescing after major surgery. However, Florence cabled lilies for the altar.

"*But whosoever shall deny me before men, him will I also deny before my Father which is in heaven. Think not that I am come to send peace on earth. . . .*"

Lillian's old minister coughs; the ladies in the pews fidget with handkerchiefs and rolls of Life Savers.

"I come not to send peace, but a sword."

Ivory's fingers are woven tightly together. The shoulder of her beaver jacket is not near enough Ray's topcoat to touch it.

"For I am come to set a man at variance against his father, and the daughter against her mother, and the daughter in law against her mother in law. And a man's foes shall be they of his own household. . . ."

The old minister coughs again. He seems shriveled inside his gown like a blighted walnut in its shell; only the tips of his fingers emerge from the sleeves. His voice is in his nose, and the accent is not local. A person, like Ivory, long ago transplanted and perhaps never quite taken root.

". . . And he that taketh not his cross, and followeth after me, is not worthy of me."

The minister peers down into the congregation of mourners. As he raises his voice it cracks.

"He that findeth his life shall lose it: and he that loseth his life for my sake shall find it."

The flames of candles on either side of the lilies tremble a little in the draft; in some distant office of the church a telephone begins to ring. Ray crosses his legs, so that his body is shifted farther away from Ivory's. There's a slightly ominous smell of forced hot air in the sanctuary, like a scorched pot or some appliance overheating, but no noticeable warmth comes out of the floor registers. Somebody sighs.

"In the midst of life we are in death," the minister is saying.

The ladies, sensing the conclusion of the service, begin to draw on their gloves.

"Earth to earth, ashes to ashes, dust to dust; in sure and certain hope of the Resurrection unto eternal life. . . ."

"Amen," a few of the ladies mutter, in a ragged and uncertain way, as the minister nods to the organist, turns off the pulpit lamp, and shuffles down the steps from the chancel. A shrill "Abide with Me" whines out of the organ.

At the sanctuary door Ivory and Ray stand with the minister to greet the mourners: members of the choir, the Ladies Aid, the Christian Outreach Society. Several peck Ray's cheek. "A tragedy," a lady says, squeezing Ivory's hand. "Nobody watches where they're going anymore," another lady remarks, and they all agree, but whether they are talking about Lillian or about the pizza van driver it is difficult to tell. Since Lillian was cremated two days ago, they are unable to exclaim over how well she looked in her coffin. In hushed tones someone wonders whether anybody's signed up to supply plastic forks for the pancake breakfast on Saturday.

As Ivory and Ray walk over crushed stone in the parking lot he says, "Interesting text the old buzzard chose."

"It didn't have a thing to do with Lillian. He must be senile."

"What was that about a man's foes being his own household?"

Ivory shrugs. "He didn't know what he was saying."

On the way back to Westwood Road, Ivory thinks about the question that was unspoken as Lillian sank closer to death: Why was Lillian in Union Square, not a dozen yards from the door of the toy shop, when the van hit her?

The next day there is a high wind, and thunder and lightning, and eight inches of soggy snow fall on top of the crocuses.

Not long after the memorial service Ray brings home a stack of brochures from Fratto's Travel in Davis Square, "honeymoon packages," as the agent at Fratto's referred to them. He has decided that he can get away from the bank for a week or two, after all. After dinner, as the dishwasher hums and swishes through its cycles, he and Ivory sit at the kitchen table and study the crisp shiny folders.

It is difficult, Ray realizes, not to look at these folders without thinking of Muriel's Aruba trip, Muriel's Monument Valley trip. Even the name "Monument Valley" makes Ray cringe; it might be the name of a memorial park laid out on what was until recently a swamp or a railroad yard.

What all these honeymoon packages seem to feature is sun and sand. There is even a ten-day tour of Egypt, illustrated with a photograph of a young couple, apparently ecstatic to the point of hysteria, seated on a pair of camels. Ray has no desire whatever to ride a camel or climb a pyramid. It's not that he is too old; even as a child, paging through the Book of Knowledge, he knew he'd feel foolish suddenly plumped down in the midst of somebody else's country. Just as foolish and miserable as those Laotians and Cambodians and Sri Lankans look wandering around Union Square in ski hats and earmuffs; and they, at least, have some *reason* to be out of place, poor devils, forcibly uprooted from their homelands.

"Do you have a preference?" he asks Ivory. "Does one particular vacation spot especially appeal to you? Bermuda? Miami Beach?"

"No," she says; she can't decide. After a while she gets up from the table and wanders off to another part of the house. Ray foresees that the brochures will continue to sit on the kitchen table. They will become buried in the same sort of debris that used to collect around Lillian: cents-off coupons, bus schedules, shopping lists, advertising supplements out of newspapers. Also, in Ivory's case, toast crumbs and tea bag wrappers.

Ray has been doing his best to be patient with Ivory's untidiness. She is not used to running a household, and Lillian's accident was a shock to her. Well yes, they *were* gruesome, those five-minute visiting periods in the intensive care unit. The visible parts of Lillian were puffy and yellow; her mouth sagged open; there was an odor about her body, unmistakable even with the antiseptic and disinfectant smells, of something rotting. She was in fact rotting before their eyes. No wonder Ivory is distracted; no wonder she finds it hard to take over Lillian's tasks as though nothing has happened.

It's why they should have a vacation, but perhaps a honeymoon package is not quite the thing in the circumstances. They might consider a week in New York City, as he was always urging on Muriel, without success. The more he thinks about it, though, the more the idea wearies him: a week packed with museums, concerts, and theater, figuring tips and double-checking restaurant bills to be sure he hasn't been overcharged and hailing taxis and keeping a sharp eye out for hustlers and muggers. . .

He does feel extraordinarily tired, he thinks, as he takes a carton of milk from the refrigerator. Run-down, he might as well face it, and not only by what happened to Lillian. He pours milk into a saucepan and lights the burner under it. The point is, he's a man of fifty-three years, with a young wife. Naturally it takes its toll.

Perhaps he should suggest to Ivory that they sleep apart for a while, until they both catch up on their rest. It is always difficult to come to sensible decisions when one is overtired. In fact, it is unwise and even dangerous to attempt to do so, he thinks, taking a bottle of blended whiskey out of the cupboard over the refrigerator and measuring a jiggerful into a highball glass.

"Peculiar word, 'highball,'" he says to Ivory, who has returned to the kitchen dressed in a red silk kimono. There's a gold dragon embroidered on the back, and the hem drags on the none-too-clean linoleum.

"I heard the refrigerator door open," she says.

"That's Sam's trick."

"I crave something, but I don't know what." She gazes into the refrigerator.

"I have the impression people don't use the word anymore," he says, pouring warm milk on top of the whiskey. "Highball."

"Maybe they don't drink them anymore." She's carrying to the table pimiento cheese spread, salami in a wax paper wrapper, and a cucumber.

"Aren't you afraid you'll have nightmares?"

"No, I'm not *afraid*," she begins, and then says, "You're right. I probably will."

She slices the cucumber without a plate between it and the enamel-topped table; the metallic scratching sound makes Ray wince. "As a matter of fact," he says, "I was just thinking that we might try sleeping in different rooms for a while."

She looks up from the cucumber. It's been a long time, Ray realizes, since he paid attention to just how lopsided her face is, how oddly warped the perspective. The two halves don't quite match. He thinks about having sex with her, and deliberately pushes the thought from his mind.

"You could sleep in my mother's bed," he goes on. "I helped Lillian turn the mattress only last summer. It seemed in good condition. My mother was proud of it; one hundred percent horsehair, she always said. Of course, it wouldn't be any good for somebody with allergic tendencies."

For a time Ivory doesn't say anything. She has spread pimiento cheese on a piece of oat bread, has covered the cheese with a layer of salami, and is now overlapping slices of cucumber on top of the salami in a sort of wave pattern.

"Are you listening to me, Ivory?"

"I don't have any," she says. "Allergies. That I know of."

"Well, doesn't it seem to you like a good idea?" he asks, pulling a chair up to the table and taking a sip of hot milk and whiskey.

The wide red sleeves, too long for her arms, flop down over her hands. "But why, Ray?"

He doesn't really want to admit to her how exhausted he feels; perhaps he fears her pity. They've never once mentioned the twenty-two years that separate them, not even when he explained to her about his changing his will and various insurance policies to make her the beneficiary, and he's not inclined to start now.

"I haven't been sleeping well," he says, truthfully enough. "I've been upset by . . . everything that's happened."

She studies the completed sandwich without biting into it, as though it is a sculpture or an artifact. "All right," she says finally.

"Is that all you have to say, just 'all right'?"

"I know you've been upset. If it will make you feel better, I'll sleep on your mother's horsehair mattress."

"I think you're distorting what I said."

"Could very well be," she says, flippantly almost, and takes a bite of her sandwich.

He feels his cheeks heating up. There's an indefinable tightness under his scalp and beneath his breastbone as he takes a breath before speaking. "I don't understand, Ivory, why we can't have a normal, logical conversation."

"Sometimes it's hard to talk to you, Ray," she says, emitting a whiff of garlic.

"So I gather."

"You do?"

His milk has become tepid; he sets the glass down on the

table. "You conceal things. You make me drag them out of you."

"For instance, what things?"

"For instance, whatever it was you said to Lillian before she went rushing into that delivery van."

"I didn't say a single word to her, Ray."

"I wasn't implying that you meant to hurt her. I'd simply like to know what it was the two of you were talking about, just for the record. I think I deserve that much, don't you?"

She gets up from the table, takes a juice glass from a cupboard, splashes some whiskey into it. "I never even laid eyes on her, Ray. The first I knew she was in the square was when I heard the ambulance siren and I went out and saw her lying in the street. I picked up her hat."

"Her *hat?*"

"It was the navy felt one with a veil."

He seizes on this, as though it might be a piece of evidence of some kind. "What became of Lillian's hat, Ivory?"

"I threw it away."

"I see."

"I put it in a barrel outside the emergency room. It was ruined, Ray. She couldn't have worn it again, even if . . . *Anybody* would have thrown away a bashed-in hat, Ray."

Once again she has managed to twist a conversation away from the point. The girl has a positive genius for it. "Look here, Ivory. Lillian never used to go to Union Square, even when she had errands there. She'd find some excuse to get me to do them for her. The truth is, she couldn't stand the retarded people, or the refugees, or the teenagers and their radios."

Ivory shrugs. "Maybe that's true and maybe it isn't, but she wasn't in my shop. You'll just have to take my word for it."

She goes upstairs, leaving the remains of her snack on the table. He sweeps everything into the trash bin, including salami

rinds, coupons, bus schedules, and honeymoon package brochures.

Lillian's room, up under the eaves, has shrimp-colored café
curtains on the dormer windows and a piece of tan bound
broadloom, curling at the edges, on a linoleum floor. The
linoleum is speckled, like a bird's egg. The paper on the slop-
ing walls is grayish, with a waving fernlike vegetation faded to
a sort of queasy pink; in a certain mood those fern fronds
would look like tentacles. The room, unaired for weeks,
smells of stale bath powder and sweat. Ivory opens both
dormers as far as they will go. A pale April sun shines on the
slate roof of the house next door, and the air, though dusty,
is almost warm. Lillian just missed spring, Ivory thinks, feeling regret for that and pity that she had to live all those years
in this depressing room.

Ivory has brought up with her a box of plastic lawn bags; she
separates three from the roll and arranges them in the center
of the carpet. One for trash, one for donations to the Salvation
Army, one for items to be packed and shipped to Cousin
Florence in Wisconsin.

She had thought disposing of Lillian's effects would be a
daunting task, but as she looks around, she finds that Lillian left
surprisingly few possessions in her wake. There are no out-of-
style or rejected outfits carelessly shoved to one side of the
closet, no shoes that need reheeling or umbrellas with broken
spokes or useless Christmas gifts languishing on the shelf. She
folds the dresses and suits and places them, with Lillian's good
coat, inside the Salvation Army sack, and then begins to empty
the drawers of the dresser. She removes piles of brassieres
neatly stowed with one huge cup tucked inside the other;
girdles all made by the same manufacturer and in the same

style; slips; Orlon cardigans; scarves in various colors and fabrics.

Even though she's not really unprepared, it's with a queasy feeling that she opens the bottom drawer and discovers the small items she's been missing: the single argyle sock, the comb, the earring, the plastic charm. Well, the woman may have been able to walk through walls, Ivory thinks, but in the end her magic didn't work. Or did it? Ivory ought to be relieved that she has Ray all to herself now, but relief isn't what she feels.

In the bottom drawer are also a pile of letters written in green ink. The top one is signed Flo. Ivory doesn't bother to look at the others or to read any of them.

The only photograph in the room, framed in imitation gold on the dresser, is of a thin young woman with a sailor hat perched jauntily on her head. She's clutching the arm of somebody who had been cut off the edge of the picture. Even subtracting some forty years, Lillian could never have been that girl. Flo, no doubt, her gentleman friend excised after a spat or when he was replaced by some other beau. A pretty girl, in a pert sort of way; she would have had lots of beaus, Ivory imagines.

Nothing in the room connects Lillian in any way to Ray. Ivory doesn't know why, but she feels sure now that Ray never visited this room, not even as a youth. Perhaps it's the wallpaper that makes her so certain; Ray would not have cared for waving fern fronds.

Into Cousin Flo's bag goes Lillian's quilted jewelry box, though as far as Ivory can tell, there's nothing of value in it. Ivory doles out to her a candy box full of fancy handkerchiefs, several of the nicer scarves, and a plate commemorating the seventy-fifth anniversary of the founding of Lillian's church, though Ivory can't quite picture what Cousin Flo will do with

the plate out in Wisconsin. She also puts in the framed snapshot and the letters, in case Flo has a sentimental streak.

Besides the clothes and a portable television set the Salvation Army does not stand to profit much by Lillian's death.
Ivory hesitates over the enema bag and then decides it's not
the sort of thing a person, even a person well below the poverty
line, would want to use secondhand.

In the end the third sack, the one for trash, remains empty
except for the enema bag and some bottles of prescription
medicine with expired dates and a handful of curlers.

So now it's done. Amazingly easy, Ivory thinks, to dismantle
what's left of Lillian's life. After fifty-eight years nothing remains but three plastic lawn bags, only partly filled, and some
ashes in a memorial park in Tewksbury.

The sheets that fit the horsehair mattress are worn where
they've been folded and are patched with iron-on tape; apparently someone in the household deemed it wasteful to purchase
new sheets given the finite time Mrs. Bartlett had to live. Ivory
can feel one of the tapes, which has come partly loose, under
her spine; Ray's hand rests lightly on her belly. He doesn't
know that she is knotted up under his hand, clogged with scar
tissue; it doesn't occur to him that at this very moment his
frustrated sperm are searching in blind alleys.

He's never had a Rubin test. He's never lain on his back with
his legs open and his feet up in stirrups, never had carbon
dioxide under pressure pumped inside him. He's never even
heard of a Rubin test. Though she knows it's unfair she resents
his bland innocence, his calm assumption that he can plant a
child in there. At times she's tempted to blast him with the
truth: *bilateral obstruction of the cornual and interstitial por-
tions of the fallopian tubes.* But she doesn't dare. She sees in

her mind two astronauts connected by cables to a spaceship; one is cut loose and tumbles slowly away in the dark. It is herself.

Downstairs in the hall the clock makes three hollow pinging sounds. Ray is roused from a half sleep and nestles his head in her armpit. If his sending her out of his bed was intended to limit their sexual activity, it was a failure. In the middle of the night he creeps under the blankets; often he tells Ivory about whatever dream awakened him, before beginning to touch her. His dreams are about mundane things: a bookkeeping muddle at the bank, a dispute over the price on a jar of sweet pickles in the supermarket, a conversation with a filling station attendant. His unconscious does not seem to have noticed any violent deaths in its vicinity.

He wheezes a little as he fondles her nipple; it's his sinuses. Spring fever. She observes the same sound when he's concentrating on cutting the fat from a piece of meat or tightening a screw in some appliance; there's a sort of tick or snap somewhere in his nasal passages as he exhales. She finds it irritating that he's apparently unaware of it, considering how sensitive he is to *her* idiosyncrasies and quirks.

His fingers are inside her crotch now, but after a few moments he thinks better of the whole thing and wipes his hand on the towel he's brought with him. Perhaps he is husbanding his resources; perhaps he's offended by his own sticky discharge. He lifts her bangs to kiss her forehead, puts on his slippers and pajama bottoms, pads away to his own bed.

Eighteen

....

TIM CARNAHAN from Sherman Hardware comes into the toy shop and puts his hat on the counter. The hat is an old gray fedora with grease spots, something like the one Ivory's father used to wear, and it has made a red band across his freckled forehead.

With her teeth Ivory opens the cellophane wrapper on a package of Kools. "What can I do for you?" she asks Carnahan, working the first cigarette out of the pack.

"Tomorrow is my daughter's birthday," he says.

"How old?"

"Fourteen."

"If she's fourteen, you're in the wrong store," Ivory says, striking a match. "What she wants is a cassette or a rock poster."

"Nancy ain't no punk," Carnahan says.

"Who said she was?"

"She's a little . . . slow."

"Oh."

"Can I bum one of those?"

She slides him the pack. He fumbles under his jacket for a lighter, one of the throwaway kind, and lights the cigarette with strangely bluish fingers. He must have terrible circulation, Ivory decides.

"I saw what happened to the old girl who was tailing you," Carnahan says. "She got squashed pretty good by that pizza van."

"I guess you could say that."

"She die, or what?"

"Eight days later, in the hospital."

"I thought about it, you know? I thought about the doctors finding falsies and balls when they cut her clothes off." Carnahan laughs, but there's very little humor in it. "You got to wonder why some old dame you don't know from Adam would watch you that way. It's enough to give a person the creeps."

She doesn't particularly want to confide in Tim Carnahan, but these questions are connected to the ones that have been eating away at her, and there's been nobody she could talk to. Certainly not Ray. For some reason Carnahan's having a retarded daughter makes her more inclined to trust him. "Actually, it turned out I did know her," she says warily, wondering what he'll have to say to that.

"No bull."

"She was kind of a member of the family. On my husband's side."

"I didn't know you had a husband."

"Since February."

"Congratulations."

"Thank you."

Carnahan taps a length of ash into a chipped dish full of butts on the counter. "So why the secret-agent act?" He's leaning toward her in a confidential way; the broken vessels in his nose look like tracks left by tiny worms.

"That's what I can't figure out."

"A screw loose, maybe?"

"She seemed all right. I guess you can't always tell."

"Let me tell you, the world's full of screwballs. My wife's

sister had a boyfriend who shot her. Here's what makes it crazy. He shot her with a bow and arrow."

"How come?"

"He musta thought he was Tonto."

"Yes, but what made him want to shoot her?"

"He got it into his head she had the hots for some other guy, and if I know Joyce, he was probably right."

"What happened then?"

Carnahan forces one last drag out of the filter. "She took a taxi to the hospital. Imagine being a doc in the emergency room and here comes Joyce waltzing in with an arrow sticking out of her arm."

"What happened to the boyfriend?"

"Joyce didn't prosecute."

"Maybe she thought he had a point," she says gloomily.

He laughs, though the pun hadn't been intentional. "Joyce isn't one to blame herself. She figured he was going to come to a bad end sooner or later without any help from her, so why make the lawyers rich? He was a screwball," he says, shrugging. "Like the old dame that got flattened."

"I don't think Lillian was planning to shoot me."

"Well, now you'll never know."

"I guess not."

Carnahan sighs, picking up his hat, then remembers what he came in for. "Nancy likes baby dolls," he says. "Like that one there in the case."

"It's kind of expensive."

"You think I can't afford it?"

"It's not really meant for kids to play with."

"She's not going to hurt the damn thing. I said she was slow, not mean."

"I'd have to charge you fifty dollars."

He takes a wad of bills out of his pocket and counts out the money in wrinkled and dog-eared fives and ones. Why is it the oldest, rattiest bills gravitate toward Union Square? Ivory wonders.

"It's ugly as sin," Carnahan observes as she's tucking the doll tenderly into a gift box.

"You can change your mind if you want."

"You got a ribbon bow to put on the box?"

"I can probably dig one up."

"Nancy gets a charge out of ribbon bows," Carnahan says.

Ivory takes a pack of Kools from the pocket of her overalls and puts a slightly crumpled cigarette in her mouth.

"I thought you weren't going to smoke, in case you might be pregnant," Ray says. Busy piano music is playing on the phonograph.

Her hazel eyes narrow; she half suspects he knows she's sterile and is waiting, like a fox at a rabbit hole, for her to give herself away. "I changed my mind."

"You're not only harming the child. You're harming yourself, you know," he says, beginning to clean his fingernails with an attachment on his nail clippers.

"Ray, is it possible to kill a person by wishing that person would die?" She doesn't know why she has blurted this out. Already he's suspicious enough of her.

"What kind of question is that?"

"Like putting a curse on them."

He studies a fingernail, detects some roughness or irregularity, delicately clips a corner. "Well, I don't know, Ivory. Isn't a curse getting God to do your dirty work for you? Would your God be apt to take your word for who ought to be eliminated?"

Ivory turns this around in her mind, staring at the very

cobweb she once imagined herself and Lillian struggling over. No, her God wouldn't. But on the other hand, she has a dread that *somehow* she killed Lillian with her thoughts, and Muriel, too. In *spite* of God, even.

"The day my father died I thought for sure my mother was responsible," Ray says with a wry smile. "She would have brought a curse down on him if she could have."

"Your mother?" she asks, startled.

"She detested him."

"Did she tell you?"

"Never in so many words, but a child always senses things like that. My father worked for import companies as a sort of agent; he traveled a great deal, to Central America and other places. Naturally, he found many opportunities."

"For messing around?"

"Once I answered the telephone and there was a woman with a foreign accent on the line, asking for him."

"She could have been a secretary or a telephone operator."

Ray folds the nail cleaner into the clipper and snaps the gadget shut. "I knew she wasn't."

"So your mother hoped he'd die?"

"It wouldn't surprise me. Obviously, I never asked her point-blank."

"Maybe she didn't care about the sex at all," Ivory says, stubbing out the Kool. "Maybe, if she wished him dead, she had other reasons."

"Yes?"

The record comes to an end, but he doesn't get up to flip it; she hears the needle droning on the record's blank inner band. "Maybe he dropped crumbs on the carpet. Or his feet smelled. Maybe something that at first she loved about him— some little tic or habit, like the way he blew his nose—began to get on her nerves."

For a time Ray is silent. He lifts the needle, removes the record, presses a button so that the tiny green light blinks off.

"She was a lonely woman in her old age," Ray muses.

"She had you—and Lillian."

"I'm not sure she thought very much of either of us."

Ivory says nothing. Pensively she taps her wedding ring on the brass daybed railing.

Now that Ivory takes the Oldsmobile to do the grocery shopping on her own, Ray has his Saturday mornings to himself. He gets the hedge shears out of the basement, oils them, adjusts the tension pin. Ray doesn't much enjoy yard work; he rather resents being forced by the whims of nature to prune before the new growth starts or to cut the lawn when it's dry. On the other hand, he reflects sourly, his whole career in life insurance is dictated by similar whims. Clients drop dead in all manner of circumstances, any old time they please, whether they conform to the actuarial tables or not. And so why not his spare time as well?

He begins with the front hedge, working from the sidewalk side, hoping that this early on a Saturday morning all the neighbors will still be in their beds and therefore not offering him advice about hedge-clipping, or making prying references to his new young wife or to Lillian's unluckily public demise. For the *n*th time he wonders how anyone could have been so misguided as to plant a barberry hedge around this property. An untidy plant, prickly and deciduous and apt to die out, leaving gaps. He's strongly tempted to have it all dug up and replaced with chain-link.

It's not so much the expense that stops him as the headache of dealing with contractors. As she lay on her deathbed his mother ordered the kitchen repainted, even though she'd never see the results herself. Ray doubts that she had his or Lillian's sensibilities in mind; rather, she did not care to stand before St. Peter with a greasy kitchen on her conscience. Ray thought he was going to acquire an ulcer before the struggles with the larcenous painter and his lunatic assistant came to an end.

It was strange talking about his mother to Ivory, and even stranger talking about his father; over the years he has not been in the habit of thinking about him very much. Yes, she would have put a curse on him, all right.

Ray remembers a picnic by a lake. He wouldn't be able to say now where the lake was. They seemed to drive for hours and hours before reaching it—although a child's perception of time is distorted. Perhaps it was no farther than Lynn or Saugus, one of those towns that afterward turned into suburbs. His father had recently returned from Guatemala. He'd brought bolts of handwoven cloth home for presents, Ray remembers, and his mother was . . . Yes, she was pregnant, Ray is almost sure of it. How queer to have forgotten, not to have thought of it all this time.

Ray pauses with the hedge shears in his hand, thinking. He remembers her high-waisted cotton dress, made out of some checked material; she worried about getting grass stains on the skirt. His father's face was red—sunburned, perhaps. He kept wiping it with a handkerchief. They were arguing over something, his mother in a tight, pinched little voice. She opened the picnic basket and began to set out the food as she spoke. There was fried chicken on a real plate, not a paper plate. A yellow jacket settled on it. Ray watched the yellow jacket crawl over the pieces, its antennae trembling, moving from a wing to a thigh. His parents paid no attention; they were too busy with whatever it was they were talking about.

Soon there were more yellow jackets, Ray remembers, not

only on the chicken but inside the bowl of potato salad, crawling over the grapes. Ray couldn't understand why neither his father nor his mother noticed them. A long time seemed to go by. He wasn't supposed to eat until grace was said, but nobody said it, and anyway he felt more than a little sick from the car ride, and the oily smell of the chicken, and the hot sun, and the sight of the insects on the food. There was now a yellow jacket moving on Ray's sleeve. Dazed, he watched as it seemed to search for something in the fold of his shirt above the cuff. He thought there might be another on his neck, near his ear, but he felt too sick to brush it away.

Suddenly his father swore, yanked him to his feet, pulled him stumbling through weeds and marsh grass into the cold lake water. His father shoved his head under the water and held it there for what seemed like many minutes, but could not have been, of course.

He remembers his father standing in the mud, his shirt dripping, his hair stuck to his head in strings. He remembers his mother sitting impassively on the grass, her checked skirt spread around her, as he and his father thrashed back through the cattails.

"I sickled into a nest once," his father said to her. "Little bastards damn near killed me." Miraculously the yellow jackets were gone, lifted by a breeze, perhaps.

It must have been soon after the day of the picnic that his mother miscarried. Ray was sent to stay for a while with his grandmother in Braintree. He can't think now how he knew his mother was pregnant; he has no memory of anyone telling him to expect a sibling, and certainly no one in the family referred to it afterward. Perhaps she wasn't pregnant at all. Perhaps it was only the cut of her dress.

Ray feels the beginnings of a blister on his thumb. Brand-new garden gloves, too. He wishes Lillian had bought a slightly less cheesy pair.

Ray is telling her something about yellow jackets, but he doesn't have her full attention. She's attacking the range top with cleanser and a plastic scrub pad, getting her elbow into it, a premenstrual cleaning jag.

"She complained about grass stains on her skirt," Ray says. "She was pregnant."

"Who was pregnant?"

"My mother," he says, in a patiently pained tone.

"Your mother was pregnant when you went on this expedition?"

He's rearranging cans in the pantry according to some filing system at odds, apparently, with her own. "It seems to me now that she was, that somehow I knew it the day of the picnic but forgot it until today."

"Well, if she was," Ivory says, sponging sludge out of a drip plate, "what happened to the kid?"

"I suppose she miscarried." He removes a can of pilchards from a stack of salmon and places it on a stack of chunk tuna.

"Maybe she had an abortion."

"Don't be ridiculous."

"People did, you know. Even back then."

"Not my mother."

She replaces a burner grate, jiggling it to make it fit. "What if the kid wasn't your father's, and he knew it? He'd been in Guatemala, you said. Maybe that's what they were fighting about at the lake."

Ray studies the label on a can of corn chowder as though he could read what really happened then in the list of ingredients.

He looks tired and his hand, holding the can, seems to tremble. There are brown spots on the back of his hand, old-age spots; he has a Band-Aid on his thumb. "I can't imagine her doing such a thing," he says finally.

"Having an affair?"

"No. The other."

Lillian's words come back to her: *People do what they have to do.* "Well, it doesn't matter now, does it?" she says, taking a towel from one of the stiff spokes next to the sink. "It all happened such a long time ago. Even if the kid had been born, he might be dead now anyway. Killed in a war or something."

He can't find a spot for the corn chowder; he gives up and shoves it in with the canned tomatoes.

"Maybe you cut too much hedge for one day," she says, not very kindly.

"You might have helped."

She turns to stare at him. "I never thought you'd *want* my help."

He doesn't answer that. "I wouldn't mind a cup of tea."

Biting her lip, she runs tap water into the kettle and sets it on one of the scrubbed burner grates. It won't stay scrubbed long. Everything about this kitchen is inconvenient and hard to clean. Lillian undoubtedly liked it that way—it gave her a purpose in life—but Ivory has one or two other things to do. "I hate this linoleum," she says, scooping loose Earl Grey tea into a special spoon with a hinged perforated cover. Ray does not approve of tea bags. "Look how old and worn and cracked it is. Now they have new kinds of floor coverings you don't even have to wax."

Ray doesn't say anything but his expression is not enthusiastic. He's pressing the soil the nasturtium seedlings are in to judge whether they need watering.

"We can afford it, can't we?"

"That's not the point," he says, clearly annoyed. Perhaps she blundered using the word "we"; even though they have a joint savings account, hardly a penny in it was saved by her.

"Would you like to tell me what the point *is*, Ray?"

Now he's at the table, hunched over his teacup. "It's too soon to be tearing things up, changing things," he says in a wearied way, as though disappointed that his own wife needs an explanation for something so obvious. Disappointed, but not in the end too surprised, really.

"Too soon after what?"

"I'd just as soon not talk about it at this moment, Ivory."

"*Please*, Ray," she begs, though it's not the linoleum that's worrying her now. She has the panicky feeling that things are slipping out of her control, that in this house she could be as helpless and muzzled as Lillian was. At this moment she almost hates him.

But he seems to have forgotten she's there at all. "I think it's because of the yellow jackets," he says to himself, "that I never learned to swim."

The tap is dripping, but she can't turn it off. No, it must be outside, something melting or leaking, or rainwater in the gutter.

She's standing on a pier. She has the box with her mother's ashes in her hand. A man says something she can't quite make out. It's not Richie or her father, it's Ray. He's on the very edge of the dock, his back to the water, his face white with fatigue —or fear. She moves toward him; he falls. When she looks over the side, she sees only oily seawater lapping against the pilings.

Nineteen

....

BUT NOTHING BAD happens. Ray's stone plant suddenly puts out a flower like a yellow daisy in its yawning cleft; buds appear on the crab apple tree; Sam goes hunting and catches a mole; a crew of men come and dig up the splintered stump in front of Sherman Hardware and replace it with a new bandage-wrapped sapling.

Almost in spite of herself, Ivory finds her gloom lifting. She makes up her mind to fix up the spare room—not for a baby, but for herself. She'll paint all the walls, and the ceiling, and the black wicker chair. And make a new cushion cover for it. Maybe, she thinks, Fogel has some suitable material for it in his box of odd bits and scraps.

She walks through Union Square whistling in her teeth, her tote bag swinging from her shoulder. She's licking muffin crumbs from her fingers. A pack of orange DPW trucks rumbles by, grinding garbage on the move, and though none of the men clinging to the backs of the trucks is Richie, she gives them a wave. Out of a drugstore comes a woman who in high school clogged a toilet with Ivory's gym suit. Ivory gives her a big grin and hello as she passes, leaving the woman gawking after her, trying to figure out where she knows her from.

She crosses Washington Street to cut through the parking

lot next to the fire station. She's not particularly paying attention to her surroundings—mentally she's ripping down the musty old drapes in the spare room—so it takes her a minute to realize that Fogel's shop isn't where it's supposed to be. A building is there all right—it's an auto parts retailer and distributor—but there are no Grand Opening signs in the window, no congratulatory potted plants. This auto parts store is as shabbily lackadaisical as any other store in Union Square, including her own. It could have been on this spot for years, for decades.

She steadies herself against a parking meter and blinks in the sunlight. She must really be going round the bend this time, she thinks. Maybe Fogel was only a figment, in which case there's the possibility that the gold spectacles and the brass daybed and Raymond Bartlett are also figments.

Unsteadily she walks back to the Triple A and sits at the counter.

"You hungry again already?" Sally says. "I thought I sold you a bran muffin not ten minutes ago."

"Sally," she says, "did you ever notice a used furniture store on Somerville Avenue across from the fire station?"

"I think so," he says, scraping wan cubes of boiled potato to one side of the grill and opening a pair of eggs in their place. The whites try to slither away from the yolks, but he thwarts them with the spatula. "Why do you ask?"

"It isn't there anymore."

"Easy come, easy go," Sally says. Next to the eggs he lays some strips of already cooked bacon, stiff and congealed out of the refrigerator.

"Now it's an auto parts store."

"So?"

"It looks like it's *always* been an auto parts store. In fact, I can sort of remember it being there, even though it's in the exact same place I know the used furniture is. Was. Are you following me?"

"You been working too hard, kid?"

"Holy Moses," Ivory says.

"Did you say up or over?" he asks the man on the stool next to hers.

"Over," the man says. He is wearing a tie with z's like lightning bolts on it.

"Am I going nuts or what?" she says to Sally as he flips the eggs.

"How long since you last saw this junk shop?"

"A couple of months, I guess."

"A lot can happen in a couple of months," Sally says, sliding the bacon and eggs and home fries onto a plate and setting it in front of the man in the lightning-bolt tie. "People are born, people shuffle off. That's life."

"I'll tell you what life is," Lightning Bolt says, shaking a catsup bottle over his home fries. "Life is Union Square in the middle of rush hour."

"Listen, kid," Sally says, ignoring him. "You want junk, I can help you out. The wife's got knickknacks on top of knick-knacks. She'd never miss a ton or two."

"The main thing I want is to find out what happened to Fogel's used furniture store. If there actually *was* a Fogel at all."

"Sure there was," Lightning Bolt says, buttering a limp piece of toast.

"You know him?" Sally asks.

"Made him a set of dentures," Lightning Bolt says. "What he said was, if he lived long enough to pay for them he was going to retire to a mobile home park in Florida."

"Did he?"

"He paid for the dentures, yes. Took him a while, though. See, used furniture isn't steady, like dentistry. In an economic downturn people around here sell junk but they don't buy. In the upswing they buy but don't sell. Of course, out in the burbs it's the exact opposite. See what I'm driving at?"

Sally, not even trying to sort this out, crosses his eyes.

"Teeth, on the other hand," Lightning Bolt says, pointing a fork at Ivory, "teeth tend to rot no matter what the state of the economy."

"So that solves the mystery," Sally says. "Your friend Fogel is probably sunning himself in front of his mobile home right this minute."

She can't quite picture it, and besides, it doesn't explain how the auto parts store sprang up that way, without anybody noticing.

"How about a Megabucks ticket?" Sally asks as she's sliding off the stool. "This could be your lucky week."

"Somehow I doubt it," she says.

It's strange to have Fogel gone. He *was* her friend, she realizes, too late.

Ivory pokes her needle into a double thickness of material, pulls the thread through, contemplates the stitch she made, makes another. The way her eyes are cast down, Ray can't see their color but he knows it is called hazel, a rather inadequate word that does not describe their tiny individual flecks of brown and green and, in some lights, a quite catlike yellow. The variety in them attracts him, though he suspects it's a result of miscegenation. Not the interbreeding of different races, perhaps, but of peoples from various climates and habitats, from over the hill and yon, joined together more by whim and accident than considerations of bloodlines and alliances. A peddler passing through a village and impregnating a laundress, a soldier raping a farm girl in a potato field. In fact, his wife seems to have all of medieval Europe in her face. A child by her is bound to contaminate the Bartlett gene pool in a way he enjoys thinking about; he's only sorry his mother will never know.

As Ivory sews, the sounds her needle and thread make, though homely, strike him as being extraordinarily sensual. He pretends to be reading, but really is working to maintain a curiously pleasurable suspension between relaxation and sexual desire.

But she drops the material, yawns, walks to the window. "Does that stone cactus bloom every spring?" she asks idly.

"Not every, no."

"Every other? Or only when there's thunder and lightning in March?"

Folding his reading glasses and laying his book aside, he shifts in the leather chair. "I haven't detected a pattern," he says.

"When it's in the mood?"

"I doubt very much whether succulents have moods."

"Maybe because I fertilized it, then."

He wishes she'd put her hand between his legs but it would shame him to ask her to, and she stays at the window examining the various plants, entirely unaware of the mood she's aroused in him.

"How did you fertilize it?" he asks.

"One time I used its saucer for an ashtray."

Although he's vaguely offended, he senses he shouldn't reveal his reaction to her. "Desert plants thrive on ill treatment," he says.

"Lucky them."

"What do you mean by that?"

"It was just a joke, Ray."

He remembers the time Janeen put her hand between his legs under cover of a newspaper on the Seventh Avenue subway. He was shocked but didn't tell her to stop. It's been years since he's thought of it.

Now Ivory is talking about her birthday. "It's coming up soon," she says. Part of the difficulty in having a rational conversation with her is the way she hopscotches randomly from topic to topic. She does not have an orderly mind and never will. He'll just have to get used to that, come to terms with it.

"We'll celebrate," he says, making a special effort to be agreeable.

She turns from the window, smiling. "How will we?"

"We could go to a restaurant. Do you like seafood?"

"I like any kind of food."

"There's a restaurant near Commonwealth Pier I used to go to sometimes."

"You mean in the harbor?"

"It's built on a dock. From your table you can look out at the boats, and the lights on the harbor islands. It's really very pleasant."

She sits and picks up her sewing; her head is bent over it so he can't see her expression. "I don't think I want to go to that restaurant," she says abruptly. Now when she pushes the needle in and out, the sound is not arousing but irritating, the rhythm of the stitches altered in some subtle way.

"Why not, my love?"

She seems to search her mind for a plausible explanation. No doubt she guesses that he took Muriel, and before Muriel other women from time to time, to that restaurant. Her problem, he decides, is that she doesn't care to be one more pea in a pod.

"It's near where we scattered my mother's ashes," she says finally. "I told you about it."

"Frankly, I don't see what difference that makes."

"I'd feel like I was dancing on her grave."

"I admire your scruples, Ivory," he says. "But I suspect what's really going on here is something rather different."

"What?" she says, raising her head. She looks stricken. Perhaps he shouldn't have been so hard on her: jealousy is in a woman's nature, after all, and he hasn't always done everything he could to discourage it. Still, he wishes for once she'd say what she means. Women and their secrets.

"Never mind," he says, cutting off any protestations of innocence she might make. "We don't have to go to the seafood restaurant if you'd rather not." But he doesn't say where they *will* go. The truth is, he's not especially familiar with other restaurants, of the kind suitable for birthday celebrations, and he loathes being taken for a sucker. "We'll settle on some nice place when the time comes," he says, opening his book to where he left the marker.

Ivory is spooked by the image of Ray backing away from her into the sea. She knows it's nonsensical: even if they went to that fish restaurant on her birthday there would be no need for them to walk along a pier, or if they did, Ray would not be likely to take any silly risks or to forget himself so much he'd make a misstep. And yet the vision keeps coming back into her mind. The worst part is the fear that if they really were on a pier together, some demon inside her might drive her to give him a push, for no other reason than to complete the vision. How else will she ever get rid of it?

Often now she feels he has qualms about her, somehow senses the lurking demons. She watches him closely in their lovemaking; at his moment of orgasm he rears up from her body, his face clenched in what looks like pain. It's almost as though he wants to get away from her but can't. Then he whimpers, exhausted. She wants to comfort him by saying,

"Don't worry, I'm not going to harm you," but of course, that would sound foolish.

Instead she holds him in her arms, her mouth near the back of his delicate neck, her hands on his breast. It takes a long time for his heart to stop pounding under her hand. Sometimes she's asleep before he recovers himself enough to retrieve his towel and water glass, button his pajamas, turn out the hall light on his way to bed.

She loves his body still, but there's no question that it's aging. His buttocks are shriveled slightly; his hair is sparse; the flesh along his jaw is loosening. At times his breath is foul from indigestion or some other imperfectly operating bodily process. There's the partial blockage in his nasal passages, the weakening eyesight. Some of his fussiness Ivory chalks up to age, too; often he is too weary to be patient, she thinks.

In spite of these flaws he's a handsome man: well preserved, as they say. When Ivory used to linger at the deposit slip counter watching him handle the telephone, swivel lightly in his chair, click the button on his ball-point pen, she'd think: If only I could possess that man, I could make him love me. He doesn't, though, not the way she had in mind then. What he wants from her is not the same as what she wanted to give.

It doesn't matter, she tells herself. In her life she has not been surrounded by people jostling and elbowing one another in their eagerness to love her; nevertheless, she's managed to survive. There are different kinds of love. His may be peevish, frugally given, forced through a very fine sieve. On the other hand, maybe it's enough.

The situation is precarious, she thinks. It wouldn't take much to knock it out of whack, and she is a clumsy person, always has been.

· · · · · · · ·

On this drizzly evening Ivory is again working at her sewing; it's a cushion cover, and she cut up an old paisley shawl to make it. Rather a silly idea: the cloth already has worn spots and moth holes, and sitting on it will not improve it. However, Ray has refrained from pointing this out to her. For one thing, it's too late; she went right ahead and cut into the shawl without consulting him. For another, it occurs to him that her sewing is like nest-making and he'd be churlish to question or criticize the instinct, however misguided and impractical the execution.

"What is the story of that shawl?" he asks in a friendly way, as he sets down on the coffee table a bottle of Scotch and the glasses he's been juggling.

"Story? No story," she says, unwinding some thread from a spool and snipping it off.

He remembers the way his mother used to cut material. She would measure a yard between her nose and the end of her outstretched arm. He'd have to try it sometime, though of course his mother's arm would have been shorter than his own. And Ivory's somewhere in between. Another of those slightly ambiguous rules of thumb.

"It wasn't handed down in my family, if that's what you mean," Ivory says.

He takes a silver jigger out of his jacket pocket and pours an ounce and a half of liquor into each glass. The Scotch, Teacher's, is a self-indulgence; once in a while he feels he deserves it.

"A man gave it to me." Licking her thumb and forefinger, she puts a knot in the thread.

"A man?"

"A dealer. He's in Florida now."

"Ah, Florida."

"That's what I hear, anyway."

It strikes Ray as odd that Ivory should know somebody living in Florida and be receiving news about him from yet a third party. Not that he minds, of course; it's just that he himself rarely talks to anyone other than Madelyn and other bank employees and clients, and even in those cases he does not make the mistake of discussing their private affairs any more than absolutely necessary.

Ivory takes a sip of Scotch. Resuming her sewing, she says, "I heard he lives in a mobile home park."

The wind changes direction, and rain begins to strike the bay window behind the cacti; he can hear it trickling down the small panes of glass from sill to sill.

"He had the strangest fingernails, Ray. They looked like they were made out of unicorn horn. Something you'd see in a museum."

He sighs, thinking of the Saturday afternoons with Muriel in the Fogg or the Busch-Reisinger. He thinks about the way he and Muriel would be looking into a glass case full of Chinese bronzes or carved reliquaries, and her shoulder would move against his, and he could hear her breathing, *feel* her breathing, and he'd be so certain that she wanted him.

"I don't think he ever cut them," Ivory says. "He couldn't have. They'd have been too tough."

Well, Muriel was worried about her heart, he supposes, a heart that was frailer, in the end, than her hymen. At least she might have given him some hint. He never claimed to be able to read minds.

All those afternoons spent inspecting virgins in the company of a virgin. The models for those wooden virgins, it occurs to him, were in all probability the wives or mistresses of the wood-carvers. The Holy Ghost would hardly have been first in line with *them*.

"Are you all right, Ray?" Ivory is asking. "You look kind of feverish, or something."

"It must be the Scotch."

He looks at her; she is wearing some sort of knitted cotton sweater and he can see her apple breasts under it.

"The proof," he begins to explain.

"Proof?"

"It's a little higher than I'm used to."

He moves toward her and takes the sewing out of her hands so abruptly that the needle slides off the thread and falls on the carpet. Her mouth tastes smoky. He has her trapped in the corner of the daybed. One of his hands grips the rail, the other pulls her sweater out from her waistband and fumbles underneath.

"Stop, Ray," she says.

His mouth reaches for her breast.

"I'm bleeding, Ray. I got my period."

He jerks away from her and feels brass knobs hit his back just under the shoulder blades. Surprisingly, he catches sight of the needle where it landed on the carpet; the light from her sewing lamp just strikes it. It is sharp and shiny, painfully shiny.

Now he feels the needle pierce his eye and begin to work its way, pitilessly, deep inside his brain. It is there on the carpet and in his head at the same time. Very queer that is. He tries to look away but finds that his neck won't turn.

"Ray," Ivory is saying, "it's okay. I'll go upstairs and get a towel if you want me."

"My head," he says carefully. "It's awry."

"It's what, Ray?"

The needle, he tries to say, but the word won't come out of his mouth. If only he could get her to pick up the needle and put it away, he would be all right and the pain would stop. He can't see her now; he fears she has gone upstairs. She doesn't understand he's in trouble. He tries to call her name, but he can't quite remember what it is, and then it doesn't seem to matter anymore.

Twenty

....

THE EXECUTOR of Ray's will is a man named Hooks. His office is an inner room of the bank that Ivory has never seen before. He is younger than Ray, and he is missing the little finger of his left hand.

"I thought you and I should have a chat, Mrs. Bartlett. Friend to friend."

Ivory has never seen Hooks before, either. He must hide out in here. She notices that he neglected to remove the dry-cleaning tag pinned just inside the sleeve of his brown suit jacket.

"I took the liberty of speaking to your husband's doctor," he goes on, when Ivory doesn't say anything.

"Oh, I see."

"Naturally, he wouldn't go out on any limbs, so far as your husband is concerned."

"No."

"However, in view of what I learned about the typical prognosis in similar cases, I felt it was my duty to bring certain matters to your attention."

Ivory wonders what happened to his little finger. Could he have been born without it? Or lost it in an accident? Or maybe he cut it off himself. The year they lived in Terre Haute she heard rumors about a boy who'd cut his pecker off with a bread knife. She wrenches her mind away from the thought.

Hooks is saying something about disability insurance. Ivory makes an effort to pay attention, since she doesn't want to embarrass Ray by appearing stupid. Solemnly she gazes at computer printouts and photocopies of documents as one by one he hands them to her across the expanse of his steel desk. He moves on to medical insurance and then to the subtleties of the Employee Pension Plan. It is all as abstract and puzzling as Ray's description to her, half a year ago, of the advantages of savings bank life insurance. Except that now, she senses, if she let it sink in she might panic.

"It is not a fortune," Hooks says, smiling thinly. "Nevertheless, with intelligent management, the two of you can expect to live reasonably comfortably, even in the event that he is never able to return to work. What I'd like to suggest is that you put yourself in the hands of a competent financial manager. I'd be happy to recommend—"

"Excuse me, but what are you talking about?"

Mustering his patience, he says, "An individual trained to advise you on budgeting. Investments, possibly. The ins and outs of the tax code."

"No. I mean about Ray not going back to work."

"Surely you've considered the possibility."

"His doctor never said—"

"A stroke, Mrs. Bartlett, is a serious proposition."

Hooks's smile is gone. All along, Ivory realizes, he's been blaming Ivory for Ray's stroke and has only been covering up out of manners or tact. A gold digger is what he thinks she is. But the joke's on her, he figures, because there isn't any gold, just a stack of papers disgorged from a copy machine.

"It's usually best," he says, "to expect the worst."

Ivory wants to laugh. He may wear a suit and tie and sit in

a private office, but he has the same philosophy of life as any short-order cook or meter reader in this town.

"Mr. Hooks, I have a business. I don't have to depend on Ray's pension and I don't need a manager to manage it."

"Well then, I can stop worrying, can't I?" he says in a patronizing way. Now Ivory knows he must have gone around to give her store the once-over and to tot up its visible assets and income-earning potential. He's not a banker for nothing. "Of course," he goes on, "my guess is that what your husband would prefer is for you to put your efforts into getting him on his feet again. I have the impression he doesn't have anybody else."

"That's right," she says, gathering the bundle of papers awkwardly together. "Just me."

His voice softens. "He'll need to depend on you."

"I know that," she says.

They are in the kitchen on Westwood Road. She seems to like to have him nearby as she goes about her chores. She's poking in corners with a sponge on the end of a stick. Gradually the water on the linoleum creeps closer and closer to his chair; at last it is as though she is on an island. But now the far edges of the linoleum have dried, and she is poking again with a different sponge, and now the floor glares under the fluorescent ring in the ceiling. She has a red cloth like a cowhand's kerchief on her head and she is whistling in her teeth.

Or perhaps it is the kettle that is whistling, after all, because he sees that she is filling the tea strainer with Earl Grey. Dry black curls of tea sprinkle onto the table and also the floor, where they will stick in the fresh wax. Ray tries not to care, because the next time the floor is washed they will be soaked up again, and then something else will stick in their place. He tries to think of the process as being like the tides, which leave nasty things underfoot on the beach, but are in the end natural and good.

His teacup is steaming on the table, and her queer crooked face is flushed with steam, too, red under the gay kerchief. She is peeling a tangerine for him, and smiling. He finds that a paper napkin has appeared, tucked into the neck of his cardigan. His mother would put a linen napkin around his throat and attach it to two tiny silver clothespins on a silver chain. That is what bibs were, in those days.

He thinks of telling her about those doll-size clothespins, but somehow now he is in his study, and she is busy tidying. The sun is flooding in the window, past the cacti, and he is feeling overwarm in the cardigan. Summer has come on with more of a rush than usual this year. They had hardly any spring at all.

She pummels the cushions, and dust and cat hair fly about, making him sneeze. She reaches for a tissue in the pocket of her overalls. Suddenly he feels on his fingertips what it is like inside her pocket: lint and grit and pencil shavings. This thing that has happened to him has made him excruciatingly aware of all kinds of sensations. He doesn't know where they come from or when they will strike him. Sometimes it is very difficult. Carefully he folds the tissue so that the unused part is on the outside and wipes his nose and eyes.

She is talking about her family. She has an astonishing number of family members, or so it seems to him, and they do improbable things. He doesn't always take in everything she says. His mother would call what he does woolgathering, but inattention is not exactly the problem. He is made weary by all these fractious people who come verbally tumbling out of her life right into his. He tries not to mind, because he knows she doesn't mean any harm.

She's watering the little cacti, overdoing it, but he doesn't like to say so. Sometimes he wonders what it is, precisely, that she's doing in his house, but he doesn't like to ask. There's always been somebody here. It's in the nature of things.

"If you see the Tiki Hut coming up on your left," Roselle said over the telephone, "you've gone too far."

But Ivory doesn't, and in fact finds the house without trouble: a flat gray Cape on an unpaved dead-end road east of 3A. The house has a blank sleepy look because the shades on the sun porch are pulled down halfway, like eyelids. A pair of waist-high evergreens lean away from the cinder-block steps as though to avoid being abraded.

"You got here early," Roselle says, opening the screen door. "How's the birthday girl?"

"You give great directions."

"You beat Rich home. He's the chef. He's going to grill stuff out back later."

"That sounds like fun," Ivory says, looking around the sun porch. "Hey, you got a piano." It's an elderly upright with the ivory gone from several of the keys.

"The piano came with the house," Roselle explains. "They wouldn't pay to have it moved." With thumb and forefinger she lifts her cotton duster, damp with sweat, away from her huge belly, as if to let the baby have some air. "The girls play 'Heart and Soul' on it."

" 'Heart and Soul'? Do kids still play 'Heart and Soul'?"

"Some things don't change. On the other hand, some things do."

"That's deep, Roselle," Ivory says, following her into the living room. It is a murky little room, its natural light cut off by the porch. The furniture from Granite Street, mismatched before, now looks clumsy as well, squeezed into the spots ordained by two radiators, three doorways, and a hideous fire-place made of shiny brick the color of creamed corn.

"The latest change," Roselle says, "is Diane got a punk haircut."

"Her hair is so fine. How does she get it to stand up in spikes?"

"I think she puts glue in her shampoo. Not that she'd tell me, even if I asked."

The dining room is also stuffed with furniture, in a style the manufacturer calls "country cottage": there are hearts cut out of the chair backs and ruffled gingham cushions tied to the seats. The set looks as though it just came out of the cartons.

"Now Arlene wants one, too," Roselle says. "Her father says 'no way,' but he'll give in sooner or later."

"Do the girls like living out here?"

"Oh sure," Roselle says, straightening one of the cushions.

"What about you?"

"I never had a dining room before. You want a beer or a diet Coke?"

"A beer would be perfect."

"Of course, the kitchen's a lot smaller than the one on Granite Street."

The old kitchen table is crammed into a breakfast nook, no room for legs or elbows, but Ivory can tell from the paper napkin holder and the salt and pepper shakers that this is where they eat. Out of habit, probably, or so as not to mar the finish on the new dining table.

"But I've got a dishwasher now," Roselle says, prying the caps from a couple of bottles of Miller Lite.

"And a good thing, too, since you don't have me."

Roselle goes on chattering as if she hasn't heard that remark. "It's a Kitchenaid. You have to be careful not to use it and the washing machine at the same time, on account of the septic tank. I didn't know about septic tanks before. I thought water just came and went, like in Somerville. You know, a part of nature. I sure as hell don't miss going to the Laundromat, though."

She shakes some nachos into a plastic salad bowl grained to look like wood.

"Rich is planning on fixing up the basement," Roselle says. She holds the back screen door open with her foot so Ivory can pass through with her bottle and glass and the bowl of nachos. "Putting up paneling and that. For the girls. Get them out of our hair."

"This is great," Ivory says, meaning the little yard. There's a square of lawn with dandelions starting to go to seed in it, an outdoor fireplace, a weathered picnic table set in cement, a small garden patch tangled with last year's dead vines and stalks, a prefabricated metal shed with an eagle over the door.

"Rich bought some tomato plants from the Kiwanis Club," Roselle says. "They were selling them in the supermarket parking lot. But then he forgot to water them and they kicked the bucket before he even got them in the ground." She sits across the splintery table from Ivory. With a dandelion leaf she scrubs at a couple of fresh bird droppings, a look of faintly baffled disgust on her bland face. "Men are all the same. You got to watch them like a hawk. Oh well. I can take tomatoes or leave them alone."

"I remember," Ivory says, pouring beer into her glass. Roselle's idea of a vegetable is a frozen french fry.

"Well, cheers."

"Cheers."

"So," Roselle says. "I want to hear all the details about you-know-what."

Ivory looks into a straggly forsythia bush. The blossoms are long gone and the branches now in full leaf. "It was awful, Roselle," she says.

"Did he just keel over, or what?" Absently Roselle scratches a mosquito bite on her inner arm.

"He was trying to tell me something but couldn't get it out. Then he sort of flopped down sideways."

"God. What did you do?"

For a long time, a nearly endless time, she didn't do anything at all. She couldn't make herself move, but she doesn't tell Roselle about that. Instead she talks about the two firemen in hats and boots and rubber raincoats, and the container of oxygen, and how the firemen put air into Ray's nose through a plastic tube. She must have called the fire department, but she has no memory of it.

Roselle's nose twitches when she hears about the plastic tube. "Then what?"

Ivory tells her about the ambulance pulling up outside, and more men running in with a stretcher and blankets, frightening the cat. And how they buckled Ray onto the stretcher, and rolled it out to the ambulance, and off they all went to the hospital.

"Sirens and all?"

"He would have hated it. The commotion. If he knew."

"Lucky he was out cold."

"I thought he was dead, Roselle."

"Oh, Jesus."

"The emergency room doctor said to me, 'Not *you* again.' "

"Why'd he say that?"

"I'd just been there with Ray's housekeeper. He meant I must be a jinx."

"Wise guy."

"I was terrified he was right. That I *was* a jinx."

Roselle, impressed by this, bites thoughtfully into a nacho.

"But he's going to be okay."

"Is he . . . you know. A cripple?"

"I wouldn't leave him alone if he was."

Roselle looks relieved.

"They've got him on a low-salt diet and a bunch of pills. His doctor says he'll probably live to be a hundred."

"Then the spell must be broken," Roselle decides.

Ivory drinks some beer. Yes, it's broken: she has him now. And there are no more secrets she must keep.

"I hear from Rich you're thinking about shutting the toy store."

"You hear right."

"Rich is kind of disappointed."

"How come?"

"Because he had a stake in it."

"What? I paid him back every cent I owed him."

"I'm not talking about that kind of stake," Roselle says. "Rich liked it that *one* person in the family didn't have to take shit from some supervisor."

"The thing is, there's plenty to do just in the house, now that Lillian's gone."

Roselle gives her a shrewd look. "So *you'll* be the housekeeper."

"If you want to put it that way."

"Well," Roselle says after a silence, "you get bored, you can always take up ceramics."

"Ceramics?"

"Like me. I'm taking lessons. I paint these little figurines—poodles and ballet dancers and Easter rabbits with eggs in their baskets—and the shop, it's up in North Billerica, fires them for me. You'll see when you open your birthday present."

Ivory has so much trouble imagining Roselle earnestly painting ceramic poodles that she can't think of anything to say.

Roselle drops her butt into the weedy grass and gives it a swipe with her flip-flop. "Stupid waste of time, right? But there isn't another damn thing to do out here." She sighs. "It's your fault, you know." She looks gloomily at the cinder-block fireplace in a thicket of ragweed. "You got a house, so *I* had to have a house. But I don't blame you, Ivory."

"I'm glad."

"Nobody needed to put a whammy on me. I whammied myself."

"You could always move back," Ivory says.

"Nah, it's too late now. Rich loves the sticks and the girls have all new friends. I'll tell you something, Ivory. Things never come out the way you expect. Or if they do, you wish they didn't."

Ivory smiles. "That's deep, Roselle," she says.